Praise for

Georgie Summers
and the Scribes of Scatter

"*Georgie Summers and the Scribes of Scatterplot*
unforgettable journey that explores the power c
and the magic that lies just beyond our wor

—NEIL BLAIR,
literary agent of J.K. Rowling and chairman of Pott

"A wildly imaginative ride into an outlandishly fa
world—perfect for fans of *Harry Potter*!"

—SAM COPELAND,
best-selling author of *Charlie Changes Into a Chic*

"A story full of heart, mystery, and magic—
an exhilarating read!"

—JENNY PEARSON,
Waterstones Children's Book Prize Finalist

ISAAC RUDANSKY

GREENLEAF
BOOK GROUP PRESS

Published by Greenleaf Book Group Press
Austin, Texas
www.gbgpress.com

Distributed by Greenleaf Book Group

For ordering information or special discounts for bulk purchases, please contact Greenleaf Book Group at PO Box 91869, Austin, TX 78709, 512.891.6100.

Design and composition by Greenleaf Book Group
Cover design by Jim Madsen and Kirk Duponce

Map illustration by Jim Madsen

Publisher's Cataloging-in-Publication data is available.

Print ISBN: 979-8-88645-316-4

eBook ISBN: 979-8-88645-317-1

To offset the number of trees consumed in the printing of our books, Greenleaf donates a portion of the proceeds from each printing to the Arbor Day Foundation. Greenleaf Book Group has replaced over 50,000 trees since 2007.

Printed in the United States of America on acid-free paper

25 26 27 28 29 30 31 32   10 9 8 7 6 5 4 3 2 1

First Edition

For Frayde

Contents

—— ◦ **Part Three: Shadow and Light.
Light and Shadow.**

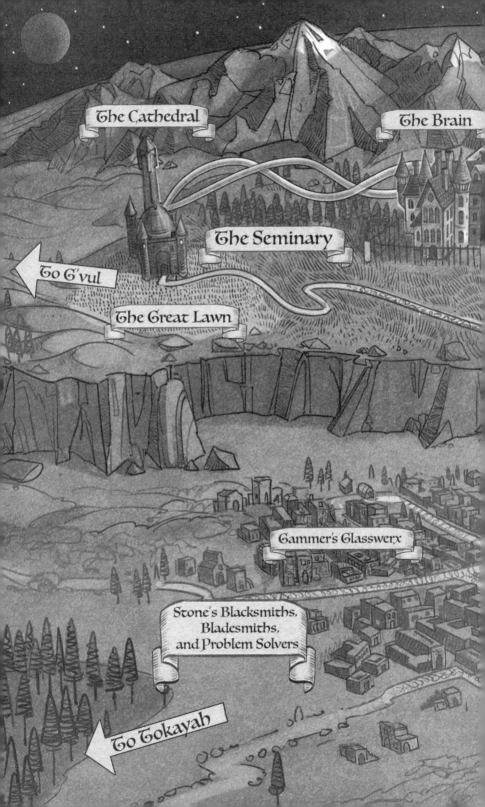

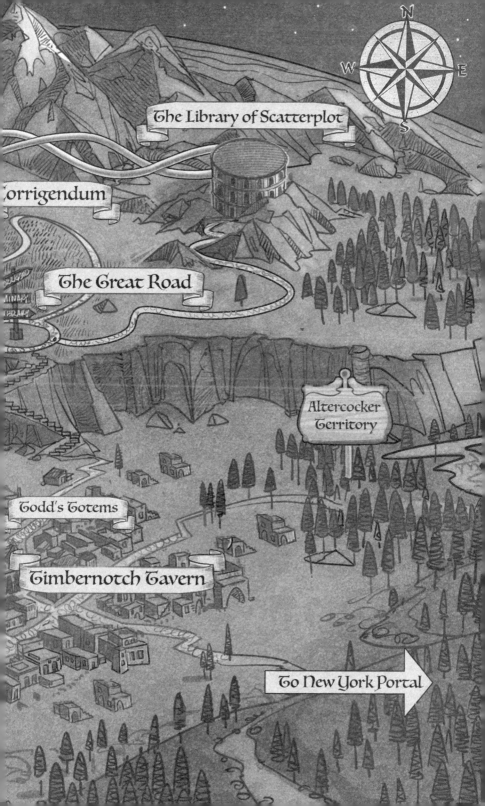

The Whisperloom Alphabet

Within these pages lies the key to this grid.
Crack the code to reveal what's been hid.

Unveil the message, send it in with your name,
incredible prizes will be yours to claim.

PART ONE

One Pen,
Two Portals,
and
Three Friends

Chapter 1

The Aetherquill

eorgie Summers adjusted his weapon.

THIP-TWANG!

The metal slingshot marble gleamed as it sped through the air, not as fast as a real bullet, but *definitely* fast enough to kill someone.

CRACK!

The satisfying sound of metal piercing metal. Out of all of Georgie's slingshots, this one was his favorite. He'd sanded the grip three times until it was extra-smooth, making a groove that fit his hand perfectly. He had also taken the time to paint the rubber bands a shiny black, which didn't make the slingshot shoot any better; it just looked super cool.

Georgie put the slingshot down on the grass and reached for his binoculars.

Bullseye.

Two hundred feet away, at the very edge of the lawn surrounding Georgie's small but tidy little home, the third can of Cherry Coke was still standing, but now it sprouted two thin streams of fizzy soda.

Four more cans to go.

Georgie checked his left pocket and felt four more metal marbles. Most kids couldn't shoot a slingshot even *half* this distance. Barely anyone could hit a bullseye from this far away, and Georgie figured he was likely the only sixth grader in all of New York who could hit seven cans with just seven bullets.

He had *thought* it would be a good idea to bring his favorite slingshot to school today.

He *thought* Apurva Aluwhalia might think it was cool.

What a mistake *that* had turned out to be. Miss Ellipsis, Georgie's English teacher, loved to shout, especially if she was aiming at Georgie. "*That's not a toy!*" she had shrieked when Georgie pulled the slingshot from his backpack. "*That's a WEAPON!*" Then she sent Georgie to the principal's office, and before Georgie could explain that he hadn't even brought any ammunition, he'd been suspended for the rest of the day.

Georgie dropped a metal ball in the leather pouch and pulled back on the rubber band until it was taut.

THIP-TWANG!

Another crack of metal. Another bullseye.

No kidding it's a weapon, Georgie thought. *But it's not like I was going to use it on anyone.*

Georgie sighed and turned back to his house. It was a small house, even for the standards of Bridget, New York, but Georgie didn't understand why anyone would need anything bigger. He had his own bedroom with a workstation for his slingshots. He had to share a bathroom with his dad, but overall, it wasn't a bad deal. The orange extension cord he'd snaked from his bedroom window powered his first-gen Xbox sitting on the grass beside him. His dad had been sleeping when he got home from school, and when Georgie checked the fridge after washing the dishes, he saw that the lunch he'd prepared for his dad—a turkey sandwich with the crusts cut off—hadn't been touched. Georgie's father *always* ate his lunches.

Until recently.

Georgie hit the eject button on his Xbox and out whirred the disc tray, which he had preloaded with the all-time greatest hits: Jolly Ranchers, Nestle Crunch, and Sour Patch Kids. He stared at all the candy, but couldn't decide what he was in the mood for. Maybe he wasn't in the mood for anything right now.

Maybe he was just worried sick about his dad.

The screen door on the side of the house creaked open and snapped shut. A moment later, his father rounded the house and slowly made his way across the lawn. John Summers walked with a cane, his body tilted and his shoulders slumped, making him seem a lot shorter than he actually was. He wore his usual checkered button-down shirt and dark jeans, and Georgie could see how much weight he'd lost recently.

"Hey, kiddo," John said, slipping the leather loop attached to the top of the cane off his wrist. Georgie had made that strap himself a few years ago and painted it the same shiny black as his slingshot rubber band. It didn't quite make his dad's cane *cool*, but it sure was better than nothing.

"Dad, you didn't eat your lunch."

The walk across the lawn hadn't been easy. John Summers breathed out heavily, staring inquisitively at Georgie's sling-shot on the grass between them. "You were home early today, weren't you?" he finally said, sitting down with a groan beside Georgie. "I thought I heard you downstairs."

"Yeah, I got suspended. Again." Georgie knew there wouldn't be any follow-up questions. There wouldn't be any anger. There wouldn't be any punishments.

There never were.

"That's okay," John said. He smiled brightly, and his eyes wrinkled in just the way Georgie remembered them wrin-kling before his father got too sick to take care of himself. "Hey, Georgie! Why do golfers wear two pairs of pants?"

Georgie's heart sunk. "In case they get a hole in one, Dad."

John rubbed Georgie's earlobe gently. "What's wrong, kiddo?"

"Nothing," Georgie whispered. "You told me that joke yesterday. And the day before that. And the day before—"

"So what?" John asked. "What law says your dad can't tell the same joke twice, huh?"

Georgie started tugging at the blades of grass. Just because there was no law against repeating the same joke didn't make any of this *normal.* It didn't make his father's mysterious illness any better.

Whirrr.

John Summers plucked a Jolly Rancher out of the Xbox tray and grunted as he threw it into the air as high and far as he could (which wasn't very high or very far). "Hit it, Georgie!"

Before he had a chance to think, Georgie had his sling-shot loaded and the band pulled tight.

THIP-TWANG!

The shot went high *and* wide.

His father threw another Jolly Rancher, beads of sweat forming on his brow.

Georgie missed again.

"Great marksmen can hit *moving* targets," John Summers whispered weakly.

Georgie never thought of himself as a *marksman.* "But I suck at moving targets."

John Summers exhaled a rattling breath. "Don't aim at where the target *is.* Aim at where the target is *going.*" He put an arm around Georgie and pulled him close. "It's the same thing with *stories.*"

"Stories?" Georgie asked, wondering if his dad was just going off on something totally random, which he had been doing a lot these days.

Georgie's father smiled weakly. "Yes, stories. The stories we believe are the stories that show us a path to where we most truly want to go. To where we *believe* we're going."

Georgie considered that. It did sound sort of totally random. But at the same time, it sort of made sense.

What didn't make sense was the sudden gust of cold wind that blew across the yard on this scorching-hot summer day. Clouds were building in the sky, which a moment ago had been blue and cloudless. The day had gone quiet. *Eerily* quiet.

"Dad, did you feel that wind—" Georgie stopped cold, seeing something in his father's eyes that he'd never seen before.

Fear.

John Summers looped his wrist through the cane strap and struggled to his feet, glancing around the yard. Georgie followed his father's eyes until they settled on the detached garage. Every hair on the back of his neck stood ramrod straight, prickling with electricity.

"Back into the house, Georgie." Georgie couldn't remember the last time his father gave him an order.

Then his father was hobbling across the lawn, the grass squishing under the cane's rubber foot. Georgie watched his father awkwardly descend the first few stairs of the garage cellar. He heard the *beep beep beep* of the electronic keypad.

Back into the house? Georgie thought, grabbing his slingshot and hurrying after his father. *No way.*

By the time he reached the stairwell, Georgie could hear muffled voices.

He palmed his slingshot, his intestines tightening into a knot, and continued down to the concrete landing. He spat onto his sleeve and rubbed a small triangle of grimy glass between two planks of wood boarding up the window beside the garage door. Stretching on his tippy-toes, he could see his father's dim outline through the smudged dirt.

Someone else was there too.

A woman, dressed like no woman Georgie had ever seen. She wore some sort of thick cloak, and—Georgie blinked twice because he couldn't believe his eyes—a giant wooden archer's bow slung around her back.

Georgie pressed his ear against the glass.

"The clock's ticking, John." The woman's voice was low and sure. "He's coming for the pen."

Gooseflesh sprouted up and down Georgie's arms. *Who's coming? What pen? Who is this strange woman and how'd she get into the garage?*

His father spoke next, his voice thin. "Every bone in my body aches. I can feel him getting stronger."

"He *is*," the woman said, her voice like cold steel. "He attacked a library two nights ago looking for the pen. Destroyed half a bookshelf before disappearing again. People are going to lose their minds. They're gonna forget who they are, John."

Georgie heard the rustling of cloth, and then the woman spoke again. "Take it."

Georgie turned his head and squinted through the grimy glass. The small oblong object the woman held in her hand emitted a flickering amber glow, casting strange shadows in the darkened garage.

"I don't want it!" John Summers gasped, taking a step back. "If he gets his hands on it—"

"Take the Aetherquill, John." She stretched her arm out. "Hide it for now. Give it to Georgie when he's ready. It's not safe with me. If he finds out I have it, I won't be able to stop him."

What was this woman talking about? Aetherquill? That was a strange word Georgie had never heard before, although "quill" did seem connected to "pen."

CLINK!

A slingshot marble had fallen from Georgie's pocket, striking the metal drain in the center of the landing. Georgie leaped down, squatting to find it, but just then, the garage door swung open.

"Georgie?" John Summers steadied himself against the doorframe. *"What're you doing out here?"*

Georgie stood up on wobbly legs. "Dad! What's going on? Who's—"

Something moved inside the garage.

"Who's in there?"

"No one," John replied. "Just me."

Georgie tried to see around his dad, but John Summers kept shifting his weight, blocking Georgie's view.

"I *saw* someone, Dad!" Georgie was becoming very frightened. "We don't hide things from each other, *right!?"*

His father moved shakily out of the way. "You can see for yourself."

Georgie stepped slowly into the garage, his heart racing.

The garage was empty, save for the overlapping rugs, a framed picture of his mother on the far wall, and a small, sagging bookshelf stuffed with bins of old clothes against the back wall.

There was nowhere to hide. Especially not for a woman with a giant bow and arrow.

She'd been *right there* a few seconds ago.

And now she was gone.

Chapter 2

Miss Ellipsis's Trains to Indonesia

eorgie slept straight through his alarm the next morning. He rubbed his eyes and checked the time on his flip-phone. Missed the school bus. What a way to start the day.

He jumped out of bed, took the stairs by two, and hurried into the living room.

John Summers was on the sofa, just as Georgie had left him late yesterday afternoon, fast asleep.

Yesterday!

The strange woman in the garage. The glowing tube-shaped object. Was that the special pen the woman had mentioned? The one that seemed to terrify his dad when the woman urged him to take it. What was that all about? And how did she *disappear*? How did she get there in the first place?

Georgie had helped his father up the garage stairs, and once they were inside, John Summers had slumped straight into the living room sofa. Georgie had gently slid his father's wrist out of the cane's leather loop, his mind racing, debating whether he should shake his dad awake. He needed to understand what that was all about back in the garage, but the dark and puffy bags beneath his father's eyes made Georgie think his father was too tired to talk even if he *wanted* to.

John Summers had stirred just before Georgie shut the living room light. "Georgie?" His father's voice was weak and scratchy. "Georgie . . . I . . . I didn't want to take it. It's too dangerous . . ."

"Take *what*, Dad!?" Georgie whispered. "*What* was too dangerous?"

"Tomorrow . . . Georgie . . . I'm so tired . . ."

And then John Summers was asleep, the blanket Georgie had spread over him rising and falling with the raspy rhythm of his breath.

Georgie had gone back to his room and spent the next two hours sanding the handle on a new slingshot. He thought about texting Roscoe Harris, his only friend, who happened to live across the street. But what would he have told Roscoe anyway? That a mysterious stranger had showed up in his garage with a glowing pen and then disappeared into thin air? Roscoe would've had a field day with *that*.

Now, Georgie pulled open the blinds. Sunlight drenched his father's pale forehead peeking out from beneath the blanket. His father's eyes opened—but just barely. He stirred and shifted his weight and then he was snoring again.

Seriously? You've been sleeping for like thirteen hours!

A few minutes later, Georgie was showered and changed and downstairs in the kitchen, trying not to make a racket. Georgie never skipped breakfast, but today he wasn't hungry at all. He made a turkey sandwich for his father and left it in the fridge in a ziplock bag. Then he grabbed a pen and a sticky note from the tray beside the kitchen phone.

Made you lunch. It's gonna be another scorcher. Drink lots today. Georgie sighed and rubbed his temples, as if that would make the uncomfortable knot in his belly go away. *Love you lots. Your number one (and only) son, Georgie.*

He stuck the sticky note on the turkey sandwich, grabbed his backpack, and headed for the front door.

❖ ❖ ❖

Bridget, New York, was a small town only two hours by car from Manhattan, but it felt much farther away. The mom-and-pop shops along Main Street were actually run by moms and pops, and most of the shopkeepers were so old they farted dust when their bells rang. Georgie pedaled along Main Street, past the hardware store and Carvel Ice Cream, thinking about the strange conversation—

He's coming for the pen—

—he'd overheard.

Georgie pedaled as fast as he could and didn't pump the breaks until twenty minutes later when he arrived at Bridget Elementary. His t-shirt was still plastered to his back with sweat when he opened Miss Ellipsis's classroom door.

He usually sat in the back of the classroom, but today the only empty desk was the one right next to Apurva Aluwhalia, the smartest girl in the entire sixth grade. She volunteered at the Bridget Planetarium and had even been named Young Astronomer Ambassador Worth Watching last year. Not really the type to think hand-carved sling-shots were particularly cool.

"Georgie Summers?" Miss Ellipsis cawed as the class-room door shut behind him.

Georgie winced.

"You're *late*." Miss Ellipsis was the new sixth grade Earth Science teacher at Bridget Elementary, and today her bun was tied so tight that it pulled her eyebrows halfway up her forehead. "What do you say when you're late?" Her eyebrows didn't move. It was unnatural.

"I'm sorry," Georgie muttered, sliding into the empty desk next to Apurva.

"Yeah, you *should* be sorry," taunted a pudgy boy with a pigtail sitting a few desks away. "And nice backpack, by the way," the boy continued, pointing at Georgie's second-hand

JanSport. "I used to have one like that, but then my dad got a job."

The other boys thought this was hilarious.

"It holds my things all right," Georgie muttered quietly. He looked at his torn backpack, slumped and spineless, unlike Apurva's backpack, which Georgie now saw had constellations embroidered on the outside pocket in golden thread. It was pretty neat.

"Essays *out!*" Miss Ellipsis shouted. There was a ruffle of paper as Miss Ellipsis shuffled through the rows of desks snatching up assignments.

Georgie pulled his essay from his backpack.

"AHEM!"

Georgie looked up to see Miss Ellipsis staring down at him from a thousand feet up.

Georgie hadn't finished his essay. He had written just three sentences and filled the rest of his paper with drawings of slingshots. Miss Ellipsis picked up his assignment by the corner, holding it out a safe distance as if Georgie's blatantly incomplete homework was hazardous material.

"Nice *fart*work, Georgie," snorted the bully in the pigtail, "or did you steal those from a first grader?"

The boys sitting around him laughed again, but went quiet very quickly when Miss Ellipsis snapped her head in their direction.

She turned her attention back to Georgie.

"Georgie, this is sad—"

Then something very strange happened. Miss Ellipsis's

eyes glazed over, and she stared at the paper in her hand like she didn't know what it was or how it had gotten there.

"Where am I?" she whispered. "Dwarf mobs quiz lynx. jpg, kvetch! *Click. Click. Click.* What day is it today?"

Miss Ellipsis looked up—her eyes red and vacant—and gazed blankly over Georgie's shoulder.

Then her eyes cleared. She shook her head and looked once more at Georgie's assignment.

"Yes, very sad," Miss Ellipsis muttered under her breath, not sounding very sad at all (but at least sounding herself again), and then shuffled away with Georgie's assignment.

Georgie felt that uncomfortable knot in his belly cinch tighter. *People are going to lose their minds,* the woman in the garage had said yesterday. He looked around the classroom to see if anyone else had noticed Miss Ellipsis's strange behavior, but the boys nearby were busy passing around what looked like a peanut butter sandwich.

He turned to Apurva, whose black hair fell like a waterfall over her shoulders and down her back.

"Hey," Georgie whispered. "Did you . . . did you *hear* that?"

Apurva nodded slowly, the color gone from her cheeks. "That was remarkably bizarre." A wisp of hair fell over her eye, and she tucked it back behind her ear. "That first part about dwarf mobs was a perfect pangram, a sentence that uses each letter of the alphabet exactly once. It loosely translates to 'a crowd of midgets question an image of a wildcat . . . then complain.' Grammatically correct, although not very meaningful at all, wouldn't you agree? Sounded like a case of transient amnesia!"

"Huh?" It sounded like Apurva had said "Trains to Indonesia," but that couldn't be quite right. Georgie likewise had never heard of a pangram, let alone a *perfect* pangram.

Apurva leaned closer to Georgie, about to say something else, when—

"What is the OBJECT orbited by EVERY planet in the solar system?" Miss Ellipsis shouted.

"Me!" shouted the idiot in the pigtail, once again pleased by the obligatory laughter from the boys sitting around him.

"Georgie Summers?" Miss Ellipsis asked.

Of course, she just *had* to call on him. But Georgie no longer wanted to sit around here and wait. He wanted to find out who the stranger was in the garage last night. He wanted to find Roscoe and ask him to Google "Trains to Indonesia." It all seemed connected, even if Georgie had no idea *how*.

"Miss Ellipsis?" Georgie asked, standing up. "I need the bathroo—"

"No," Miss Ellipsis sighed, "it's the sun, Georgie."

"What's the matter, Georgie?" taunted Pigtail's sidekick. "Your mommy didn't potty train you?"

Georgie's mother had died in a car crash when he was two years old, and he had no idea if she'd ever potty-trained him or not. Out of the corner of his eye, Georgie saw one of the boys moving toward his desk.

"Miss Ellipsis, can I *please* go—"

"You didn't raise your hand, Georgie. Sit down and try again."

Georgie looked up at his raised hand, rolled his eyes, and sat back down—

SQUISH.

Something soft and mushy flattened between the hard plastic desk chair and the seat of his pants. The snickering from the boys around him became uncontrollable giggling. Georgie jumped back up and craned his neck around to find a single slice of white bread glued to his butt with chunky peanut butter.

Everyone was looking at him now. Even Apurva.

"GEORG-EE MADE A POO-POO IN HIS PANT-EE!" the boys began to chant.

"Oh, shut up!" Apurva shouted.

"GEORG-EE MADE A POO-POO IN HIS PANT-EE!"

"Stop that right now!" Miss Ellipsis howled. "Georgie Summers, go clean yourself off."

Georgie peeled the bread off his pants and raised his arm to throw it at the boy who'd put it there. He wouldn't miss—that much was for certain. But instead, he launched the bread across the room where it landed in the trash.

He wasn't like the rest of them.

The class was still chanting and pointing at the splotch of peanut butter on Georgie's pants as he navigated the maze of desks. He banged his hip on the corner of one, sending the class into a fresh bout of laughter. Georgie laughed too, because he imagined laughing would make him seem like less of a loser.

◇ ◇ ◇

What had Apurva called it? Georgie thought as he walked out of Bridget Elementary and into the muggy June heat. He'd spent the last twenty minutes scrubbing the peanut butter from his pants with soap and water. They were—no, *had* been—his only good pair of school pants.

He wished he had a smartphone like everyone else. Then he'd be able to search Google himself, starting with that word the woman in the garage had used: Aetherquill. He rounded the building, thinking that a smartphone *still* wouldn't make him half as smart as Apurva, then stopped short.

Apurva was right there, leaning against the brick wall, her face in her hands.

She was crying.

Georgie tried taking a step backward, but Apurva gasped and looked up. "Hey! Were you watching me cry?"

"Yes," Georgie began, his mind spinning like a turbine. "I mean *no* . . . I was, but not on purpo—"

"It's okay," Apurva said, wiping her nose. "Those boys were awful. *So* disgusting."

Georgie looked down at the pavement.

Apurva stepped closer to Georgie. "I used to get pranked all the time in my last school. Before my parents moved us here. The girls in Vermont can be just as mean as the boys in New York."

She slipped a sheet of paper from her backpack and held it up. "Last week's assignment."

A big "A-" was stamped in red ink at the top of the paper. Below it, Miss Ellipsis had scrawled: *Do better! Nobody's perfect!*

"That's why I was . . . upset! Miss Ellipsis said if I don't get straight As, she'll recommend someone else for the summer position at the planetarium."

Georgie nodded. "That makes sense."

"That I'll lose my job at the planetarium because of an A-minus?"

"No! That you're upset."

"Oh." Apurva slipped her essay back into her backpack. "Anyway, that was really bizarre back there with Miss Ellipsis, right!? I was *about* to tell you that my mother just started having episodes of transient amnesia. Two days ago. It's when someone suddenly experiences severe memory loss. Do you think that's what happened to Miss Ellipsis? Because it really looked that way to me."

He attacked a library two nights ago looking for the pen, the strange woman had told his father yesterday. *People are going to lose their minds.*

"I don't know . . . ," Georgie said, confused. "This is gonna sound really stupid . . . but my dad was talking to someone . . . yesterday . . . in my garage. Something about an attack on a library and how people are gonna forget who they are."

Georgie looked up at Apurva, who was staring at him intently. "Never mind—"

"No, go on," Apurva said eagerly. "It doesn't sound stupid."

Georgie heard the screech of tires around the front of the school building.

"I don't know," Georgie continued. "Something about a pen, and I may have *seen* it, and it was like . . . glowing. Look, I'm still trying to figure this out and I know how it sounds—"

"And you think all this has something to do with my *mother?*"

Georgie raised his hands up. "No, no, I'm not saying that it does or it doesn't—"

"She forgets who she is," Apurva whispered, twisting her hands together. "We thought it was Alzheimer's disease, but the doctors have done a ton of tests on her and they say it isn't. It came so *suddenly.*"

Georgie adjusted the straps on his backpack. "Something really weird is going on. Miss Ellipsis's . . . *thing* today . . . and your mom . . . you said it started happening all of a sudden." Georgie wondered if they were connected. They definitely *seemed* connected. It also seemed like he was starting to scare Apurva. "Look, I really hope you get the job at the planetarium this summer."

The idling car engine choked off, and Georgie heard a door open and slam shut.

Apurva looked away, and when she spoke again, her voice was thin, like the words were painful. "It's her *eyes,* Georgie. They remind me of how Miss Ellipsis's eyes looked today. Like they've been emptied of all the life and love and things they *knew*. It's exceedingly distressing."

They're gonna lose their minds, John. Miss Ellipsis, and now Apurva's mother.

Apurva's big brown eyes swam with tears. "She forgets who *I* am."

Georgie couldn't think of a response. He didn't have any answers. He just had good aim and a sick father and a bunch of his own issues to deal with.

"I should go," Apurva said, offering Georgie a weak smile. "We're not allowed back here, and I don't need the school finding out I broke a rule *on top* of my A-minus. Can you *imagine?*"

Just then, a familiar voice shattered the midmorning stillness.

"*Georgie!*"

Georgie spun to see his father limping around the side of the school building.

"*Du-dad?*"

How did his father *get* here? He didn't actually *drive* here, did he? His father had stopped driving a year ago after knocking over three mailboxes on his way home from the doctor.

John Summers stopped a foot from Georgie, panting. "Georgie, we . . ." he paused to catch his breath. His hair was a complete mess. "Home. Now. You need to pack a bag."

He didn't seem to notice Apurva, who was already heading toward the school's side entrance.

"Dad! I . . . can you tell me what's going on?"

Georgie's father looked afraid. Maybe even terrified. "I will. In the car."

Georgie turned to Apurva; he only caught a glimpse of her black hair before the school's door swung shut behind her.

He exhaled, then slung his father's skinny arm around his neck. "Come on, Dad."

Georgie Summers never returned to Bridget Elementary.

Chapter 3

We're Not Safe
Here Anymore

John Summers's hair nearly brushed the roof of the small car as he jerked through Bridget's mostly empty streets, rolling through stop signs like they were merely suggestions.

John Summers looked over at Georgie. "What happened to your *pants*—"

"*DAD! Watch OUT!*"

John lurched the car away from the sidewalk and back into the lane.

"It was a stupid prank, Dad. Open peanut butter sandwich on my chair. It's all good."

John Summers took a hand off the wheel and reached for Georgie. "Hey, kiddo—"

"It's fine, Dad. I cleaned them." His pants were going to be the least of his worries if his dad didn't get both hands back on the steering wheel.

"You're my best friend," John Summers whispered shakily. "You know that, right?" The puffy bags beneath his eyes were even puffier and darker than they were last night.

"This morning," Georgie began, trying to keep his voice steady, "Miss Ellipsis . . . she was looking at my homework and she started mumbling, like . . . like a crazy person or something! No one heard besides that girl in my class— her name is Apurva by the way. *Her* mom just got sick and apparently she forgets who Apurva *is* and—"

"Wait." John Summers exhaled a great breath of air. "Where are they from?"

"Miss Ellipsis and Apurva's *mom?*"

John Summers nodded.

What did Apurva say about the girls in—where was it—was it Vermont? "Apurva's from Vermont, but Miss Ellipsis . . ."

"Is she a new teacher?"

"Yeah," Georgie nodded. "This is her first year at Bridget Elementary."

His father's eyes narrowed to slits as he tried his mightiest to concentrate on the road. "So neither of them are from New York."

Georgie sighed. "I guess so?" Was his dad going all random again?

"*Our* Library is safe," John Summers said. "For now."

"Dad, you're not making a drop of sense, you know that, right? Does this have to do with the woman in the garage yesterday? I *saw* her, Dad; she said someone was coming. That people are gonna lose their minds. What—"

"Georgie, listen to me very closely," John interrupted, wiping sweat from his forehead with the inside of his elbow as the car jerked around another winding curve in the road. "I'm not from here."

The hair on the back of Georgie's neck stood up straight.

"*We're* not from here. Not from New York. Not from the United States. Not from this world."

Was his father aware of the words coming out of his own mouth? How sick was he, really?

"Dad, you're scaring me."

"I know. And I'm sorry. Someone . . . some*thing* . . . is looking for me. I'm getting sicker, Georgie. You'll understand everything when we get there—"

"*WHERE!? You keep not making any sense*—"

"To . . . to . . . to Scatterplot."

John Summers drew in a sharp breath, as if he could take back the words he had just spoken. He slapped his palm against the steering wheel, then repeated quietly, "To Scatterplot."

A throbbing frustration rose to the surface of Georgie's face, the kind that makes you want to dig your nails into the soft skin below your eyes and pull down hard. If he wasn't so confused, he may have screamed.

"There's a lot you don't know," John continued. They

swung onto Jericho Road and John gunned the engine, which sounded like it was on the verge of quitting for good. "About Mom. About *us*."

Georgie pushed the heels of his fists into his eye sockets. "You're talking to me about Mom, now?"

He thought about how he helped clear the table for two every night, always wondering what it would have been like to clear the table for three. To have a mom who'd tuck him into bed and kiss him goodnight. To have someone who helped him take care of his dad all these years. "*Seriously!?*" Georgie tried swallowing that lump in his throat. "What do I care about Mom!?"

John Summers brought the car to a screeching stop in their driveway and killed the engine.

Dead silence.

Georgie and his father stared at each other, their chests heaving, each of them fighting back the tears that sometimes came soundlessly as they lay awake in their own beds at night.

"Your Mom was so brave, Georgie. And she loved you like crazy."

He fumbled with the door handle until Georgie had to lean over to help with the latch. "Pack a bag, then we're outta here."

What about school? Georgie wondered numbly, slamming the passenger door shut. Would Apurva notice he wasn't there? Would *anybody*?

◇ ◇ ◇

A minute later, Georgie was in his bedroom, throwing two pairs of underwear into an old duffel bag. "DAD!" Georgie called. "DO I NEED MORE THAN TWO PAIRS OF UNDERWEAR?"

No answer.

Georgie raced around his room, throwing who knows what into his bag. He grabbed his favorite slingshot— the one with the black painted rubber band and custom grip—and stuffed his pants pocket with a handful of metal marbles. His pants were already too big in the waist, and the marbles only made them sag down even lower. Gosh, what a disaster. Georgie put two marbles back—not that it made any difference— then tossed a zip-up hoodie into his bag. Would it be cold where they were going?

"*Shoot!*" Georgie muttered to himself. "*I need to charge my phone!*"

"No, you don't."

Georgie nearly jumped out of his own skin. He turned to find his father standing in the doorway.

"Your phone won't work where we're going."

Weird.

"What about a jacket? Will it be cold—"

"Georgie, we need to leave."

What his father said next made questions of climate and cellular service completely irrelevant.

"We're not safe here anymore."

Chapter 4

Terror Arrives at Jericho Road

Georgie stood in the driveway, clutching his beat-up duffel bag and waiting for his father. He squinted up the embankment across the street at his best friend's house. The sun beat down mercilessly, and even Roscoe Harris's dog—who was messing about sluggishly with a spare tire in the backyard—was not immune to the heat.

Georgie pulled out his phone to see if he'd missed any texts from Roscoe and was just looking at the screen when the day went impossibly dark. He looked up to see a thick cloud blotting the sun, even though a moment ago there hadn't been a cloud in the sky. A freezing cold gust of air wrapped itself around Georgie's body, making him shiver.

Just like yesterday, Georgie thought. Only this time there was this strange sound—very faint, like it was coming from behind a stack of pillows—of crashing waves.

Roscoe's dog turned its head to the darkened sky and gave a single, shrill bark. And it was Roscoe's dog Georgie was looking at when a black line about the height of an ordinary door appeared out of nowhere. It hovered a foot off the ground at the edge of the driveway.

Georgie blinked and rubbed his eyes, but the black line hovering in midair didn't disappear.

It was definitely there.

It looked like a tear, as if someone had slit a canvas painting down the middle with a knife. The view on either side of the line curved inward, like two pages of a book meeting at the binding.

Roscoe's dog ran to the fence and snarled.

Then a hand—an actual, human hand—jutted out from the tear like a jack-in-the-box. It was gray as ash, wrapped in bloody veins. Five long, pale fingertips reached and stretched, and then clamped shut on a flap of air before pulling back.

Georgie felt a dizzying vertigo as his view of the hemlock trees and a chunk of street curved sharply inward, then disappeared entirely. If not for the man standing on the other side of the doorway-sized cavity hovering just off the ground, it would have looked like a full rectangle of reality had just ceased to be.

But there *was* a man standing there. He was paler than a bedsheet. His lips were bloodless. Eyes as black as the bottom of a well sank deep into his skull. His wrinkled skin wrapped tightly around the bones of his face like old leather stretched too thin.

He wore a tasseled black scarf around his neck.

As Georgie's eyes adjusted, he saw that the man was standing on a desolate beach. The ocean behind him was vast and gray. Waves crashed against boulders as big as houses sending eddies of spray and foam into the air.

He could hear the beach clearly now. The pounding waves and screaming seagulls.

Roscoe's dog darted across their yard, momentarily disappearing as it ran behind the doorway, reappearing a moment later on the other side. The man in the black scarf swung one leg over and perched on the bottom of the doorway, one foot on Georgie's driveway, the other on the beach. The doorway sagged under his weight like a rubber swing. Then he swung his other leg over and landed in a squat less than ten feet from where Georgie was standing. The flaps of the doorway snapped mostly shut behind him.

"Good morning!" the man bellowed. He was dressed in a burlap smock, the fabric cut open in a V across his chest. He smiled at Georgie, his barely-there lips contorting his face into something ghoulish.

Georgie dropped his duffel bag.

Thump.

"My name is Flint Eldritch. Where am I?"

He took a step toward Georgie.

Georgie willed his body to move, to run back to the house, but his legs were cement pillars and wouldn't budge.

"New York, I know," the man said, his voice thin and almost mechanical. He spread his hands and smiled, revealing rotten yellow teeth and a tongue that was nearly black with decay. "But where am *I*?"

It was only much later that Georgie realized what the man who called himself Flint Eldritch was *really* asking, but right now, all Georgie understood was that he needed to run. If only his legs would receive the message from his brain.

The man pointed at Georgie's duffel. "Is it in there? The pen. The Aetherquill. I'd like to have a look."

That word again. Aetherquill. Even in Georgie's frozen terror he remembered what the woman in the garage yesterday had called the glowing object in her hand.

"Who are you?" Georgie croaked. "Stay away from—"

In three quick strides he was standing inches from Georgie. A putrid scent of stale fish and many worse things radiated off him like heat off an iron.

He grabbed Georgie's bag, unzipped it, and stuck a hand in.

"Get out of my bag!" Georgie reached for his duffel, but the man in the black scarf swung it out of reach easily.

"*Georgie?*" His father's voice was close. "Who are you talking to, kiddo? Are you in the driveway? We're not taking the car!"

The man with the scarf tipped the duffel bag upside down, spilling Georgie's clothes everywhere. He shook the bag violently and tossed it aside. Pain shot through Georgie's face as the man's fingers clamped down on his chin, and a terrible, heart-wrenching coldness overcame him.

"Where is it?" The stench of the man's breath was unbearable. He squeezed harder, digging his fingernails into the soft skin around Georgie's mouth. "Where. Is. The. Aetherquill?"

Georgie heard the squish and clack of his father's cane on the pavement.

"I'll find it," the man breathed. "And I'll kill any Scribe who stands in my way."

"GET YOUR HANDS OFF MY BOY!" Georgie had never heard his father scream—let alone raise his voice—and the sound sent shivers running up and down Georgie's spine. He glanced to his left just in time to see his father swing his cane at Flint Eldritch's head. Flint dropped to the ground, and John Summers fell on top of him, letting loose a flimsy punch.

Flint rolled away easily, and John's fist connected with the pavement.

CRUNCH!

Georgie heard the brittle bones in his father's hand break like twigs.

"DAD!"

Georgie helped his father to his feet. His knuckles were dripping blood and his hand hung limp, like it was attached to his wrist with silly putty.

Flint was already up, standing at the edge of the driveway, the doorway hovering in the air just behind him. "*There*

I am," Flint said, staring at John Summers. He slowly uncoiled his scarf, revealing a gaping black hole in the center of his neck. A hole lined with bumpy and irregular scabs, like an infected wound.

"The Aetherquill, John." A shiny black beetle crawled out of the hole in his neck and scurried down his shirt.

John Summers clenched the one fist he was still able to use and Georgie watched in astonishment as smoky white light curled out of the cracks between his father's fingers.

"You'll never find it. Don't ever . . . don't ever come near my son again." John's chest was heaving up and down like he was on the verge of a very bad heart attack.

"Dad?" Georgie began, staring blankly at the light dissipating like steam. "What the—"

Flint cackled madly. "That's all you have left!?" An electrified purple beam flew from Flint's outstretched palm and coiled around his father's neck. John grabbed at it, straining to breathe.

"I *will* find it," Flint Eldritch snarled. "And you're going to help me." He threw his head back and laughed, and as his chin lifted to the sky, another beetle—this one fatter than the last—crawled out slowly. It stopped for a moment as if to survey the scene unfolding in the driveway, then scampered over Flint's skinny shoulder blades and down his back.

John Summers started forward, pulling himself along the purple chord tightening around his neck. His face turned from red to purple and his feet curled awkwardly inward as he pulled himself closer to the man in the black scarf.

"*DAD!*" Georgie screamed, still frozen in place. His dad was going the wrong direction . . . they should be running away!

"*Aaaaaarghhh!*" John Summers cried as Flint Eldritch grabbed his father in a death hug and *squeezed.*

And just as Eldritch squeezed, John Summers *dimmed.*

For a moment, Georgie could see straight through his father's body. Then, with a flicker like a dying lightbulb that refused to go out, his father solidified again.

"DAD!" Georgie screamed again, and all of a sudden, blood rushed back into his limbs and he grabbed his sling-shot and a marble from his pocket. He aimed at Flint's face but froze again when Flint reached behind and pulled open one of the portal's flaps.

There were creatures on the beach now; three-legged monsters with beanpole legs and razor-sharp beaks march-ing up and down the shoreline. One of them snapped a seagull out of the air with terrifying speed. Georgie heard the bird's dying shriek through the open doorway.

Georgie watched in disbelief as his father dimmed again, this time nearly disappearing entirely.

"Come!" Flint cackled. "*COME!*"

Roscoe's dog slammed itself against the chain-link fence at the top of the embankment.

Georgie's frozen terror broke, and he released. The mar-ble whizzed a centimeter past Flint's forehead and sailed straight through the portal.

Georgie tried reloading, but Flint shot his arm out and an immense force hit Georgie square in the stomach, catapulting him backward like a doll. He crashed into the headlight of his father's beat-up Toyota. Georgie coughed and groaned. A bolt of sizzling pain throbbed in his back. Safety glass crunched beneath his palms as he tried hoisting himself up.

"Stay away, *boy*," Flint snarled, and then without any further warning, he dragged John Summers through the tall seam in midair between the edge of Georgie's driveway and Jericho Road, pulling his limp body over the ledge and onto the beach. A second later, Georgie could see Flint standing alone on the shore, his father nowhere in sight.

"Dad?" Georgie blurted, sounding stupidly confused and alone and terrified all at the same time. Then the flaps of air snapped shut, leaving not even the black line that had marked the portal's center.

Clouds were building in the distance, but overhead the sky was blue and untroubled.

A bird sang.

Roscoe's dog stopped barking.

Georgie's father was gone.

Chapter 5

A YouTuber and an Astronomer

"DAD!"

Georgie ran to where the doorway-sized opening had been. He braced himself to bump against something, *anything*, but there was nothing there.

Had he imagined the entire thing? No, certainly not. His father was *here*, and now he was gone. The . . . doorway? *Portal?*—no, *impossible*. Portals weren't real. Passageways between worlds weren't real. But . . . he had seen it—whatever *it* was—open and shut with his own eyes.

And his dad was on the other side of it now.

Georgie blindly stretched his hands out. "*DAD! CAN YOU HEAR ME?*"

Georgie grabbed his flip-phone, but hesitated before dialing 9-1-1. What would he tell the police? That his father had been dragged through a doorway in the middle of the air? They'd probably check him into a psychoactive hospital. Or was it a *psychiatric* hospital? Georgie couldn't remember.

Anyway, the police wouldn't let a twelve-year-old live alone. They'd put him in child protective services! He didn't have time to think about his dad flickering back and forth, the white light coming out of his dad's hand . . . or those disgusting beetles.

Think!

The strange woman in the garage yesterday. Miss Ellipsis. Apurva's mother. And now his father was gone, missing . . . kidnapped. By a man whose neck sprouted plump beetles and who was looking for a pen.

We're not from here, John Summers had said in the car ride home from school. *Not from New York. Not from the United States. Not from this world.*

If anyone might know something about portals or a pen called the Aetherquill, it would be Google, but Georgie's flip-phone was as dumb as they came. He needed to get to a smartphone fast.

A moment later Georgie was scrambling up the sloping thicket across the street on his hands and knees, hoping Roscoe was home—hoping Roscoe's first-gen iPhone wasn't confiscated as it often was. He crept along the chain-link fence until he reached the post where years ago Roscoe had snipped the wire with a pair of his dad's cutters. He could see through Roscoe's first-floor bedroom window from here.

Roscoe was lying on his bed, his back to Georgie, covered in his dinosaur blanket. Roscoe loved that blanket. He'd say that even though it *looked* like a baby blanket, it was actually made from a super-magical fabric that fended off demons and nightmares. The blanket was actually the last thing Roscoe's father bought for him before Mr. Harris started drinking and shouting and shoving Roscoe around the house for no good reason at all. Roscoe held on to that blanket because it helped him remember his dad before all that terrible stuff started happening. Georgie knew that. So did Roscoe. Not that they'd ever talk about it.

Georgie chipped a soft piece of bark off a nearby tree and placed it in the cup of his special slingshot. He aimed in a high arc, pulled back on the rubber band, and released. The shot was true, and the bark thunked against a brontosaurus on Roscoe's shoulder.

Roscoe flipped over and stared at Georgie. He had dark chocolate-brown skin and a buzzcut so short Georgie often called him Lieutenant Harris.

Georgie waved at Roscoe frantically.

Roscoe climbed nimbly from his bedroom window and crept across the lawn, stopping twice to look back over his shoulder.

"Looks like you've seen a ghost!" Roscoe said, climbing through the seam in the fence. "Or worse, your own reflection. Anyway, long time no see—"

"You okay, Roscoe?" Georgie asked. "It's happening again, isn't it?"

Roscoe twisted his face into something between confusion and the reaction to a foul odor.

"With your dad, I mean," Georgie added. "He's screaming at you a lot again?"

"I know what you meant!" Roscoe said, his eyes cast to the ground.

"Okay, okay, I'm sorry," Georgie continued. "Listen, Roscoe, I need your phone." He didn't have time to explain everything. Not that Roscoe would believe him anyway.

Roscoe pulled his first-gen iPhone out of his pocket. "How long were you spying on me, anyway?"

"I wasn't spying on you, Roscoe!"

"By the way, I know what kids say about my old man behind my back," Roscoe rattled on, "that—"

"My dad was kidnapped!"

"—that he's crazier than a soup sandwich!" Roscoe looked away from Georgie again. "But I don't want you to think that. *Sincerely.*"

"Roscoe! Did you hear what I said!?"

Roscoe looked up, startled.

Georgie rubbed his eyes, exhaled, and punctuated every word. "My. Dad. Was. *Kidnapped.*"

"What!?"

Georgie told Roscoe everything—he didn't have a choice at this point—trying very hard to keep it together and very much aware of the simple disbelief etched across Roscoe's face.

Finally, Georgie ended with, "I gotta see what Google knows about . . . portals. Doorways. Another dimension. Yeah, I know it sounds crazy. But I'm not crazy. I *saw* it. Seriously, Roscoe. Your phone. Now. *Please!*"

Roscoe laughed. "You think I was born stupid, Summers, or do you think I got special training? Now you're gonna tell me that the clouds are spelling out the word *gullible*, right?"

"Sorry, Roscoe," Georgie sighed, then snatched the phone right out of Roscoe's hand.

"Hey! Give it back, you *wet!*"

Georgie turned and ran, leaping over brambles, and was close to the lip of the embankment when—

OOMPH!

His foot caught on a protruding root and he—and Roscoe's iPhone—went flying. He tumbled down most of the steep slope, tearing his pants open and scraping his knee hard enough to bleed. Georgie's pants were having nearly as bad a day as he was.

"*And he's doooowwwwn!*" Roscoe had his iPhone back, and now he was filming. "Ladies and gentlemen, Georgie Summers has fallen! The crowd is going *absolutely WILD!*"

Roscoe turned his phone around and spoke directly to the camera.

"For my new subscribers, welcome to episode seventeen of *Roscoe's Rag*, where Bridget's annals are plumbed daily by your host, Roscoe Harris! In today's installment, we examine a spy, a storyteller, and a thief, all rolled into one *extremely* wet noodle."

Roscoe gave Georgie a hand up. "I record every episode

of *Roscoe's Rag* on this baby. You *know* how serious my vlogging is!" He wiggled the phone in Georgie's face.

Last Georgie checked, *Roscoe's Rag* only had fourteen YouTube subscribers, a fact Georgie would have reminded Roscoe about had he not caught movement in his driveway at that very moment.

Georgie yanked Roscoe behind the trunk of a big old elm, jamming his finger against Roscoe's lips.

There must have been something about the pure terror in Georgie's eyes just then because all the color drained out of Roscoe's face like a squeezed sponge. Roscoe pulled his face away from Georgie's trembling finger. "You're really telling the truth?" Roscoe whispered. "About your father? *All* of it?"

Georgie nodded.

"Say it."

"I'm telling you the truth."

"Nah. *Say* it."

Georgie only had to invoke this particular ritual twice before, once when he and Roscoe were nine years old and Roscoe had accused Georgie of putting a small colony of dead salamanders in his underwear drawer.

"I swear on my mother's grave."

Roscoe sucked in a long breath.

Then Georgie hawked a glob of spit into his open palm and stuck his hand out.

"Jumpin' Jiminy, man, I'm really sorry. Sincerely." Roscoe shook Georgie's hand and pumped it firmly. "Shoulda been *my* dad who got violently abducted."

Georgie took a careful step out from behind the tree and slid a few feet down the embankment.

"Oh no," Georgie muttered.

"What's wrong?" Roscoe whispered excitedly, skidding down and colliding with Georgie. "Is the man in the black scarf back? Where's the portal!? Oh God, is this the sort of thing that only *you* can see!?"

Georgie ignored Roscoe because he was staring at the teal and purple bike parked against his mailbox. He slid another foot down. Apurva Aluwhalia was there, kneeling in front of his dad's car, examining the shattered headlamp.

"What's *she* doing here?" Roscoe whispered, but Georgie was already stepping onto Jericho Road, swatting twigs and dirt from his pants.

"Oy!" Roscoe called loudly, catching up to Georgie. "No touching! That's a crime scene!"

Apurva shot up and spun around. "There you are, Georgie! *Crime* scene? Hi, Roscoe. Are you okay? You look . . ." She eyed them nervously.

Roscoe shrugged. "It's not me you should be worried about." He shot a look at Georgie.

"O-kayyyy," Apurva said, scrunching her eyebrows. "Georgie, you left your backpack at school. You also left your bike . . . but I'm sure you can understand that I couldn't realistically return your bike. Here, hold on." She hurried to the mailbox, where Georgie's backpack was hanging from her bike's tasseled handlebars.

"You like her, don't you?" Roscoe whispered in Georgie's ear.

"I—no. Can you *shut up?*" Georgie hissed. "And don't say *anything.*"

The spokes on Apurva's wheels went *tick tick tick* like the giant Wheel of Fortune game at the Bridget County fair as she walked her bike over to Roscoe and Georgie. "I should get going. I've got a lot of homework." She handed Georgie his backpack, then hesitated, her arm suspended. "Did you find out what that glowing pen was all about?"

"How does *she* know about that?" Roscoe cried, facing Georgie. "You two have *secrets* now!?"

Georgie pushed Roscoe aside gently. "We were about to look it up on Google."

"Well," Apurva began, "if we're talking about . . . supernatural phenomenon here, our technology may not be equipped to investigate it accurately. Have you considered that possibility?"

Roscoe rolled his eyes very noticeably, but Apurva ignored him. "But maybe I can help?"

"No need!" Roscoe snorted, waving his hands and turning to Apurva. "And besides, all of this is seriously dangerous. Georgie's father was kidnapped!"

Georgie slapped his palm against his forehead. *Seriously, Roscoe!?*

Apurva looked disbelievingly at Roscoe.

"Tell her," Roscoe said. "Then we can get on with it. And by 'we' I mean just you and me. Copy?"

Apurva laid her bike down on the driveway. "I'd really appreciate it if one of you could tell me what's going on."

When Georgie finished telling Apurva everything that had happened, Apurva looked at Georgie and Roscoe as if some part of her desperately hoped they were just playing a mean trick on her, but deep down knowing they were not.

"Miss Ellipsis," Georgie began, "and your mother. I think they're connected."

"It's all true," Roscoe said. "We spit on it."

Apurva ignored him and looked back at Georgie. "Back at school, your dad said you needed to pack a bag." Her voice was barely a whisper. "Where were you going?"

Georgie looked at his dad's car and the twinkling shards of the shattered headlamp. "Scatterplot."

"Where's *that?*" Apurva asked. "I never heard of it. Must be a *very* small country. You were going to *fly* there?"

What had his father said while Flint Eldritch was dumping his duffel bag out?

Are you in the driveway? We're not taking the car!

"The garage!" Georgie whispered, mainly to himself. "My dad said we weren't taking the car. And the woman yesterday . . . *she* was in the garage. And then she just, like, *vanished.*"

Apurva glanced dubiously at the garage. "Can I have a look?"

"*Fine,*" Roscoe groaned, as if some invisible committee had elected him president. "But don't touch anything in there." He looked at Georgie. "And I'm coming with. You two ink-stains are going to need my help."

Georgie wasn't sure about bringing Apurva and Roscoe into the garage. What would happen if they came face-to-face with Flint Eldritch again? Maybe Roscoe was right, maybe it *was* dangerous. And while Roscoe could be annoying sometimes—*most* of the time, if Georgie was being honest—he was also pretty tough. Maybe having him around wasn't the worst idea in the world.

"Let's go, Summers," Roscoe said, giving Georgie a shove toward the garage. "The suspense is killing me."

As they passed the side of the garage opposite the door and stairwell, Roscoe stopped short. "Do you hear that? *Who's in there?*"

"No one," Georgie replied. "It's empty." His father had locked the door behind them yesterday.

Or had he?

Georgie pressed his ear against the garage wall.

Now he heard.

Voices.

Voices coming from inside the garage.

Chapter 6

Secrets in the Garage

They hurried around the back of the garage, then descended the stairwell on the other side. Georgie reached the landing first, and now he stood there, staring at the red light on the keypad.

"Are they there?" Roscoe breathed into the back of Georgie's neck. "Can you hear 'em?"

Georgie could not. The garage was silent.

"They're waiting to ambush us," Roscoe continued. "That's what I'd do!"

Apurva reached past Georgie and wiggled the knob. "Locked."

"And only I know the code," Georgie said, only partially relieved. "Trust me."

"*Trust you!?*" Roscoe whispered, spitting into Georgie's ear canal. "Any decent criminal knows how to lift fingerprints! All you need is some fluorescing powder and an iodine fuming kit. They have this stuff on Amazon!"

Georgie and Apurva both looked at Roscoe, his database of unusual and mostly useless knowledge never ceasing to amaze.

Georgie held his breath and brought his hand to the keypad.

3-5-9.

Beep beep beep.

His fingers left sweat marks on the rubberized keys.

Georgie exhaled.

1-1-2.

Beep beep beep shwirr–LUNK!

The red light blinked green, and the deadbolt disengaged. Slowly, he stepped inside, one hand on his slingshot. The overhead bulb was still on from last night. The garage was empty.

Apurva followed behind.

"What's the report, soldiers?" Roscoe called from the landing. He had his phone out, filming again. "Something strange is happening in Bridget. According to one Georgie Summers, a mysterious man from another universe, perhaps even a *monster*—"

"Stop live streaming!" Georgie hissed. Where was his father right now? Getting further away with every passing minute? *If he's still alive*, Georgie thought, then shoved that terrible idea out of his mind. If anything, he wished Roscoe had caught the portal opening in midair on camera—at least that way he'd have some footage to review! By now, Georgie was quite certain he *hadn't* imagined the entire episode . . . that the portal *was* real. But neither Apurva nor Roscoe had been there when it all went down.

"I'm *not* live streaming," Roscoe replied, pausing the video but remaining right where he was. "I'm a *creator* now, which requires sophisticated post-production. Sound effects, captions, the *works*. Besides, what if something happens to us? This video is evidence that we were here—"

"*Seriously?*" both Georgie and Apurva exclaimed at the same time.

SHOOOP! Apurva's phone buzzed in her pocket.

"Oh no, sorry," Roscoe whispered. "Apurva, I think I just accidentally AirDropped you a video of Georgie tripping over a branch a few minutes ago—"

Apurva arched her eyebrows.

"—never mind, just delete it," Roscoe breathed, stowing his phone. "My fingers are sweaty and shaky, okay!?"

Georgie could tell Roscoe was afraid. Georgie didn't blame him; the voices were gone, but the garage had taken on a creepy quality they were all feeling in their bones.

"It's okay, Roscoe," Georgie said. "You can come in now. It's empty." He thought of Roscoe's silly dinosaur blanket. Maybe it *was* some sort of monster-fighting magical quilt. Georgie had never believed in magic . . . but that changed about twenty minutes ago. If only Roscoe had brought the blanket with him now, Georgie would have told Roscoe to drape it over the three of them . . . just in case.

Roscoe took a few uneasy steps into the garage but when the door swung shut behind him he screamed and jumped a foot off the floor.

"You'll need to be a lot steadier than *that* behind the camera," Apurva said, half-smiling at Roscoe, "if you *really* want to become a famous YouTuber."

"*Whoa!*" Roscoe exclaimed, ignoring Apurva. He was pointing at the wall opposite the garage door, next to a framed portrait of Georgie's mother. Her hair was wavy and dark. Her skin was golden copper. She was standing in front of a mansion with at least nine chimneys. But that's not what Roscoe was pointing at. "What's *that?!*"

There was a big bulge in the concrete wall. It definitely hadn't been there yesterday.

"Looks like the wall is giving birth to a soccer ball!" Roscoe said.

Georgie stepped to the wall and was just about to put his hand on the bulge when, with a slow cranking sound, the bulge rolled upward about a foot.

Roscoe threw one arm around Georgie and the other arm around Apurva. All three of them retreated until their backs were against the opposite wall.

"Did you see that?" Roscoe panted. "It *moved!* The thing *moved!*"

They stared at the bulge, waiting. It was like a giant, bruised eyeball, watching them.

"I hear them again!" Roscoe panted.

Georgie heard them, too. Now he could make out two distinct voices. Fragments of naked words drifting sluggishly from the wall.

"Hello?" Georgie called.

"Are you *nuts*?" Roscoe whispered from behind him. "What if they hear you?"

The voices went silent.

"Great. You scared them away," Roscoe said, his back still pressed against the wall opposite the bulge.

Georgie exchanged a perplexed glance with Apurva, then reached into his pocket and scooped out a handful of small metal marbles. He dropped a few into Roscoe's hand, then gave the rest to Apurva.

"What're these for?" Roscoe asked.

"My slingshot."

"Right on. And where's *my* slingshot!? You're armed up to your eyebrows and I'm a sitting duck! Thanks a lot!"

"You have no idea how to shoot a sling—"

"*Shhh!*" Apurva whispered. The garage had gone eerily still, and the only sounds that could be heard were the throbbing buzz of the overhead bulb and the beat of blood in their own ears.

What happened next happened quickly.

There was that cranking noise again as the bulge in the concrete wall receded. At the same time, a tall black line appeared on the wall, running right down the center, as if the wall was made of canvas and someone standing behind it had slit it open with a knife. It stopped three feet from the floor, just like the line that had appeared in Georgie's driveway.

Right before his father was abducted by Flint Eldritch.

"I'm finished," Roscoe whispered. "They'll take me first. The defenseless one!"

The tear widened an inch, like a mouth.

Georgie took a step forward, trying to see what was on the other side. And what *was* the other side? Another world? Georgie had no idea, and if not for the fear rising in his throat like a sharp metallic burn, he wouldn't have believed his own eyes. But he remembered the three-legged monsters he saw on the beach, the ones with the razor-sharp beaks and legs like stilts. He wondered if those monsters could travel between worlds. He wondered if they'd be able to stand in the garage, or if they'd need to duck their heads while their eyes rolled in their sockets.

"Oh, oh, oh," Apurva panted. "It's all *true!?* Is *that* what you saw in your driveway? That actually . . . *happened!?* I . . ." Apurva shuffled a step backward. "I don't think I really believed you," she finished in a whisper.

"Yeah," Georgie whispered. He didn't blame Apurva for not having believed him. Who in their right mind *would* have? "Looks the same."

"What is it, Georgie?" Roscoe panicked. "Who's there? What do you see? Are we outnumbered? Are they armed? Is it my dad? They're armed, aren't they? We've been *ambushed!* Ambushed! Oh God, just like I said we would be!"

Georgie squinted through the tear. He couldn't make anything out.

"Let's make a run for it," Apurva whispered, but didn't move—didn't even twitch—like someone had dunked her in a bucket of glue and stuck her to the wall.

"Yeah, yeah," Roscoe wheezed. "We'll each go a separate direction!"

Georgie had just enough time to think what a dumb idea that was when a puff of snowflakes the size of pennies drifted lazily through the portal and into the garage.

Georgie took another step forward, desperately hoping his father would appear on the other side, but at the same time terrified Flint Eldritch's long, bony hand would jut out from the darkness instead.

The voices, muffled and vague earlier, were now clear and distinct.

Then, out of the dark slit in the wall, a hand reached into the garage.

Chapter 7

The Seven-Thousand-Lingual Twins

Apurva screamed, rushed forward, and yanked Georgie backward. They bumped into Roscoe, and all three fell clumsily to the garage floor.

"Stop pushing me . . . you go first!" The voice of a young girl.

"Hold these—" The voice of a boy.

Four hands gripped the tear now, wrinkling the concrete flaps like stage curtains. The tall black line opened wider.

The voice of the girl: "Are you sure about this?"

The impatient voice of the boy: "*Ja, ja . . . Vamos!*"

"On the count of three," said the girl. "Remember, we need to grab him fast! In and out."

"Oh *God,*" Roscoe whispered in terror, "it's me, isn't it? It's me they're here for!"

The boy counted down from three, and then the flaps of the garage wall pulled back like saloon doors made of heavy fabric. There was no beach or three-legged monsters on the other side of the portal this time. Through the opening in the garage wall, Georgie could see the dark outline of birch trees, their thin trunks illuminated by a bobbing source of flickering light. It was nighttime over there.

The girl was dressed in a cream-colored velvet smock with shiny copper trim. Hanging from her neck was a chain made entirely of sapphires. She stuck her head into the garage, her long, braided hair dangling to the floor like a rope.

Roscoe lifted his arm slowly and gave Georgie a fabulous smack across the face.

"What was that for?!" Georgie yelled, holding his hand to his stinging cheek.

"To make sure I'm not dreaming!"

The girl turned around. "There are three of them!" she said to a figure standing behind her. "One of them smacked another in the face. Is that normal?"

Now the light from the garage illuminated the boy's face, who looked the same age as the girl and was dressed identically to her. He knocked one of the girls' arms down, and the flap of the garage wall she had been holding open sprung back into place, hitting her in the back and sending her tumbling into the garage. She bumped her shins on the bottom of the portal, let out a surprised shriek, and landed in a tangle on one of the rugs.

She shot up, wiped the dust from her velvet smock, and looked back at the boy who was still standing in the forest. "You . . . are . . . so dead!"

The boy was now holding the flaps open himself, and in one smooth-as-a-cowboy motion, he hopped through the portal and landed in a squat beside the girl. "Whoa! Did you *feel* that, Edie!? That was *so* cool—"

"I'm telling Momma the second we get back," the girl said sternly.

"It was a joke, Edie! I'm sorry, oka—?"

A marble whizzed past the boy's face, missing his forehead by centimeters. Georgie had his slingshot drawn, but it was Roscoe who had thrown the marble.

"Whoa!" the boy shouted. He threw his arms up. "Do NOT attack!"

Roscoe fired another marble, this time striking the boy on the shoulder.

"*Ooovwwwww!*" the boy yelped, hopping from one foot to the other. "*That hurt!*"

The girl—Edie, if that was her name—stepped between Roscoe and the boy, her hands spread. "CEASE FIRE!"

Georgie aimed his slingshot at the girl. "WHERE'S MY FATHER!?"

"Don't you dare." She let the words hang there for a moment, eyeing Georgie. "I'm Edie Obey. Spelled like Oh-*bay* but pronounced Oh-*bee*." She pointed to the boy.

"This is my brother. His name is Ore. We're from Scatterplot. We are *not* your enemy."

She looked at Ore for support, but Ore was rubbing his shoulder and glaring at Roscoe.

"*Gai cocken of'en yam, you little mamzer,*" Ore seethed.

Georgie had no idea what the boy had said. It sounded like a foreign language. He wondered which one it was, or if it was even a language from this world to begin with.

As if reading his mind, Ore smiled at Georgie. "That was Yiddish." He glared at Roscoe again. "It meant, 'Go poop in the ocean, you little bas—'"

"ORE!" Edie cried.

"How many languages do you know?" Apurva asked, still on the floor. Georgie had a million of his own questions, and that one didn't even break the top fifty.

"All of them," Edie and Ore replied at the same time.

"But Yiddish is my favorite," Ore added. "The insults are—" he looked up at the ceiling, as if searching for the right word. "Splendiferous."

"Surely you don't mean *all* of them," Apurva said wondrously. "There are over seven thousand languages—"

"It's part of our training," Edie interjected, sounding like a museum tour guide who had better places to be. "How else would Scribes know which memories are key memories and which ones are not?"

Georgie, Roscoe, and Apurva had matching looks of bewilderment on their faces, but the girl carried on anyway. "You lower-realmers have a saying: 'Sticks and stones may break my bones, but thine words will never hurt me.' Do you know it? But words *do* hurt, and Scatterplot's analysts have measured the impact of enough long-term memories to know that hurtful words hurt *much* more than getting cudgeled by a stick or a stone, which, by the way, is actually a vanishingly rare occurrence, statistically speaking."

She finally lowered her arms, keeping a careful eye on Georgie, who still had his slingshot drawn.

Ore took a step forward. "Let's get down to business. Which one of you is Georgie Summers?"

"Him!" Roscoe yelled, pointing at Georgie. "It's him you want!"

"*Oui*," Ore said.

"We *what?*" Roscoe looked like he was on the verge of panic attack.

"*Oui. Bene.* Correct. We're only here for Georgie."

"Slow down!" Georgie cried, standing up. Nobody was taking him anywhere just yet. "What's on the other side of that . . ." Georgie pointed behind the twins at the tall slice running down the garage wall.

"Portal?" Ore asked, calmer now. "Some people call it a doorway. *Doorway.* A means of access. A passageway or opening into a room, building, or in this case, another world."

"Another *world?*" Apurva repeated.

Edie nodded. "On the other side of *this* particular portal is a place called Scatterplot. Where we're from. Where we live. Where we're *going*."

Scatterplot! Georgie took a step forward. That's where his father said they were headed! "Do you know what happened to my father!?"

A great clap of thunder slammed across the sky and all five children jumped. Then a windswept downpour began to fall, battering the corrugated tin roof of the garage like a steel drum.

"We don't know where your father is!" Edie shouted, raising her voice over the rain. "But you might be the only one who can save him!"

Relief washed through Georgie. He didn't know if he could trust these two strange, multilingual children in matching pajamas from another world, but the girl just implied that his father was still alive.

"*How?*" Georgie asked, looking between the girl and the boy. "How do I save my father?"

"Look, Georgie," Ore said, "we don't know all the details, but first, we need to see if you're a Scribe or not. Because if you're *not* a Scribe, the plan is dead in the water."

I'll find it, Georgie remembered Flint saying. *And I'll kill every last Scribe who stands in my way.*

"If you *are* a Scribe," Ore continued, "which would quite honestly be very impressive and extremely surprising, you'll need to be officially ordained at the Coronation Ceremony, which is *tomorrow* by the way, so yeah, we need to hurry."

"ORE!" Edie shouted. "We're not supposed to say anything! We've already been here too long. In and out, remember?"

Georgie's mind clogged up with a traffic jam of questions. Was the woman in the garage yesterday *also* from this place called Scatterplot? What was a Scribe and why was it so important to finding and helping his dad? Was this all connected to Miss Ellipsis and Apurva's mom? What was this special pen, the Aetherquill, that Flint Eldritch was after?

And finally, where was his father right now?

The rain battered against the garage's roof as all five children regarded one another.

Then Roscoe took a step forward, keeping his eyes on Edie and Ore. "Why should we trust you?"

"Fumbluff said you might be spectacle at first," Edie said.

"*Skeptical,* you mean," Ore corrected. "Spectacles are eyeglasses, usually with a piece of wire that loops around the ears. It can also mean a public show or display, as in 'the stars make a fine spectacle tonight.' My sister struggles with her vocabulary sometimes—"

"Enough!" Edie cried. "This is your father's orifice—"

"Office," Ore corrected.

"—Yesterday, your father tried teaching you how to shoot a moving target with your . . ."

"Slingshot," Ore finished.

Georgie felt like he'd been punched in the stomach. How could they know that?

"Georgie," Edie urged, "I know you have a lot of questions—but we need to go. *Now.* And only you. We have orders."

"I'm not coming without my friends," Georgie said.

"Thank you very much," Roscoe said weakly, slapping Georgie on the shoulder. "But you got this. You can tell Apurva and me all about it when you get back."

Another ferocious clap of thunder went off like a cannon. Roscoe didn't even flinch; he was staring intently through the portal, his forehead creased.

"We're *really* not supposed to bring anyone back other than you," Edie said to Georgie, "but if you'll only come with a friend, you can bring—" she pointed at Apurva.

"Apurva," Apurva said. "Apurva Aluwhalia."

"—Apurva," Edie continued. "Girls are *much* braver and smarter. She'll be more useful if we run into trouble on the way back to Scatterplot."

"Braver *and* smarter?" Ore asked sarcastically, rolling his eyes. He grabbed hold of a flap and pulled back. "Whatever you say." The portal opened halfway. "Single file! Apurva and Georgie!"

"*Wait!*" Apurva cried. "I can't. I can't go through that . . . portal. I can't leave my mother." Apurva's bangs fluttered away from her eyes in a rush of cold air from the forest. "Unless," she continued, her voice cracking, "unless there's a cure for my mother over there? If what's been happening to her is connected to . . . to all of *this*, then I *have* to go, don't I?" Her voice trailed off, transfixed by the swirling snow-flakes on the other side of the portal. "Oh," Apurva sighed, "I really don't know. People will be looking for me!"

Roscoe shuffled his feet and stuffed his hands in his pockets. "No one'll be looking for me. And besides, whatever creep show is waiting for us over *there* can't be worse than what's waiting for me at home." He looked up at Georgie and Apurva with a weak attempt at a smile. "And let me just say this, okay? If *she* goes"—Roscoe jabbed a finger in Apurva's direction—"*I* go." He crossed his arms over his chest and turned to Edie and Ore. "You just *try* to leave me behind."

If Georgie hadn't been friends with Roscoe since they were four years old, he would have been amazed at how quickly Roscoe changed his mind. But that was Roscoe.

"So, you're in?" Georgie asked, facing his best friend.

The wind outside screamed, and the rain fell in sheets against the tin roof.

"Dumb question," Roscoe breathed. "I'm *always* in." He hawked a glob of spit onto his palm and stuck his hand out to Georgie. "Besides, you two wet noodles won't last five minutes over there without me."

Georgie smiled. Then he shook Roscoe's hand hard, three pumps, then let go.

"Gross!" Apurva cried, but then she was standing between the two boys, spitting a small—but still impressive—wad of saliva into her open palm. Georgie and Roscoe exchanged amazed looks and then each of them took turns shaking Apurva's hand. Three pumps each.

"All *three* of them!?" Ore shouted at Edie.

Edie shrugged and raised her palms, which meant the same thing no matter which of the world's seven thousand languages you spoke, or even what world you came from.

"Squadron! Single File!" Ore shouted. "Let's make like bees and leave!"

Georgie was pretty sure it was 'let's make like *trees* and leave,' but he wasn't going to hold that against a boy who spoke seven thousand languages.

"I'm going first," Roscoe said, shaking his arms and bouncing on the balls of his feet. "Catch me if you can, *suckas*, I'm OUTTA here!"

Then Roscoe took off, covering the distance between where he was standing and the portal in two giant strides, and dove headfirst through the tear. It was a clumsy dive, and the second flap of concrete pushed forward against his hips before snapping back into place.

Roscoe was gone.

Apurva and Georgie hurried across the garage.

"I can't see Roscoe!" Apurva exclaimed, but she was already climbing onto the portal's ledge, holding Georgie's shoulder for support. As she balanced between two worlds, Georgie had an urge to say something to her, something she'd remember, just in case—in case what? In case they never saw each other again?

But just then, with a long, high-pitched shriek, Apurva jumped, and just like Roscoe, disappeared.

It was only Georgie, Edie, and Ore in the garage now, and all Georgie could see through the portal was the faint outline of trees stretching into the darkness. Images of Flint Eldritch choking his father scampered across his mind like a hellscape. But this time, the fear didn't paralyze him.

Georgie felt a mysterious sense of calm (his father would have told him this was the calm that descended upon great warriors in the moments before battle). His father was over there, in Scatterplot, whatever *that* meant.

He pulled himself up onto the bottom of the portal. It felt rubbery, and it sagged like a swing beneath his weight.

He closed his eyes and breathed in through his nose. The freezing winter air stung his nostrils.

Georgie jumped.

He felt giant hooks grab him under his armpits and whisk him through a vortex of color and twinkling light.

Then, he was falling.

Falling through the darkness.

PART TWO

Welcome to Scatterplot

Chapter 8

Serious Trouble
in the Forest

"Wel ... um ... ooo ... atter ... ot," Ore said.

Georgie found himself lying face down in knee-deep snow. He cleared a clump of snow from the inside of his ear with his finger. "What!?"

"I said, 'Welcome to Scatterplot.'" Then his hands were under Georgie's arms, pulling Georgie up.

Georgie brushed snow out of his eyes and nose and spun around. Roscoe and Apurva were shakily getting to their feet. Georgie looked for the portal, for the way back home.

The portal was gone.

Just an uninterrupted forest of tightly packed birch trees unfolding into the darkness, with deep marks left by harsh weather marring the tree trunks.

"There's no reception!" Roscoe cried suddenly, jabbing at his phone screen. "How am I supposed to back up my footage with no *RECEPT*—"

"Shhhh!" Ore hissed. "I mean it!"

Deep drifts of snow piled high against the tree trunks.

Georgie looked up. Snowflakes landed softly on his eyelids and cheeks. The tree cover was dense; no stars or moon or other features of a night sky. And it was *freezing*.

"How do we get back!?" Apurva asked nervously.

Ore put a finger to his lips. "*Tranquilo!* Quiet! And stay close."

"We mustn't get caught," Edie whispered.

"Caught?" Roscoe asked. "What do you mean 'caught'? Are we trespassing?"

"We're in Altercocker territory," Ore whispered. "Rollie D and the Altercockers do *not* get along with people from Scatterplot. Rollie D is a legend, by the way, but not in a good way. I've never met her, and I don't intend to anytime soo—"

"The Alter*who?*" Apurva interrupted, hugging herself against the cold.

"Altercockers," Edie whispered. "*Meshugenas.* Bad people. The tribe Rollie D formed after she was exiled from Scatterplot. Avoid them at all costs."

If Georgie hadn't been so amazed at just having traveled through a portal to another world, he might have been sufficiently worried about a tribe of unfriendly exiles patrolling the forest.

"Take these," Edie whispered, handing out thick squares of fabric from Ore's backpack. "Wrap up." A luxurious warmth radiated from the fabric. Georgie slung the fabric over his shoulders and was soaked in a toasty heat.

"Warmkins," Ore said, shouldering his backpack, which had a glass box attached to the leather shoulder straps. Inside the glass compartment was an oil lamp with a slowly pumping mechanical arm and a tiny wicker flame. "Let's go catch our ride."

Roscoe, Apurva, and Georgie followed Edie and Ore single file through the deep snow, the light from Ore's backpack bobbing up and down. Georgie wasn't sure what sort of ride Ore intended to catch out here in the snowy forest, but something told him it wasn't a car . . . or anything else with four wheels and an engine, for that matter.

"Hey, Ore?" Georgie whispered. He needed more answers. He needed a *plan*. "What can you tell me about my dad?"

"Your dad?" Ore began quietly. "Well, for starters, your dad was a Scribe. So was your mother. Two of the best Scatterplot ever had. John and Penelope Summers. Absolute legends. The *good* kind."

Hearing his parents' names mentioned so casually—so *normally*—felt very weird. "And—"

"—what's a Scribe?" Ore asked.

"Yes," Georgie said, careful to keep his voice low.

"Glad you asked," Ore carried on in a whisper. "Scribes

are recorders of memories. There are many baronies in our world, sort of like how you have many cities in *your* world. Scatterplot is the name of the barony we're from. Each barony has seven active Scribes responsible for recording the memories of everyone under their jurisdiction. Scatterplot covers New York, New Jersey, and most of Connecticut. The Scribes record your memories on pages of whisperleaf and—"

"Wait a second," Apurva interrupted, exasperated. "Did you say, 'record memories'?"

"I did," Ore said, as if this all should have been quite clear.

"Like a memoir?" Apurva asked. "Or a diary? Our world has lots of those."

"We call them authors," Georgie added. "And they don't just write about themselves. We have blogs and magazines and comics."

"And fiction," Apurva added. "You never heard of J. K. Rowling? Or Jeff Kinney?"

Edie and Ore shook their heads slowly.

"What's fick-shun?" Ore asked. "Hey . . . I don't know that word." He sounded perturbed.

"Fiction is . . . you know, make-believe?" Apurva answered, sounding rather perturbed herself.

"Stuff that never happened," Roscoe added. "Stories!"

"*Stories!?*" Ore spat, sounding disgusted. "Your Scribes—sorry, your *authors*—write *pretend?*" The color had drained from his face. "Our Scribes don't write any of this fick-shun. Over here, it's super-dangerous. Not to mention, a serious crime."

Georgie, Apurva, and Roscoe exchanged confused looks.

"Because our Scribes aren't writing their *own* diaries," Edie said. "They're writing *yours*."

Georgie opened his mouth, then closed it again.

"All the important things that happen to you," Ore continued. "So you can *remember* it all! We don't deal in stories or make-believe or fick-shun. Our work is *muy importante*. If the Scribes stopped writing, or if their books were destroyed, you'd *literally* lose your mind as your memories disappeared from your head. *Poof!* Gone. You'd go crazy."

Georgie felt goosebumps crawling up his arms as he remembered what the woman in the garage had said. *He attacked a library two nights ago looking for the pen. Destroyed half a bookshelf before disappearing again. People are going to lose their minds.*

"*Your* Scribes record *our* memories?" Apurva asked suspiciously. "That sounds ridiculous for several obvious reasons, no offense."

"Agreed!" Roscoe said.

Ore chuckled. "You'll see."

They continued single file through the snow. Georgie wondered about Miss Ellipsis and Apurva's mother. Neither of them were from New York. "There was an attack on a library recently, wasn't there?"

Edie and Ore exchanged puzzled looks. "How do *you* know about that?" Ore asked. "Someone very bad is apparently looking for something very powerful and he attacked a neighboring barony just a few nights ago. He destroyed an entire *shelf* of Great Books, but Dullwick—Fumbluff's butler—caught me spying before I could get any more details."

I think I've met this very bad person and I think I know what he's looking for, Georgie thought, not sure if he should say as much.

"So, one of your libraries got attacked," Apurva began, "and my mother's memories were *actually* destroyed? And *that's* why she's been sick and forgetting who I am?"

"It's possible," Ore said. "Likely, even."

"That must be what happened to Miss Ellipsis!" Roscoe added with some excitement. "Oh man, this is creeping me out. Sincerely!"

Georgie kept walking, his feet crunching lightly in the snow, wondering about his own father. His father didn't often mumble nonsense, and he *never* forgot who Georgie was. He'd just always been . . . *weak.* What happened suddenly to Apurva's mother and Miss Ellipsis was not at all like that. And if his father's illness wasn't connected to Flint Eldritch's recent attack, what *was* it connected to?

The group of children had gone quiet, letting their thoughts and wonder swirl like the occasional gust of snow dislodging from the tree cover, until Georgie broke the silence. "What's an Aetherquill?"

"A *what?*" Edie and Ore asked at the same time.

"Aye-thir-quill," Georgie repeated, not really sure if he was even pronouncing it correctly. Eldritch was after it. His father was afraid of it. That strange woman *had* it.

"Don't know *that* word either," Ore sighed. "Something from your world?"

"No," Georgie said. "It's something from *your* world . . . at least, I think it is. I didn't get a good look at it, but I think it's some sort of pen. I think it's what the man who kidnapped my father was looking for."

A shadow passed between two trees twenty feet up ahead.

Georgie stopped short. Apurva and Roscoe stopped.

Edie and Ore stopped.

More shadows moved in the darkness. Just a shade blacker than the darkness between and beyond the tree trunks, but unmistakable: Someone—or *something*—was moving between the trees.

"An ambush!" Roscoe moaned. "Just like I said there would be!"

Snow crunched behind them. Snow crunched in front of them.

And then they came, stepping out from behind the tree trunks. Figures, silhouetted against the very outer rim of light from Ore's lantern, steam curling from their noses.

Georgie and his friends were surrounded.

𝍣𝍣𝍣 𝍣𝍣𝍣𝍣𝍣 𝍣𝍣𝍣𝍣

Chapter 9

Rollie D and the Altercockers

Georgie's fingers trembled as he reached into his pocket and palmed his slingshot's sanded handle. Four more marbles left. Good thing he hadn't given them all to Roscoe.

He'd missed Flint Eldritch back in his driveway.

He wouldn't miss again.

"*Stay back!*" Ore shouted, his voice no longer confident but quivering mightily. "We're not here to make trouble with Rollie D!"

A group of men and women came forward, out of the

shadows. They wore great coats of fur cinched together with leather shanks. Some wore vests made of cowhide, their meaty arms exposed.

Georgie swiveled his head. Nineteen. Nineteen men and women surrounded them.

Beyond the ring, Georgie noticed one figure standing back, still cloaked in darkness, draped in a coat longer and thicker than anyone else's.

"Go away!" Ore shouted, spinning around. He stuck two fingers in his mouth and blew. Two high-pitched notes rose straight through the tree cover and into the sky.

"Are you *whistling?*" Roscoe hissed. "You plan to get us outta here by *whistling?!*"

Ore paid no attention to Roscoe . . . he was staring up at the trees.

The figure who had not come forward fidgeted with something on their back and inched into the clearing, just enough for the light from Ore's lantern to illuminate long red hair and a fur cloak pinned above her chest.

Georgie's breath caught in his throat.

It was the woman from the garage. The woman who'd urged his dad to take the Aetherquill and give it to him. Was *that* Rollie D!? The legend? The criminal?

Ore whistled again, this time even louder.

But now there was a man stomping forward through the deep snow, his eyes locked on Roscoe. Georgie could see an ancient gun—a dueling pistol—holstered in a leather pouch on his waist.

"Roscoe!" Georgie shouted, but it was too late. The man

with the gun, whose speed was impossible for someone so stockily built, took two leaping steps toward Roscoe and grabbed him by the shoulders.

Roscoe screamed and flailed, his eyes insane with terror.

"Just cuz yer a Scribe means ye think yer better'n us?" the man holding Roscoe growled. He spun Roscoe around and held him like a hostage. "Ye think you can be out in our forest jus' walking about?"

Roscoe kicked and clawed at the Altercocker—but he was like a blade of grass trying to overpower a boulder.

"It's not *your* forest!" Edie bellowed. She was standing shoulder to shoulder with Apurva.

The ring of men and women murmured—some laughed, some shouted. Georgie heard all of it. Every intake of breath and every snotty nose sniff. He drew his slingshot and a metal marble from his pocket, dropped the marble in the leather cup, and drew back on the rubber band.

"Let him go!" He had his slingshot aimed at the man holding Roscoe.

Everyone went quiet.

The man holding Roscoe smiled. His teeth were dark and crooked, like a cobbled street.

"Ye can't make that shot!" the man exclaimed, but still he ducked his face behind Roscoe's head.

"No, sir!" Roscoe agreed eagerly. "You're absolutely right, sir! He most definitely cannot make that shot!" Roscoe stared wildly at Georgie: *You're not gonna shoot that thing at me, right pal?*

"Hey, Yooker!" a woman standing nearby cried. "Scribe boy got the drop on you, looks like it to me!"

This was met with laughter from some of the other women in the ring.

Yooker turned red in the face. "No Scribe kid gets the drop on Yooker Tenderfoot!" he said, pulling the gun from his leather holster. It was older than antique, with a long rusty barrel. Georgie thought his slingshot was probably a more reliable weapon.

Probably.

Yooker pointed the gun at Georgie—then, rethinking things a bit, aimed the barrel at Roscoe's head.

"Let him go," Georgie said again, his voice steady. Even though it was freezing, his hands were starting to sweat and his grip was starting to slip.

"Sir," Roscoe said, trying to crane his neck up to look Yooker the Altercocker in the eyes. "Let me apologize on behalf of my friend over there, sir. You see, he's not all there in the head, not to mention a pain in the neck and a blister on the butt—"

"SHUT YER MOUTH!" the Altercocker shouted, and then turned his attention back to Georgie. "You've got one more chance, boy," he waved his gun in the air. "Lower yer weapon, or I'll teach you a lesson or two." Yooker smiled, but his eyes showed just how nervous he was. "Scribe kids have a tendency to disappear fer good in yon forest."

Georgie lowered his slingshot, but just a drop, the rubber band still pulled tight.

"I lowered it," Georgie said.

"All the way," Yooker the Altercocker said.

"When you let my friend go."

And then Yooker made his move. He hoisted Roscoe off his feet and plunged backward toward the rest of the Altercockers.

He was fast, but not faster than Georgie Summers with a slingshot. Georgie adjusted his angle—just a millimeter—and released, the hand holding the slingshot steady as stone.

THIIIIIP-TWANG!

"*OOWWWWW!*" the Altercocker howled, holding up a bloody hand. "*ME FINGERS!*"

His gun was gone, buried somewhere in the snow. The top thirds of his pinky and ring fingers were also gone. Blood dripped from his hand, down his arm, and off his elbow in a steady trickle. Roscoe's mouth hung open. Yooker—now short two fingertips—still held Roscoe around the shoulders with a forearm as strong as a bundle of steel cables.

"*LOOK WACHOO'VE DONE! ME FINGERS!*"

Georgie loaded another marble and drew back. "Let him go!"

Another Altercocker rushed forward and grabbed Ore around the neck.

"Get off me!" Ore shouted and tried to kick the Altercocker in the shin, but the Altercocker, whose legs could be mistaken for tree trunks, barely noticed.

Edie shrieked and began shambling through the snow.

"Next one goes between your eyes," Georgie said calmly.

Then something sharp and cold pressed against his lower back.

"It's over," a woman said in his ear.

Georgie glanced to where the woman with the long red hair had been standing.

She was gone.

"Drop the slingshot," the woman said. "All the way. Do it now. Do it slowly."

The sharp tip of the blade pressed further into the skin of Georgie's back, drawing a pinprick of blood, and Georgie knew it was over. He lowered his slingshot and caught the marble in his hand.

Just then, a great rustling came from high in the trees. Growing louder until the sound was directly overhead. A high-pitched horse's whinny erupted from above.

"RETREAT!" yelled the woman standing behind Georgie. She grabbed him by the shoulders and yanked him backward.

As Georgie passed a tree trunk, his feet just skimming the snow, he realized he had made a mistake earlier. The scratches on the tree trunks were not marks left by harsh weather.

They were claw marks.

Chapter 10

The Pocket Horsemen

"**R**ETREAT! RETREAT!"

The Altercockers scattered, stumbling back into the trees.

Georgie looked up and saw two small animals leap off a branch high above.

Their heads were horse's heads, lozenge-shaped, with chestnut manes. But from the neck down, they looked like miniature gorillas, with leather chests and black fur carpeting their bodies. As they fell through the air, they *grew*. Their heads enlarged to the size of full-grown Shire horses. Huge sinuous muscles popped, bulging and rippling from their backs, legs, and arms. Their coarse black fur grew longer and thicker, and then—

BOOM! BOOM!

The two giant animals landed on all fours, shaking the forest floor. Bricks of snow dislodged and thumped like debris all around. Even on all fours both animals were taller than any of the men and women now shrieking and stumbling away.

"*Phiz!*" Ore screamed, still trying to free himself. "*Bugle! Here boys!*"

Saliva flung from their open mouths as the two creatures roared something ferocious. The larger one reared up on its hind legs and beat its heaving, leathern chest . . . then took off toward Ore, kicking up a violent spray of snow. Georgie was no expert on Earth's animals, but he was certain there was nothing at all like these creatures in *his* world.

The Altercocker forgot all about the Scribe boy and turned to run.

But before he took half a step, the animal swung one gigantic arm and sent the Altercocker flying—heading straight for one of the largest tree trunks in the forest.

The red-haired woman let go of Georgie's shoulders, unclipped her thick fur cloak, and threw it high into the air. Then, in an actual blur, both hands went over her shoulders and came back, one hand holding a giant wooden bow and the other hand already drawing two arrows across it.

She released.

The double arrows punctured her cloak and propelled it like a torpedo into the very tree trunk the Altercocker man was headed for. An instant later the Altercocker thunked against the furry cloak and fell fifteen feet into the deep snow.

She can't *possibly* have been that fast, Georgie thought, amazed. *And her aim . . . it was perfect! More than perfect. It was art.* The woman holstered her bow and ran to the man. She lifted his head and slapped his cheek, her sunset-orange hair drifting down in curls all around her.

The two giant creatures stood in front of Edie and Ore, their knuckles curled, chests rising and falling rapidly. They brayed low and slow, expelling twin jets of steam from their nostrils and bared their horse's teeth.

The eighteen remaining Altercockers stumbled into a messy group behind the woman with the red hair.

Yooker Tenderfoot still had Roscoe around the neck.

And, for once, Roscoe was speechless.

The woman drew another arrow from her quiver. "Children," she said, tapping the arrowhead against Roscoe's arm. "My name is Rollie D. If those Pocket Horsemen take one step forward"—she swung the arrow and pointed it at the two animals—"your friend here will sleep at the bottom of the river tonight."

Georgie reloaded his slingshot and drew back on the rubber band.

The woman twirled the arrow in her fingers, slipped her bow from the pouch and drew back, aiming between Georgie's eyes. "You're a good shot, dear, you really are. If you *land* your shot, my dying fingers release this arrow. So gamble on my aim and accuracy if you wish."

Georgie only needed one quick glance at the arrow still

impaling her cloak to realize she was right: It would be suicide. Georgie lowered his slingshot and Rollie D stowed her bow.

She squeezed Roscoe's arms and gave him a couple not-so-gentle smacks across the face. "He'll come with us. He's strong. Whines like a little child, but we'll straighten that out. We're going to need more warriors, and I'll make a warrior out of this one yet."

"*What!?*" Roscoe cried, struggling in Yooker's grip. "Miss, I *AM* a child! You . . . you don't *want* me! I couldn't blow my own nose if my brain was dynamite! I'm harmless, I swear! Tell her, Georgie! Tell her I don't need to be punished! *Sincerely!*"

But Georgie was staring at the woman who stood in his garage yesterday. The woman who almost seemed like his father's *friend.* And if they *were* friends, maybe she knew something about what had happened to his dad.

Georgie shuffled in place, no longer even noticing the snow and ice water pooling in his sneakers. "I saw you. *Yesterday.* Talking to my fa—"

Swifter than a hawk, Rollie was suddenly in front of Georgie, a hand clamped tightly over his mouth. She backed Georgie up against a nearby tree, her face inches from his. Her chest rose and fell, and Georgie could see a thick gold chain around her neck glinting in the moonlight.

"*Quiet, boy,*" Rollie breathed.

Georgie could feel her warm breath on his face.

"I was never in your garage, *Georgie Summers.* Do you understand?"

Georgie didn't need to be asked twice. He nodded with his eyes.

"You need to go see Fumbluff," Rollie continued, her voice a whisper, but not any less commanding. "You'll be tested. Those tests are important. *Crucial.*" Rollie took her hand off Georgie's mouth. "Now, listen closely kid," Rollie breathed, her eyes darting this way and that, presumably to make sure no one was listening. "Fumbluff will have a plan. But there is never just one way to solve a problem. Come find me before you decide to do something stupid."

Georgie drew in a breath but Rollie stilled his questions with a finger pressed over Georgie's lips. She shook her head gently. "No talking. Get tested. Then come find me." Even in the freezing cold, her last words sent icicles running up Georgie's spine. *"You've never met your full father."*

And just like that, Rollie stepped backward through the snow, her eyes locked on Georgie's, until she was gathered with her people.

"Let our friend go!" Apurva shouted in Rollie's direction, but Rollie ignored her.

Georgie's mind was blazing as he hurried over to Roscoe. *'You've never met your full father?' What was that supposed to mean? What tests am I supposed to take!? How do you know my father? Where are you taking Roscoe!?*

"Don't leave me!" Roscoe panicked, struggling uselessly in Yooker Tenderfoot's grip. "I mean it, Summers!"

Georgie tried to think. The Altercockers didn't seem very safe *or* very nice. Edie and Ore said to avoid them at all costs. But his father clearly trusted Rollie D. It sounded crazy, but they really did sound like *friends*.

And Rollie, for some reason—

(don't do anything stupid)

—wanted Georgie to find her.

"Go with Rollie," Georgie said finally. "It's gonna be okay."

He knew how hollow that promise must have sounded to Roscoe. They hadn't been through the portal for an hour and already they were splitting up.

Roscoe's jaw dropped. "Gonna be . . . *okay?* You think I'm the village idiot you cabbage-brained *wet!?* Nothing's gonna be OKAY! Do NOT leave me with these—"

"Roscoe!" Georgie exclaimed. "Shut up for a second, would you? I think you can trust Rollie D. I'm going—"

"You *think!?*"

"—*I'm going to find you.*" Georgie glanced at Rollie, then back at Roscoe. "And *her.*"

Roscoe got quiet and stared Georgie straight in the eyes while he spat into his palm. "Swear it."

Georgie shook hands. "I swear it on my mother's grave."

Yooker pulled Roscoe back further into the shadows, following Rollie D and the rest of the Altercockers.

"She's going to turn you into a warrior, Roscoe!" Georgie called, although he could barely see the outline of Roscoe's face anymore. "Lieutenant Harris! For real!"

For a moment there was no reply, then drifting from somewhere deep between the trees came Roscoe's voice.

"Find *meeeee!*" His voice trailed off as the Altercockers drew further and further away.

A minute later, there was no sign of the Altercockers ever having been there in the first place. And now that Roscoe was really gone, Georgie wasn't sure at all if he'd done the right thing. As tough as Roscoe was, he was probably terrified. Georgie would be too, if *he'd* been dragged away by a gang of vicious strangers in the middle of the night through an unknown forest of untold depth.

"Was that Rollie D!?" Ore asked aloud.

Edie was livid. "Ore! We're . . . going . . . to be . . . in SO MUCH TROUBLE! We brought TWO extra kids back through the portal and now the Altercockers have one of them!? What a mess!"

"But . . . was that Rollie D!?"

"I can't believe this!" Edie cried. "I can't!"

"That . . . *that was Rollie D!*" Ore shouted. "We saw her! Did you see that shot? She's a legend!"

"She's a kidnapper!" Edie shot back. "And a criminal!"

Apurva, who was still trembling, raised her voice. "What about Roscoe!? *Criminal?* Georgie, what *was* that? What did Rollie say to you? We have to save Roscoe! What are they going to do to him!?"

Ore cleared his throat. "They won't kill him."

"Oh!" Apurva blurted. "Well, *that's* very reassuring!"

"What do you suppose she meant by 'needing warriors'?" Ore asked Edie.

"I haven't a clue, Ore!" Edie shot back. She patted the smaller of the two Pocket Horsemen. "This is Bugle." She gestured to Georgie and Apurva. "You two will ride him. Ore and I'll ride Phiz." She looked up at the sky. "I just can't believe this mess!"

"I'm sorry about your friend, Georgie," Ore added, "but we still need to get you to Fumbluff and the Scribes, like, an hour ago."

The creature's muscles flexed and tensed as Georgie swung his leg over its back. Georgie buried his hands into the tufts of tangled black fur and found a knob of bone with a comfortable pocket for his fingers. Apurva swung up behind him, and when she was barely steady, Bugle reared up.

Edie kicked her heels, sending both Pocket Horsemen charging through the snow and trees.

Georgie closed his eyes. The cold air rushed past him, hugged him, slapped him, and stung his cheeks with its cold, dark palms. He felt Apurva tighten her hold around his waist and bury her head between his shoulder blades.

He thought about Roscoe, wondering if he'd be okay. If something happened to Roscoe, Georgie would never forgive himself.

They rode through the forest for what felt like an hour—not nearly enough time for Georgie to process or make sense of all the miraculous and dangerous and downright strange events that had taken place since the portal opened in his garage. Then the two Pocket Horsemen exploded from the trees at the same time, cutting a streaking path across a snowy plane, until after a while, the Pocket Horseman's knuckles protruded from the thinning snow and came to a full stop.

Edie, Ore, Georgie, and Apurva dismounted. They were standing at the crown of a hill where the ground descended steeply before leveling out into a dirt road lined with miniature houses far below. The road wound into the center of a small city, where light twinkled brightly against the night sky.

"Downtown Scatterplot." Ore brushed his blond bangs away from his eyes. He pointed to the sparkling village and handed Georgie a pair of golden binoculars. "Where we live. Have a look."

Through the binoculars, the city, which had looked like a thousand flickering lights before, was now rich with detail. Cobblestone streets wound through tightly packed buildings, some made of stone with iron balconies, others made of wood and clay with roofs that looked like castle towers. A steep ridge rose behind the city, and beyond it, the peaks of a mountain range punctured the dark purple sky like daggers.

Georgie panned the binoculars up a stone staircase carved into the ridge and followed a dirt road until it ended at a set of iron gates.

Behind the gates stood a castle.

It had at least nine chimneys.

"The picture of my mother," Georgie whispered, lowering the binoculars. "In my garage. That's the castle she was standing in front of."

Chapter 11

The Road to Corrigendum

Georgie handed the binoculars back to Ore, letting this all sink in. His mother had been here, maybe was *from* here. His father, too. What had he said in the car? *We're not from here. Not from this world.* Why didn't his father ever *tell* him about this world of Scribes and Altercockers, hovering just behind a magical portal in their garage? And why, all of a sudden, after Rollie D had paid him a visit, had he decided that they needed to go to Scatterplot?

Once the Pocket Horsemen had enough of the feather grass sprouting from the snow, they kneeled low for their riders, and soon got moving again, walking like silverback gorillas over the brow of the hill.

"So . . ." Georgie wondered aloud, once they were past the steepest part of the decline. "Who's Fumbluff? The guy you're taking us to?"

"Our Editor in Chief!" Edie exclaimed excitedly, as if that was supposed to mean anything to Georgie or Apurva. "Leader of the seven Senior Scribes! Dean of the Seminary! Master of events at the Coronation Ceremony!"

The ground below leveled out, and now they passed houses on either side of the narrow dirt road. Some were shanties with wooden porches and some were larger cottages with second-floor balconies and colorful glass windows.

"Look up there," Edie continued, and Georgie followed her finger above and beyond the looming ridge surrounding the village of clustered buildings and windy hills. At least a mile away, he could see the darkened outline of a domed building, not unlike the Bridget Planetarium. Only this dome was much, much bigger.

"That's the Seminary," Ore said. "Where the apprentices study." He pointed beyond the domed roof. "Can you see the tower?"

Georgie thought he could make out the outline of a tall, narrow tower rising into the clouds.

"The Cathedral," Ore said. "Where the Scribes *write*."

Georgie wondered what it was like to be a Scribe, to write memories. And what if a Scribe made a mistake? Is that why he sometimes forgot where he put his slingshot sandpaper?

"The Great Books travel from the Seminary all the way to the Great Library," Edie said, back in her tour-guide-with-better-places-to-be voice. "Every few batches go to Fumbluff for an edit. What we call a once-over. You know when something is on the tip of your tongue . . . just out of reach—"

"And *blam!*" Ore interjected. "You remember it later? That's Fumbluff catching a typo! A misspelling, or bad grammar, stuff like that. *All* the Great Books eventually wind up in Scatterplot's Library where they stay forever. Guarded and protected. *Never* to be edited or altered."

Georgie looked at Apurva and was pleased to see the expression on her face was exactly the same blend of confusion and amazement that he felt. He was happy she was here. At the first intersection, the dirt road became a cobblestone street, and the buildings grew more tightly packed. Cast iron lanterns polka-dotted the main drag in soft candlelight.

On their left, they passed a barn with a sign that read: GAMMER'S GLASSWERX. Through the window Georgie could see glass bowls, pitchers, and water pipes hanging upside down from their ears. A wooden placard nailed to the archway above the door on the next building read: TODD'S TOTEMS. A number of handcrafted totems stood on the covered porch. The biggest one was a replica of a Pocket Horseman with snow accumulating on its ears and nose. Then they passed a two-story building with a bluish-green door. Carved into a wooden signpost hanging from the second-floor balcony was: STONE'S

BLACKSMITHS, BLADESMITHS, AND PROBLEM SOLVERS.

"We live up this hill," Ore said, pointing past the blacksmith's shop with its multicolored shingled roof. Atop which hill Edie and Ore's house was situated ranked on the very bottom of Georgie's scale of Important Things, maybe even less important than missing Miss Ellipsis's class tomorrow, which itself was of literally zero importance. Rescuing his father was important. Finding this Fumbluff guy and getting some answers was important.

They continued north through the city, until the crowded buildings thinned out and the street widened into a bumpy dirt road. The giant ridge loomed over them, like a colossal stage curtain of vertical rock. A short while later, Ore brought Phiz to an abrupt halt and slid smoothly off the creature's back.

"We gotta huff it by foot from here," Ore said. He rolled up the sleeves on his velvety pajama top then gave Georgie and Apurva a hand dismounting Bugle. They were at the base of the stairs now, which were much steeper than they had appeared from a distance. "Too steep for the Pocket Horsemen to carry you . . . only expert riders can handle the staircase." He gave Bugle and Phiz matching pats on their matching rumps, and the giant creatures shrank to the size of monkeys no larger than a house cat with a mini horse's head and sprang nimbly up the first few stairs.

"I don't think I'll *ever* get used to seeing that," Apurva said wondrously, then grabbed Ore's hand and hoisted herself onto the first ledge. Halfway up the staircase, Georgie's legs and lungs were on fire, and he had to stop to catch his breath. Roscoe probably would have flicked his ear and skipped right ahead, calling him a french-fried couch potato or something like that.

But Roscoe *wasn't* here. He was with Rollie D now.

They continued up in silence—even Apurva sounded winded now—until Georgie took a giant step and his foot came down flat in front of him, nearly knocking him off balance. Far below, the lights from the city twinkled like a clockface.

Edie and Ore were a little way ahead at a roundabout illuminated by an enormous half-moon hanging low in the sky. Three wooden arrows attached to a signpost in the center of the roundabout pointed in different directions. TO THE GREAT LIBRARY: TOURS MEET AT HAMPSHIRE HUMP (ROUGH ROAD, WATCH YOUR STEP!) was carved into the sign pointing right. TO THE SEMINARY was carved into the arrow pointing to the left. Georgie squinted in the direction of the Seminary and could make out a white tent partially constructed in the Seminary's courtyard, off to the side of the giant dome.

"For the Coronation Ceremony," Ore said, pointing to the tent. "Remember, it's tomorrow, right? It's a *biiiiig* tent. Hard to tell from here, but you'll see. Every Scatterplotter comes. It's a big deal, you bet."

The third arrow, which pointed straight ahead toward a wide dirt road, read: TO CORRIGENDUM. FREE MEALS FOR ALL TRAVELERS. Georgie could see the very tips of the nine chimneys from here. And it was on that road, which cut through fields of feather grass, that they mounted Bugle and Phiz once again and continued through the nightscape until they reached Corrigendum's iron gates.

The mansion rose like a mountain. Georgie stared up at Corrigendum as armed guards, clad head to toe in metal armor, rolled the heavy gates open. The roof was steep and shingled and curved balustrades made of stone underlined arched windows. He wondered if his parents ever stood on the same patch of ground currently below his own two feet. It was a weird thought. It was also a weird feeling.

Halfway across the mansion's plaza, a shooting star with a glittering blue trail zoomed through the air, passing between two chimneys before curving sharply out of sight.

"Books in transit!" Ore shouted excitedly.

Two more sparkling bundles of books—yes, now Georgie could see they were humongous *books*—shot across the sky, traveling at high speed through a network of semi-translucent pipes.

"What in the world—" Georgie whispered.

Georgie followed the crisscrossing, snaking pipes in and out of moonlight as the books in their tubes wove around craggy outcroppings all the way to the high tower behind the Seminary's dome, a great distance away. Wood beams supported the pipes like the arms of buried giants rising up from the ground.

"You think we *carry* all those heavy bundles of whisperleaf?" Ore asked.

Georgie wasn't thinking at all about *how* the books traveled from the Seminary to the Library. He was thinking about how, at least according to Edie and Ore, these books contained the living memories of all the people in his world. *His* memories. Roscoe's and Apurva's memories. The idea itself was crazy. *Crazier than a soup sandwich,* as Roscoe would have said.

Georgie and Apurva followed Edie and Ore up a short marble staircase, and now Georgie could hear snippets of chatter and the muffled sound of a piano. Shuffling blocks of color moved about through two windows opaqued with frost on either side of the mansion's double doors.

Butterflies swarmed in Georgie's stomach.

Edie and Ore pulled the double doors open and the chatter and the music were all of a sudden very loud indeed.

Georgie stood there, his heart pounding in his ears, until Apurva grabbed his hand, and together they stepped inside the mansion.

Chapter 12

The Aetherquill Chronicles

The chatter stopped.

Heads turned.

"I did it!" Ore proclaimed, his voice echoing across an enormous entrance hall surrounded by second- and third-story balconies. The floor was a gleaming checkerboard of black and white marble beneath a chandelier made of emerald gemstones.

Edie was outraged. "*You* did it!?"

"*We* did it," Ore corrected. "*Curtsy*, Edie. Come on! We brought Georgie Summers! Through the portal!"

Edie didn't curtsy.

Twenty or thirty pairs of eyes stared at the four children—some from the balconies, some from a grand staircase, some from fur sofas flanking a fireplace where a steady, healthy fire burned.

Georgie's cheeks prickled, defrosting. He scanned the place for exit routes but only saw more torchlit corridors and arched doorways leading further into the mansion.

"Georgie?"

A man with receding brown hair and a gray robe approached. His robe had a long tear down his right arm, repaired with red thread. He smiled and grabbed Georgie's hand.

"Georgie, son of John and Penelope?"

The man put a hand on Georgie's cheek as if to confirm he was real.

"I'm Dullwick Ratriot, Corrigendum's caretaker and personal assistant to our Editor in Chief. I speak for all of Scatterplot when I say thank you for being here!"

Apurva cleared her throat very loudly. "And I'm Apurva Aluwhalia," Apurva said. "Also of the New York . . . barony."

Dullwick tapped his throat three times. "A friend of John's son?"

"Yes," Apurva said with great confidence. "Georgie and I are friends."

Apurva looked at Georgie. "Right?"

Georgie nodded enthusiastically, then turned back to Dullwick Ratriot and the crowd of robed men and women. "Does anyone know what happened to my father?"

A gigantic man—taller and wider than any of the

Altercockers—shuffled into the entrance hall through a doorway near the fireplace. He wore an emerald robe trimmed with copper and had a messy shock of black hair above a round, clean-shaven face.

He tapped his throat three times. "Scribe Fenton! One of the Seven!" His voice was deep and emphatic. "But everyone calls me Fenton . . . or Charles!"

"Fenton!" Ore cried. "We did it! Just like I told you we would!"

Fenton gave Ore a noogie, then thrust a hand the size of a couch cushion out to Georgie.

"Good to meet you, boy! I'm sorry about your old man!"

He released Georgie's hand, which had disappeared inside Fenton's pulverizing grip. Georgie shook his wrist and wiggled his fingers, happy that at least *someone* here knew something about his father.

"You alright, boy?" Charles Fenton then turned to Apurva. "Is he alright?"

"Yeah," Georgie said. "Good to meet you, too—"

"Speak up!" Fenton grumbled, before wiggling a pinky finger the size of a pickle in his ear. "I'm hard of hearing. Only one good ear. This side."

"NICE TO MEET YOU!" Georgie shouted.

"Not that loud! I'm not deaf!"

Ore cracked up at that.

Georgie exhaled. "I'm trying to find my father. He was kidnapped by . . ." Georgie blanked on the name. God, why would he blank on the name at a time like this?

"Eldritch?" Charles Fenton grumbled, as if just saying the name left a nasty taste in his mouth. "*Flint* Eldritch?"

Georgie nodded. "Do you know where he is? Where my *father* is?"

The questions spilled from Georgie like a faucet.

"What does Flint want from my father? And what does he want with the Aetherquill? AY-THUR-QUILL? Rollie D wanted—"

Georgie snapped his mouth shut, remembering what Rollie D told him not too long ago in the forest: *I was never in your garage, Georgie Summers.*

"Flint Eldritch was looking for it, I mean," Georgie corrected.

The grand entrance hall erupted in crisscrossing conversation. Georgie looked from Apurva to Edie to Ore, then back to the crowd beneath the chandelier.

"Can *anyone* tell me what's going on!?" Georgie shouted.

A single voice rang out, from nowhere and from everywhere.

"I CAN."

It was the piercing voice of authority.

At once, Corrigendum fell silent.

A man stepped into the entrance hall from an arched corridor lined with torches. A short man, with deep black skin and a prickly gray beard. A black topcoat fell to his ankles and he held an overturned velvet top hat in front of him.

The cavernous space had gone so quiet that the only sound now was the occasional crackle from the fireplace.

The man with the top hat smiled warmly at Georgie and Apurva. "You two must be ravenous, yes? That means very hungry. My name is Fumbluff. I know what happened to your father." His blue eyes blazed like an ocean of wisdom. "And I will tell you all about the Aetherquill. We've prepared dinner."

Fumbluff turned to Edie and Ore. "Impressive, the both of you. Your work tonight. Impressive indeed."

Edie and Ore positively beamed.

"Back home now," Fumbluff continued. "A sentry will walk with you."

"Aww, come on, Fumbluff!" Ore cried. "Let us stay! We want to stay! At least for dinner . . . Edie—tell him you want to stay!"

Fumbluff shook his head. "Your very first Coronation Ceremony is tomorrow—"

"And I can't friggin' wait!" Ore exclaimed, his eyes alight. "We can help set up the tent tomorrow after school, right? *Right!?* Promise, Fumbluff! *Promise!?*"

Fumbluff chuckled again in his rusty hiccups.

Crestfallen, Ore gave Georgie and Apurva a handshake. "It was a pleasure making your acquaintance." He tipped his invisible cowboy hat. "*Nadobranich.* Good night."

Edie gave them each a hug, then at the door, turned to Apurva. "It was nice getting to hang out with a girl for a change." She smiled. "Been a while since I had someone actually smart to talk to."

Ore chased her down the front staircase, the guard trying to keep up in an awkward shamble in his metal armor.

Once the mansion's doors were bolted shut, Fumbluff turned to address the Scribes and apprentices, rubbing his prickly beard. "As most of you know by now, John Summers was captured by Flint Eldritch this morning. And"—Fumbluff glanced at Georgie and took a deep, rattling breath—"*if* Georgie Summers is a Scribe, if he could read *and* write—yes, writing is the key—then Georgie might be the last person in this world *or* his who can stop Eldritch. He will need the Aetherquill, and because of"—Fumbluff paused again, this time looking straight into Georgie's eyes—"because of Georgie's connection to the pen, he is the only one left who can actually deploy its power to defeat Eldritch."

Fumbluff raised his hands, his velvet robes dangling handsomely from his wrists. "Yes, this is a very serious thing." Fumbluff looked at Georgie and his eyes were filled with a deep and inexplicable sorrow. "John Summers was my dear friend. *Is* my dear friend, yes? I don't make this suggestion lightly, nor do I propose this plan without having agonized over its terrible implications."

Make *what* decision lightly!? Georgie wondered. *What* plan? What did Fumbluff mean by "terrible implications"?

"If Flint Eldritch obtains the Aetherquill," Fumbluff continued, "it will be a catastrophe orders of magnitude greater than the destruction of a thousand libraries or a million *kef* of whisperleaf."

Some of the apprentices gasped, but Fumbluff continued, addressing Georgie directly, his voice not quite *rising* but somehow filling the mansion's entrance hall entirely.

"The Aetherquill is indeed a pen, yes? But it is not just any pen. The Aetherquill is a magical artifact of unbelievable power, from a realm even higher than Scatterplot. But an artifact from a higher realm must *never* be used in a lower realm. It's too dangerous. Too unpredictable."

Fumbluff began walking slowly across the marble entranceway. Georgie and Apurva exchanged a glance, then followed without having to be asked.

"Imagine, Georgie," Fumbluff continued, "installing an automobile battery inside a toy. Possible? Yes. Wise? No. The toy would explode. Imagine using a magnifying glass to amplify the heat of the sun to light something on fire. A sudden release of violent energy." He paused and looked at Georgie. "The Aetherquill is a high-energy artifact, and activating its magic in a lower realm—*our* realm—can lead to dangerous and unpredictable ripple effects. Do you understand, Georgie?"

Georgie nodded slowly. The Aetherquill was a magical pen from a higher realm. Too dangerous to use in Scatterplot.

"But what does the Aetherquill actually *do*?" Georgie asked, staring unblinkingly at Fumbluff. "What's its . . . magic?"

They passed through a stone archway into a torchlit corridor. Georgie was only distantly aware of the Scribes and apprentices trailing behind.

"The Scribes of Scatterplot record things that *actually* happened, yes?"

"The Obeys told us about that," Apurva said, raising her hand reflexively, forgetting she was no longer in

Bridget Elementary. "The people of Earth"—she looked at Georgie—"*us* . . . that's how we're able to remember things, at least according to Edie and Ore. But I always thought that our *brains* store our memories in the hippo-campus, which is located in the temporal lobe under the cerebral cortex."

Fumbluff chuckled, his eyes bright and blue and warm. "Yes, yes," Fumbluff said softly. "The scientists in your world certainly have sensational theories." He turned serious again as he continued down the long corridor. "If our Scribes stopped writing . . . if the Great Books were destroyed . . . the people in your world would forget *everything*. But Flint Eldritch is after an even worse type of destruction. While the Scribes use their sacred power to preserve the what-was, the Aetherquill has the power to write the might-have-beens, the could-bes, the never-weres."

Georgie remembered what Ore said about fiction. That it was dangerous. That telling made-up stories and writing pretend was a crime. "So the Aetherquill can write . . . a lie?"

"Worse than a lie, Georgie," Fumbluff said carefully. "To the recipient of the Aetherquill's words—its *fiction*—the lie is a *truth*. A false truth so powerful that it twists and per-verts the very lens through which you would see the world."

"Like misinformation?" Apurva asked. "Or fake news?"

Fumbluff laughed again. "Very much like that, Apurva Aluwhalia. A cerebral invasion. A mind virus . . . with a life of its own, quite literally."

Fumbluff turned back to Georgie. "Suppose you believed that mirrors weren't *just* reflections, but actual windows into a darker world. A world where a shadowy version of you lurks, waiting for a chance to grab you and pull you in. You'd never look into one. You'd run past every mirror like your pants were on fire. Even though, in *truth*, mirrors are just . . . reflections."

As they approached the end of the corridor, a wave of delicious smells hit Georgie hard, making his stomach grumble loudly. He hadn't realized until now how *hungry* he was.

"I think I get it," Georgie said. "The Aetherquill can make someone believe something that never happened. A made-up story. But they'll believe it as if it were true. As if they . . . actually *remembered* it?"

"Quite right!" Fumbluff exclaimed.

"Okay," Georgie continued, his eyebrows scrunched. "But what's, like, the *plan*? How will the Aetherquill save my dad from Eldritch? Why does Eldritch even *want* it?"

Fumbluff paused at the archway, the dim light from the corridor casting him in half-shadow. "To understand what Flint wants, Georgie, you have to understand where Flint *came* from, yes? What he *is*." Fumbluff closed his eyes. "When you were just a baby, Georgie, a grave error was made. *The Aetherquill was used on your father.* A fiction meant to protect your father unleashed a catastrophe. The Aetherquill's power, wielded in this lower realm, split your father in two and gave birth to a dark entity."

Fumbluff's eyes snapped open, and a dreadful current pulsed through Georgie's entire body.

"Flint Eldritch," Fumbluff whispered, "is the other half of your father."

Chapter 13

Shadow and Light

It was as if Georgie's ears and brain were working on separate tracks. From miles away, Fumbluff's voice said, "Come eat. We shall council. Talk. Palaver."

Flint Eldritch is the other half of your father.

Georgie wasn't sure if he believed what Fumbluff had said. It sounded completely crazy. Wackier than a duck on roller skates—another Roscoe favorite. But Georgie was here, in another universe, by way of a portal in his garage. Was what Fumbluff said about Eldritch being one half of his father crazier than *that?*

"Georgie? Are . . . are you okay?" Apurva's hand was on his shoulder. "You don't *look* okay. Which is okay, by the way."

What had Rollie D whispered back in the forest? *You've never met your full father.* Up until just now, Georgie thought she meant he hadn't met his *real* father. But that's not what she said, was it? She had said "your *full* father." He nodded his head numbly and dragged his feet along the polished floor as the group shuffled into Corrigendum's dining room.

"Whoa," Apurva gasped.

The dining table was longer than a bowling alley and packed with heaping mountains of food. Bowls of baked potatoes smothered in meat sauce and gravy. Juicy corned-beef roasts in earthenware bowls. Fresh loaves of bread piled high, surrounded by copper bowls of sugar, cinnamon, and maple syrup. Chicken and turkey and duck, their skins perfectly crisp. Meat cobblers with rivulets of steam rising through the scores in their crusts. Grilled-cheese sandwiches stacked on butcher boards next to wedges of fresh butter.

And the desserts! Custard and jelly donuts, chocolate banana pops, strawberry shortcake with fresh strawberries the size of kiwis, and blueberry pies dusted with sugar.

Georgie heard the scraping of dining room chairs as the Scribes took their seats. Georgie had never been at a meal with so many people in his entire life. Come to think of it, Georgie couldn't remember a single dinner when it wasn't just him and his dad. It was Georgie who usually cooked (nothing like the delicacies spread out before him right now), and even though Georgie was a terrible chef, his father would always rate his cooking five stars. When

Georgie told his dad how he got suspended for bringing his slingshot to class, his father just smiled and nodded. There were never any punishments, for *anything,* something Roscoe argued was extremely unfair. But it was true.

"Here, Georgie," Apurva said, grabbing Georgie two steaming grilled-cheese sandwiches with a pair of wooden tongs. She took Georgie by the elbow and helped him into one of the velvet dining room chairs.

He looked up, past the Scribes sitting across the table. Flickering torches lined the dining room walls, casting shadows that danced darkly against the stone. The flames burned steadily, but the shadows kept changing form, dancing like wild things along the wall, trying to reach each other but never quite making it.

You've never met your full father.

Light and shadow, Georgie thought, feeling his nerves tingle. *Shadow and light.*

"Georgie, you need to eat," Apurva said. "You look pale." Then she turned to Fumbluff, pulling her long black hair into a tight pony with the blue scrunchie that'd been on her wrist. "You said the Aetherquill makes someone believe a lie as if it were true, right? So how did the Aetherquill cause Georgie's father to be . . ." Apurva scrunched her eyebrows together, " . . . to be split into two people?"

The Scribe sitting beside Fenton had silver hair that fell to his shoulders and deep-set eyes. "Blaze Nelson," he said, peering across the table at Apurva and Georgie. "One of the Seven. May your journey here not be in vain." He tapped his throat three times. "The Aetherquill was used on John Summers here, in Scatterplot, a lower realm than the realm the Aetherquill came from, releasing a level of energy that the atmosphere here cannot tolerate."

Charlie Fenton spread a napkin the size of a towel across his lap. "And because of that, when the Aetherquill's magic struck your dad, it didn't just *confuse* him . . . it—"

"The Aetherquill's fiction," Fumbluff began, his blue eyes shining like an ocean, "its *story* . . . didn't fully stick in your father's mind." Fumbluff fingered the velvet brim of his top hat. "Part of him *knew* the Aetherquill's story wasn't true . . . and that mental contradiction tore him apart." Fumbluff sighed and cupped his wrinkled hands together. "We're all made up of two different parts, Georgie—"

"Shadow and light," Georgie said, peeling his eyes away from the flickering torchlight and staring at Fumbluff.

"Shadow and light," Fumbluff repeated in a whisper. "Quite right. The two powerful forces inside each of us." Fumbluff pushed his chair back, stood, and walked to the far wall. He took one of the torches from its holder and held it in his outstretched arm. "Light." Fumbluff waved the torch in an arc and the yellowish-red flames whooshed and flickered. "Light is good. Light is love. But what is light's *purpose*?" Fumbluff held his other hand out in front of the flame, making a shadow that looked like a rabbit on the wall behind him. "Light's purpose is to control its shadow. To direct its shadow-energy for good." He rearranged his fingers and the shadow rabbit turned into a bird. "When light controls the shadow, we are in balance." Fumbluff wiggled his fingers and the bird's wings flapped.

"But if light *loses* its shadow . . ." Fumbluff shook the torch violently. The shadow bird was gone. In its place was a horrifying black shadow-creature, with long tentacles licking up to the ceiling. "Then the light becomes purposeless, and the shadow grows stronger." Fumbluff replaced the torch in its holder. "Flint Eldritch is what became of the shadow torn from your father when the Aetherquill's magic struck him." Fumbluff took his seat again at the head of the table. "Your father remained, but his light was diminished, like a book missing half of its pages."

"Oh my God," Apurva said, and Georgie had to quickly slide his chair over as Apurva slumped into the one beside him. Georgie sat there, not wanting to believe a word Scatterplot's Editor in Chief was saying. But a deeper part of his mind knew Fumbluff was right. His father had never been *sick* . . . he was just, what? What had Fumbluff called it . . . *diminished.*

"When Flint Eldritch grabbed Georgie's father," Apurva continued, "Georgie said he saw his dad flicker." Apurva looked over at Georgie. "Isn't that what you said? That you were able to see *through* your father?"

"Yeah," Georgie confirmed, "and right after they went through the portal . . . onto that beach . . . I couldn't see my dad at all."

"Like he just vanished," Apurva finished, reaching over a vat of fresh fruit for a slice of meat pie.

Fumbluff brought his ancient hands together. "Flint Eldritch didn't kidnap John Summers. Flint Eldritch *absorbed* John Summers."

Goosebumps sprouted up and down Georgie's arms.

"The shadow has become stronger than the light." Fumbluff rubbed the grooves in his forehead and sighed. "And I fear . . . I fear—"

Georgie turned to Fumbluff. "Is he dead?"

"No," Fumbluff answered without hesitation. "Flint Eldritch wants the Aetherquill, and he believes your father will lead him to it."

"*Why* does Flint want the Aetherquill?" Georgie asked, feeling relieved that his father was alive, at least according to Fumbluff. But there was something behind Fumbluff's sparkling blue eyes that gave Georgie a sense of unease. He seemed sad. Gloomy, even. Fumbluff had said a lot of things, but what he *hadn't* said was how they were going to save Georgie's father.

Fumbluff clasped his hands together and exhaled a shaky breath. "If Flint obtains the Aetherquill, he will use it to create a world filled with shadow creatures just like him, in this world *and* in your world, driven only by guilt and pain, as Eldritch himself is. Shadow-monsters torn from their bodies—torn from their *light*. He'll destroy everyone you've ever known and loved, and their fate will be worse than death."

Georgie felt his chest rising and falling. He thought about the kids in his class. Even the idiot bully with the ugly pigtail. He thought about poor old Lorenzo, his barber on Main Street. He thought about Roscoe and Apurva.

Georgie leaned forward, his hands curled into fists. "Why didn't you guys keep my father safe? My dad was one of you, wasn't he? What was he doing in New York?"

Charlie Fenton cleared a great glob of phlegm from his throat. "After the Aetherquill tore your father in half," Fenton began, wiping a smear of gravy from his chin, "he couldn't be a Scribe anymore. He was getting weaker and weaker every day. He couldn't write, and his reading abilities were fading rapidly. The only thing that seemed to wake him up was holding you in his arms. We knew Flint would come back looking for your father, so we hid you and your dad in New York, where we hoped Flint would never find you." Fenton paused, looking down at his plate and fiddling with his silverware. "It was my idea."

"But you were wrong," Georgie said, feeling his cheeks getting hot. "You were wrong! Eldritch *found* my father."

Fenton kept his gaze downward, his messy black hair falling over his eyes. "I was wrong, indeed." He tapped his throat three times. "I'm sorry, boy."

Georgie drew in breath, but Fumbluff raised a hand. "You want answers, yes? What happened all those years ago. You want the backstory, as they say, you—"

"I want to know how to save my dad," Georgie said.

Fumbluff sighed. "We have a plan, Georgie, son of John. Yes? But first, you must eat. I insist."

Georgie took a bite of his grilled-cheese sandwich and felt the cheese oozing out of the sourdough bread, which was soft on the inside and crunchy on the outside. It was the best grilled-cheese sandwich he'd ever tasted by a mile. Georgie took another bite before he swallowed the first. He'd forgotten how starving he was.

FOOOOOMP!

A stack of four humongous books wrapped in blue velvet appeared in a large compartment in the dining room wall. One moment Fumbluff's top hat was in his hands, and the next moment it was on his head. If Rollie D's shooting hands were a blur, Fumbluff was so fast it looked like a magic trick.

"Ahhh," Fumbluff smiled, pushing his plate away to make room for the books. "Thank you kindly, Dullwick." Georgie hadn't even noticed Dullwick Ratriot, the butler, standing in the shadows all along. Georgie watched him closely as he carried the books from the compartment and placed them down in front of Fumbluff.

Their spines were stamped with strange gold lettering.

Slowly, Fumbluff opened one of the books and thumbed its pages, which were covered edge to edge in tightly scrawled lines of figures, patterns, and dots. Here and there a letter or word was smudged and written over.

"A Scribe wrote all of that?" Apurva asked.

Fumbluff nodded. "Your brains serve as an *access point* to your memories." He rubbed his hand over the thick and ragged-edged page open before him. "These pages of whisperleaf are where your memories are actually *stored*." He turned the page of the great volume in front of him.

"There are thousands of other baronies and Great Libraries—G'vul and Tokayah being our closest neighbors—each with their own jurisdiction. The Scribes write to record what you've done and what's been done to you. Your key memories, the essential memories that connect to millions of others. Who you are, yes?"

"Wait!" Apurva protested. "But don't people forget things all the time? My mother—"

"Your mother," Fumbluff said softly, "was a victim of Eldritch's recent attack on the Great Library in Tokayah." Fumbluff turned another page, running his finger over the scrawling text. "So was your schoolteacher—Miss Ellipsis she's called, yes? May their days be as long as summer shadows. Apurva, I checked on your dear mother personally. Many of her volumes remain intact—and you're in them."

"But . . ." Apurva began, tears swimming in her big brown eyes, "what does that *mean?* Can my mother get better?"

Fumbluff handed Apurva one of those giant napkins. "There is no cure or counteragent for a *false* memory, like one implanted by the Aetherquill. But to repair a *lost* memory? It's possible, yes? However, there's a very long queue at the Department of Recovery and Reclamation, and you must go through the Librarian to get anything done there. They're awfully slow, but don't tell them I said that." He chuckled in rusty hiccups, looking from Apurva to Georgie.

Georgie only caught some of what Fumbluff had said about the Department of Recovery and Reclamation. A pale yellow light had begun to curl from the pages of whisperleaf, and Georgie couldn't look away. For the moment, Georgie forgot all about monster shadows, fractured souls, and even the plan to save his father. The light curling off the pages of whisperleaf was hypnotizing.

"Georgie?" Apurva asked.

"Do you see something, Georgie?" Fumbluff asked excitedly.

Charles Fenton and Blaze Nelson pushed their chairs back in a hurry and gathered around Fumbluff at the head of the table.

"It can't be," Blaze whispered.

Georgie tried swallowing, but his throat was dry as parchment paper. The yellow light became thicker, curling off the pages of whisperleaf like tendrils of heat rising from a frying pan.

A dog barked.

But Georgie knew the sound wasn't coming from Corrigendum.

It was coming from the book.

Chapter 14

A Visit to Apurva's Whisperleaf

"Georgie?" Apurva's voice was muffled. "Are you alright?"

The light thickened into a solid column of light rising up from the Great Book. Georgie heard the dog bark again. It sounded like it was ready to play.

Georgie stepped in front of Fumbluff and bent his head into the column of light. He was in a world of golden-yellows, and when he looked down at the page of whisperleaf, he no longer saw the scrawling writing of the Scribes, but a three-dimensional scene springing to life. Miniature objects—a bed,

a desk, a rug, walls, windows, and a door—arranged themselves on the surface of the whisperleaf, everything awash in
burnt-yellow hues.

Georgie turned his head . . . only, he didn't actually turn
his head. Somehow, he was controlling the view of the scene
with his mind.

The objects had all settled in place. He was inside a bedroom. The bed was neatly made with a quilt that had lace
frills along the edges. A pillow in the shape of a microscope
was propped up against the headboard. Above the bed were
framed posters of each of the eight planets, surrounding a
neon sign that read: I NEED MY SPACE.

Tucked beneath a sloping eave was a small wicker desk
with a glass top. A grid of Polaroid pictures was pressed
beneath the desk's glass.

Georgie willed himself closer.

Now the Polaroid pictures were big enough for—

Georgie's breath caught in his throat.

Georgie recognized the girl who appeared in nearly
every picture beneath the glass.

Apurva.

This was Apurva's bedroom!

Which meant . . . if Scatterplot's Great Books were filled
with the memories of people on Earth . . . then this must be
one of Apurva's *memories.*

Georgie had never quite had an experience like this
before—today was a day *full* of firsts. He could feel
Corrigendum's dining room floor filmy beneath his feet, but
his mind was here, inside a memory that wasn't even *his.*

Did Fumbluff *want* Georgie to see this memory? Could it have been a coincidence that Fumbluff opened this specific Great Book to this specific page?

He heard Apurva's voice just then—her *memory's* voice.

Come here, boy.

Georgie's heart galloped. She couldn't have been talking to him, *could she?*

Georgie spun the mental joystick around and found himself facing Apurva's bed.

And Apurva.

She was sitting cross-legged, her hair pulled up and away from her face in a high ponytail. She was wearing sweatpants and a white tank top. A three-ringed binder was open on her lap.

Georgie's heart throbbed in his chest, and he had to remind himself that he wasn't really *there*, that this was just a memory, that Apurva couldn't see him—but was that even true? Georgie really didn't have the slightest idea how this memory business worked.

Come, boy! Apurva called again, and then a small golden puppy with floppy ears leaped from the floor onto the bed. Apurva nestled her face against the puppy's neck.

It's going to be okay, won't it? Apurva asked aloud, then exhaled deeply. When she pulled her face away, her eyes were moist with tears. Apurva tucked the puppy under her arm and walked to her desk. Written with perfect script letters on a large notepad was each day of the week, and beside each day, in the same perfect handwriting, was a list of what looked to Georgie like medications. Apurva used a ruler and a pencil to cross out one of the days with a perfectly straight line. Then she took a plastic pillbox from the shelf above her desk.

Time for mom's medicine, Apurva's voice echoed inside Georgie's head. Apurva walked to her bedroom door, carefully shaking the contents of the pillbox into her hand. Georgie didn't have to follow, because the objects in the scene disintegrated to golden dust particles. A new scene sprang to life, the particles swirling and then solidifying again. They were in Apurva's living room now, and there was Apurva's mother, sitting in a rocking chair, staring blankly at the television.

Apurva knelt down in front of her mother and rubbed her leg.

Mommy?

Apurva's mother looked away from the television at her daughter, but there was no recognition in her eyes. They seemed blank, just like Miss Ellipsis's had been.

Come, Mom, you need to take these. Apurva handed her mother a glass of water from the table beside the rocker. *The doctor said.*

But I took these already, Apurva's mother replied, her voice barely a rattling breath. *You're the new nurse, aren't you?*

No, Ma, it's me, Apurva.

Apurva took her mother's arm and gently placed the pills into her hand.

I love you, Mommy, Apurva whispered.

Georgie watched the two of them, Apurva's head rocking gently in her mother's lap, and her mother staring over her daughter's shoulders. The golden light began to fade, and the miniature objects disintegrated into billions of shimmering particles. Georgie could see through Apurva and her mother now, until they too turned to glittering sand.

With a great pain in his chest, Georgie watched it all go. He'd been so focused on his own mission to save his father that he never fully realized what Apurva was going through. He wasn't the only lonely one.

Georgie looked up and rubbed his eyes.

The scene was gone. The light was gone. One of Fenton's giant hands lay flat against the Great Book's cover. Blaze Nelson ran a hand through his silvery hair, regarding Georgie with a look of pure amazement.

"Georgie!" Apurva cried. "What *was* that? It looked like you were in a trance!"

He was suddenly exhausted, as if he'd run ten miles around the track.

Fenton handed Georgie a clay mug of water.

"Impossible," Blaze whispered. "It takes an apprentice nine years to even *begin* reading—"

"*That* was reading?" Georgie asked, looking up at Fumbluff, then to Apurva. "It was . . . I was like *inside*."

"Inside *where*?" Apurva asked.

"Inside y—" Georgie gulped and he felt his cheeks turning red. Apurva never invited him into her bedroom. Into her *memory*. What was he supposed to tell her? But before he could answer, the woman Scribe who'd been sitting beside Fenton stood up abruptly. And as she did, three white doves flew into the dining room and landed on her shoulders.

"Only the Seven can see the writing like that!" The birds fluttered their wings restlessly, then were still again.

"Yes," Fumbluff muttered, gazing at a device strapped to his wrist with tiny polished spheres appearing to orbit in midair. It didn't look anything like Georgie's Casio, but he guessed that's what passed as a timekeeper in Scatterplot. "Georgie is ahead of the game. Georgie passed the first test. He can read. Quite fluently, I might add."

"Test?" Georgie muttered. "*That* was the test?" He thought about the first thing Rollie D had said back in the forest. *You need to go see Fumbluff. You'll be tested. Those tests are important. Crucial.*

"Yes," Fumbluff chuckled. "The first part." He lifted the Great Book and carried it back to the compartment from which it had first appeared.

Georgie's mind was blinking like a switchboard—he wanted to know what the second part of the test was and he wanted to know why these tests were so important. What did passing these tests have to do with saving his dad? But he was so tired, and a little dizzy, and wondered if this was what being drunk felt like.

"*Maestro,*" Fenton began, "don't you think—if Georgie can read like that, maybe he can . . . if Georgie can write as well as he can read, he can use the Aetherquill to—" Fenton trailed off as Fumbluff turned slowly.

"Soon, Scribe Fenton. Georgie's eaten. Georgie's read. But no Scribe can write with an unrested mind."

Georgie rubbed his eyes with the heels of his palms. "Wait a second," Georgie began, stifling a yawn. "These tests, what are they for? To see if I'm a . . ."

"Yes," Charlie Fenton said excitedly. "To see if you're a Scribe. There are very few children of Scribes, we have . . . busy schedules, you know. But you're the offspring of not just one Scribe, but *two* Scribes, two of the most talented Scribes Scatterplot's ever seen. It's in your blood—we just need to see how much!"

"Writing is the most important part," said the woman Scribe with the white doves on her shoulders. She wore a pair of large plastic glasses that magnified her eyes. "The Aetherquill's magic will only work in the language of the Scribes. A language unlike any other language in the world. We call this language Whisperloom. It takes our apprentices many years to master, but you seem to have . . . a natural gift." She smiled warmly, fanning the skin around her eyes into a web of fine wrinkles. Georgie wondered why they couldn't hire teachers like *her* at Bridget Elementary.

"More complicated than any language in your world," Fenton added. "Whisperloom mixes numbers, letters, diagrams, dots, patterns, don't even get me started. I was left back two years in a row and had to wait another *twelve* years to finally be ordained at the Coronation Cerem—"

"The Coronation Ceremony!" Apurva exclaimed. "Edie and Ore told us about that. Ore said if Georgie was a Scribe, he'd need to be officially . . . *ordained* . . . or something like that."

Fumbluff smiled. "Reading and writing Whisperloom is one thing. But in order to activate the Aetherquill's magic— for the writing to *take effect*—you must be an ordained Scribe. The Coronation Ceremony is very serious business, and it happens at just the precise time, when all the realms are aligned, once every fourteen years."

"So getting coronated is like getting a degree?" Apurva asked.

"That's right," Fumbluff said. "A knowledgeable apothecary in your world may *know* the correct potions to prescribe for an infected wound . . ." Fumbluff paused, seeing the perplexed look on Apurva's face. "I'm sorry, a *pharmacist* may know the correct *medication* to prescribe a patient, but only after he or she obtains a license to practice would he or she be welcomed into the guild of apothecaries—*pharmacists*."

"This magical pen cares whether or not I have . . . a *license* to use it?" Georgie asked with more sarcasm than he intended.

Fumbluff looked at Georgie calmly. "It most certainly does. Besides, we mustn't use the Aetherquill *here*. We must travel *up*, and only Scribes who've been officially inducted into the Scribehood *can* travel up."

Travel *up?* Georgie wondered. His dad used to say you travel *up* to Maine and *down* to Florida, but something told Georgie the type of *up* Fumbluff was talking about wasn't like that at all.

"Only inducted Scribes are allowed entrance into Quillethra," Fenton said.

"The Aetherquill's origin realm," Blaze added.

Fumbluff held up his hand, and the Scribes fell silent. "We'll give Georgie his writing exam tomorrow morning. Once he's rested. *If* Georgie can write, and judging by Georgie's uncanny reading aptitude, I suspect his competence might surprise us once again, then we will induct him into the Scribehood at the Coronation Ceremony tomorrow afternoon."

Georgie gulped down the last of his water and wiped a dribble away from his chin with his t-shirt. "And then what? Let's say I *can* write. And I *do* get . . . inducted as a Scribe. How do we save my father?"

Fumbluff looked at Georgie and his eyes were once again filled with a deep and inexplicable sorrow. The great dining room was silent for a long moment, before Fumbluff began to speak in a cracked whisper. "The only way to defeat Eldritch," Fumbluff continued, "to *save* everyone you love, is to use the Aetherquill on Eldritch. To give Eldritch a memory of utter and complete defeat. Making him believe that he'd failed. That he had failed to create a world of disembodied shadows. Living with such failure would be impossible. For this mission of his is the only reason he exists. He will have no further purpose. It will destroy him."

Georgie slipped a hand into his pocket. Feeling his slingshot's extra-tough rubber band, the one that took him all day to finish with three coats of shiny black paint, helped calm his nerves. "And what about my dad?"

Fumbluff shook his head, and a single tear brimmed over and ran down a deep groove in his cheek. "It'll destroy your father, too."

Georgie felt like a giant snake was coiling tightly around his stomach. He didn't come all this way, through a portal in his garage into this strange universe in the dead of winter, only to be told that the best plan was to . . .

what? *Kill* his own father? So what if his father wasn't exactly . . . *complete*? Georgie loved his dad more than anything in the world.

"You've *GOT* to be kidding me," Georgie shouted. His head was pounding, but the exhaustion was gone as quickly as it had come. There was that, at least. Georgie glared at Charlie Fenton, whose head was hanging low. "You *CANNOT* actually be serious, right?"

Fumbluff brushed a speck of dust off the sleeve of his topcoat. "It is the only way."

"There *has* to be another—" Apurva began.

"What's left of Georgie's father is buried beneath Eldritch's shadow," Fumbluff said softly. "The *order* is all wrong, yes? Imagine placing chicken eggs at the bottom of a rucksack and then packing bricks on *top* of the eggs. It's the wrong order, can't you see, Georgie? The eggs would crack. And once they crack, there's no making them whole again."

"But my father is not an egg at the bottom of a . . . rucksack! Whatever *that* is!"

"It's another word for a backpack," Apurva whispered.

Georgie glared at her, feeling hot tears stinging the back of his eyes. He swallowed the lump in his throat. He wanted to ask Apurva for help . . . Roscoe was gone, but she was the smart one anyway! He wanted to ask *anyone* for help, but he knew that if he did, the tears would come streaming down and now wasn't the time for that. He had to *think*.

What Fumbluff was suggesting was stupid! Extremely stupid. And he was Scatterplot's Editor in Chief? The most talented of all the Scribes? Protector of memories? STUPID!

Georgie's eyes went wide.

Stupid.

He remembered Rollie D's warm breath on his face, just after she took her hand off his mouth: *Fumbluff will have a plan. But there is never just one way to solve a problem. Come find me before you decide to do something stupid.*

Maybe Fumbluff's plan was exactly the stupid thing she had been talking about. He certainly hoped so.

He had to find Rollie D.

But first, he had to take this writing test. If he couldn't write, finding Rollie D would be pointless. Rollie had said Fumbluff's tests were *crucial.*

"Georgie," Fumbluff said softly. "Rest. You've had a long day, yes? The decision is yours to make, and yours to make alone. We've prepared a bedroom for you. Dullwick has the fire going and you'll—"

"No," Georgie said.

Apurva turned to face Georgie and Georgie gave her just the slightest tilt of his head.

Georgie looked back at Fumbluff, the torches along the dining room walls casting ancient shadow figures along his ageless face. "I'm ready. I can do it. Give me the writing test."

He stood up and hurried to Fumbluff on legs that felt almost out of juice. No matter how badly he wanted to flop down on a cool mattress and sleep for a month, Apurva needed his help. His father needed his help. "Fumbluff, please. I'll . . . be careful?"

Fumbluff stared long and hard into Georgie's eyes, not moving a muscle, not even blinking. Finally, he spoke a single word. "Yes."

"Yes?" Georgie echoed.

"Okay."

"Okay!"

Fumbluff smiled and held a hand up. "If you're sure you're feeling alert enough, yes?"

"I am."

"Don an anorak or a warmkin. It's chilly outside."

Chapter 15

Georgie's Final Exam

ifteen minutes later, a small group crossed Corrigendum's courtyard and through the iron gates. Charlie Fenton followed behind Georgie and Apurva, while Fumbluff, Dullwick, and the woman Scribe with the birds on her shoulder walked ahead. They turned off the main road well before the roundabout onto a narrower path through the fields of feather grass. It was pitch black, save for the flickering cone of light from Dullwick's lantern, spotlighting the low-hanging fog curling around their ankles.

"*Georgie,*" Apurva whispered, barely louder than the

occasional gusts of wind. "*What're we doing? You're not actually thinking about—*"

Georgie shook his head. No, he wasn't about to use the Aetherquill to destroy his own father. He leaned closer to Apurva, keeping his voice down so the Scribes wouldn't hear him. "Back in the forest, Rollie D said something about Fumbluff having a plan. But *then* she said how there's always more than one way to solve a problem. And that we should come find her."

Apurva's eyebrows arched. "Ohhhh." Then she nudged Georgie in the shoulder. "*Why didn't you tell me this before?*"

Georgie shrugged. "I'm . . . I'm sorry," he whispered. "It was, like, a lot to process. I was confused." But truthfully, Georgie was more scared than confused. He didn't like the sound of a writing test. Would it be like an essay? Georgie *hated* essays. Essays were the pits. What if he could read, but he couldn't *write*?

Apurva sighed. "Okay, that's a reasonable explanation and I forgive you. But no more secrets, okay? We're in this together."

Apurva sounded plenty nervous herself, and Georgie didn't blame her. "I promise," Georgie whispered, and he meant it. Georgie remembered Apurva's golden memory-figure handing her mother her medicine. How Apurva smiled, even though she was crying.

"Rolle D will have a different plan," Georgie whispered, even though he really didn't know if that was true or not. "And we're going to help your mom, too."

Apurva smiled. "My mom used to say, 'Keep your face

to the sunshine and you'll never see a shadow.' It's an idiom about the power of always keeping a positive attitude, even when things seem really awful. It has a whole new meaning now, doesn't it?"

Shadow and light. Cracked eggs. *Flint Eldritch absorbed your father.* "Yeah, it sure does."

Up ahead, Georgie could see a giant lawn beyond the field of feather grass.

"An idiom is a saying not meant to be taken literally, by the way," Apurva continued. "Like 'it's raining cats and dogs,' or 'don't bite off more than you can chew.'"

"I know what an idiom is," Georgie replied, even though he didn't.

Apurva giggled.

They broke from the feather grass and were now walking along the edge of the lawn, which looked as long as three football fields. They passed the giant white tent, and just beyond it, the group came to a stop at the base of a long staircase.

Built entirely of limestone, the Seminary looked as if it had been carved from the very mountains it stood nestled against. A domed structure stood in the center of four towers connecting the Seminary's outer walls. A tall, windowless tower rose like a chimney behind the dome.

"Are you sure about this?" Fenton asked Georgie. "Even the best Scribes can't write worth a damn when they're pooped."

"I'm alright," Georgie replied, although "alright" would be near the very bottom of a very long list of more accurate ways to describe how Georgie was feeling. Dead tired, on the verge of a panic attack. Terrified.

Those were better.

The group climbed the Seminary's polished stone staircase, which gleamed in the moonlight. Beyond the first set of iron doors, a marble walkway lined with pillars led across a courtyard to the domed building. The Scribe with the birds on her shoulders hurried ahead and pulled the door to the domed building open.

"Thank you kindly, Scribe Hambrey," Fenton said as he and the rest of the group entered the dome.

"Thank you," Georgie said, facing Scribe Hambrey. He tapped his throat three times with two fingers. Maybe acting like a Scribe would help him with whatever was about to come next. Scribe Hambrey's birds fluttered their wings gently in response.

"This is our study hall," Scribe Hambrey continued, once the entire group was inside. "It takes years of training to become a Scribe." Scribe Hambrey paused, surveying Georgie with great interest. "For most of us."

Hundreds of teenage students—all dressed in gray robes with copper trim over dark green vests—were seated at long tables in pairs. Pens and paper were scattered everywhere, and tall stacks of books created barriers between each pair of partners. Georgie and Apurva followed Fumbluff, Scribe Hambrey, and Dullwick Ratriot down a long aisle to the front of the room where a red velvet curtain hung from a gold rod. Georgie could feel the apprentice's eyes on him.

Fumbluff pulled the curtain back.

Apurva gasped.

The room behind the curtain was cavernous—so large that Georgie couldn't tell how far back it went. From hundreds of feet above, seven pillars of light shone down from the ceiling, each pillar illuminating a workstation set up below. Each workstation contained a large writing desk, raised up on a small platform. Shelves packed with pens, ink bottles, and stacks of the leather-bound Great Books stood beside each desk. Georgie didn't remember Blaze Nelson leaving Corrigendum, but he must have slipped out earlier to make his shift because there he was, sitting behind the desk all the way to Georgie's left, the column of light illuminating his silver hair. He and four other Scribes wrote furiously as they stared into flat-bottomed glass orbs.

"That was your father's Writer's Block," Scribe Hambrey said, pointing to the third station from the left. "And that one," her voice cracked, pointing to the desk all the way to the right, "that one was your mother's . . ."

Her voice trailed off, sad and doleful, until Blaze Nelson's voice broke the heavy silence. "Georgie."

The book that had been open on his desk a moment ago was now floating up the column of vertical light. Sparkling, coruscating particles of dust parted like a whisper as the book traveled upward.

Blaze stepped off the platform and motioned for Georgie. A moment later Georgie found himself behind Blaze's desk. The glass orb sat in the center of a cracked leather map, and beneath it, Georgie recognized New York.

Charlie Fenton took a Great Book from the stack beside

the writing station, laid it before Georgie, and opened it to the first page. Georgie slumped into Blaze's wooden chair and stared down at the blank whisperleaf.

No way I can do this, Georgie thought. He remembered Miss Ellipsis's writing assignments. The pages he'd filled with doodles instead of words.

A gentle hand squeezed his shoulder. Georgie looked up at Scribe Hambrey. "Steady, Georgie. Clear your head. A Scribe does not write with his hand. A Scribe writes with his mind."

"With my mind," Georgie repeated, having absolutely no idea what that meant. Where were the instructions? What was he supposed to do?

"That's right," Fenton continued, now standing on Georgie's other side. "But you do need ink."

He uncorked an ancient glass bottle filled with rich, black ink.

"And a pen." Scribe Hambrey uncapped a heavy bronze fountain pen, dipped it into the inkwell, and handed it to Georgie.

A Scribe writes with his mind.

Georgie closed his eyes and tried to clear his mind, but his mind was clogged with fear. Fear that he would fail this writing test. That this had just been a big misunderstanding. An epic mistake. He wouldn't be able to save his dad or Apurva's mother. Not to mention the lives of everyone back home. He was just a loser who couldn't do much of anything other than hit stationary targets with his slingshot.

Fumbluff's gonna send me straight home after this, Georgie thought.

Straight to the orphanage . . . or worse, back to Bridget Elementary.

He was so tired now that it actually stung when he cracked his eyes open. Had he dozed off for a second there? A splotch of ink had pooled on the blank page.

"What am I supposed to *do*?" Georgie whispered.

"Look into the orb," Charlie Fenton said, guiding Georgie's left hand against the glass orb. The orb was cool to the touch and so smooth it was almost liquid. "But a Scribe does not see with his eyes," Fenton whispered. "A Scribe sees with his heart." Fenton let go of Georgie's hand. "For your mother's sake. For the sake of truth and for the sake of Scatterplot, *see with your heart and write with your mind.*"

Georgie stared into the glass orb, waiting for something to happen.

Fenton stepped off the platform and stood beside Blaze. "Wager?" Fenton asked.

Blaze Nelson scratched his chin. "If Georgie can write, I'll buy you dinner at the Notch."

"You two will not gamble on whether or not the boy is a Scribe!" Scribe Hambrey gasped.

Fenton nodded happily and stuck his hand out.

"But if Georgie *isn't* a Scribe," Blaze continued, "I get to tell all the apprentices that you used to have a crush on Rollie D."

"No bet," Fenton croaked. "No bet!"

"No bet?" Blaze asked. "The Charles Fenton I know never turns down a bet."

Georgie tried desperately to concentrate. "Shhhh . . . *please!*"

The Scribes went silent. The vast Cathedral breathed in and out, the way old houses breathe in the middle of the night when everyone's asleep. Georgie thought about the photograph of his mother standing in the feather grass with the nine-chimneyed mansion—which Georgie now knew was Corrigendum—in the background. He thought about Apurva tucking the loose strand of hair back behind her ear in Miss Ellipsis's class. He thought about Roscoe screaming in Yooker Tenderfoot's arms, *not to mention a pain in the neck and a blister on the butt*—

Small gray clouds formed inside the glass orb, obscuring the cracked leather map beneath it. Georgie bent his head toward the glass. A jolt of electricity shot through his fingertips and up his arm . . . but his arm felt far away now, like it was in a different room. Something warm tingled at the back of his neck. In a distant part of his mind, Georgie realized the warmth on his neck must be the column of light . . .

. . . then he was inside the orb, falling through the clouds.

Falling fast through a windless void. Falling from the sky.

Part of him was inside the orb now, just like a part of him had been inside Apurva's memory, and that part of him plummeted toward Earth.

He broke from the clouds and saw a forest racing toward

him. A network of roads and highways, cars and trucks gliding silently along, no larger than ants.

This must be what a pilot sees as he loses control of his plane in a nosedive.

He tried to scream. He was going to splatter all over the ground like spaghetti sauce. There was Dotty Pond, where his father used to take him to watch the fireworks show on July 4th. There was Bridget Elementary! Buses the size of bees were lined up in front of the brick school building.

Then, with a nauseating lurch, Georgie slowed down before coming to a complete stop, hanging about fifty feet in the air.

He opened one eye.

On the asphalt driveway directly below him, shards of a shattered headlamp twinkled in front of a red Toyota. Georgie opened his other eye.

His *mind's* eye.

It was early morning, and a light rain was falling.

Georgie was hovering directly over his house.

Chapter 16

Key Memories in the Cathedral

eorgie's garage was wrapped three times in criss-crossing yellow tape.

A police cruiser idled on the street. Satellite dishes extended from the roofs of three local news vans. Cameras were hoisted on shoulders, and the news anchors pointed and talked and stared into the cameras' lenses. Everything else looked like the world Georgie was used to and had left behind just mere hours earlier—except for the weird pill-shaped tubes hanging over each person's head. The tubes came in all different colors. Some were just an outline, yet others were colored in entirely. It was like all these people were characters in a video game, and the tubes were their health meters.

A woman was walking down Jericho Road toward Georgie's house, the tube above her head nearly empty, but it glowed and pulsed a deep amber, spilling light outward like a neon sign. From what felt like a million miles away, Georgie rubbed the pad of his thumb delicately against the glass orb. His view of the driveway zoomed in. He was close enough now to see the lettering on the news vans and the numbers on the police cruisers. And he was close enough to recognize the woman hurrying toward the group crowded behind the police barricade.

It was Mrs. Harris. Roscoe's mom.

Georgie zoomed in even closer. His viewpoint was only ten or fifteen feet up in the air now. Her eyes were bloodshot, and what little makeup she wore was smudged and runny.

Mrs. Harris pushed her way to the front of the barricade and called out to one of the police officers. The officer shook his head, said something, and Mrs. Harris began to weep.

The amber pill hovering above Mrs. Harris's head began to fill up like a tank.

Georgie remembered Fumbluff talking about key memories—the experiences that connected to millions of others. Maybe *that's* what the tubes filling up meant . . .

◊ ◊ ◊

A universe away, Georgie Summers was writing.

✧ ✧ ✧

A strong wind blew and the soft summer rain continued to fall in Bridget, New York. Slowly, Roscoe's mom looked up, directly at Georgie. She spoke then, and whether she sensed Georgie there or she was simply praying, Georgie couldn't know. *Please let my son be safe,* she mouthed. *And please, please bring him back to me.*

I will, Georgie sent back. *I promise.*

Mrs. Harris closed her eyes, letting the rain and tears roll off her face.

✧ ✧ ✧

In the Cathedral of the Scribes, Georgie sat behind Blaze Nelson's Writer's Block. He was writing feverishly, all the muscles in his fingers firing like fine pistons. His eyes were glazed over, a smoky-white film opaqued his pupils and his hair clung to his forehead in sweaty clumps. He couldn't hear anything. Not the excited whispers of the Scribes standing around him, nor the voices of the people down below on Earth.

A Scribe writes with his mind and sees with his heart, and Georgie's heart was open and his mind was ablaze.

✧ ✧ ✧

Georgie nudged the glass orb across the worn leather map. Only a fraction of a centimeter, but Georgie's view slammed into a frenzied blur and he was no longer hovering over his house. The view settled in a brightly lit playroom. Here, a little girl unwrapped a birthday present. The pill-shaped tube above the young girl's head was blue, and it glowed brightly as it filled up.

Georgie nudged the orb again and he went flying. He settled on a group of kids laughing and pushing each other, each of them carrying shopping bags brimming with expensive-looking toys.

With every memory Georgie recorded, his pen moved faster and faster. More confidently and smoothly. The lurching sense of vertigo that came each time Georgie nudged the orb no longer made him nauseous.

◇ ◇ ◇

He hovered over a graduation party now. Girls and boys were laughing and high-fiving. One of the girls was swept off her feet, and the neon green tube hovering above her head filled up as she went round and round.

◇ ◇ ◇

Georgie felt a squeeze around his wrist.

He tried fighting it, he tried to hold his concentration. The view shuddered, and for an instant, he saw the cracked leather map through a bowl of punch at the graduation.

No! He wanted to stay here. He wanted to write!

The squeeze around his wrist came again, this time

like an iron bracelet. The graduation party was gone, and Georgie was flying up, up, up, up, everything a fantastic blur of speed and twinkling carnival lights.

Then Georgie was staring through the glass orb again, the clouds trapped inside its convex dome dissipating until the orb was crystal clear. He was panting. Fumbluff was standing over him, with a hand gently clasped around his wrist.

"You did it, Georgie!" Apurva cried, jumping onto the platform and giving Georgie a mighty hug that almost knocked him clean off the Writer's Block. "You were writing!"

Fenton and Scribe Hambrey were holding hands, shock and awe etched across their faces. Georgie looked down and saw that he had written nearly two hundred pages! He couldn't believe it. He paged back through his writing and saw with amazement that every page was filled from margin to margin with strange characters, numbers, shapes, dots, and patterns.

He had written in Whisperloom.

It didn't look nearly as neat and tidy as the writing he saw in the Great Book back in Corrigendum, but then again, it *was* his first-ever go at this!

"Gee, Fenton, he can write!" Blaze Nelson exclaimed, running a hand through his hair.

Fenton's gigantic, round face broke out in a monumental smile.

"How long?" Georgie panted, then winced as he tried moving his wrist. It was killing. "How long was I down there?"

"Not long," Apurva said. "Maybe ten minutes?"

"That's it!?"

"Oh ayuh," Fenton said. "Time passes differently down there. You get used to it. The nausea, too. Most new Scribes puke their brains out their first few weeks."

Georgie took a deep breath and exhaled slowly. He was shaking all over. Was he really a Scribe? All of a sudden, he missed his father awfully. Would his dad be proud of him?

"The Coronation Ceremony," Blaze said, facing Fumbluff. "Tomorrow. We must induct the boy into the Scribehood. An eighth Scribe."

Georgie's mental processing systems were drained. Spent. Depleted. He had nothing left. He gazed out from behind the Writer's Block into the faces of all the Scribes standing before him. They looked like a group of aging choir singers in their hooded velvet robes. He didn't know if he *wanted* to be inducted into the Scribehood. He didn't *want* to travel up to Quillethra, where Fumbluff would have him destroy Flint Eldritch, *and* what remained of his father, with the Aetherquill. Fumbluff had said it was Georgie's choice to make, but did he really mean that?

Besides, the Scribes didn't even *have* the Aetherquill. He was pretty sure the Aetherquill was with one Rollie D, somewhere unknown in that dark and endless forest, with the Altercockers . . . and Roscoe.

Fumbluff took off his hat and tucked it under his arm.

"Fumbluff," Georgie began weakly, "I . . . I don't want to—" Georgie closed his eyes. This was more than exhaustion.

Fumbluff stepped up to the Writer's Block and held

Georgie by the shoulders. "*Shhhh,* dear boy, you've had quite the evening, yes?" Fumbluff looked out at the Scribes. "Yes, we'll induct Georgie Summers tomorrow afternoon, when he'll receive his very first *kef* of whisperleaf." The Scribes nodded. "But without the Aetherquill, our plan to stop Flint Eldritch is moot. Irrelevant. Unobtainable. Yes?" Fumbluff looked carefully from Scribe to Scribe. "Like I told you, Rollie D visited John Summers two days ago. I know because *I* visited John Summers myself." Fumbluff peered down at Georgie. "While you were at school yesterday."

Georgie's mind whirred through his exhaustion. Fumbluff came through the portal in the garage *yesterday?* While he was at school?

"Rollie D has the Aetherquill," Fumbluff continued. "John confirmed this. I do not blame John Summers for refusing the Aetherquill when Rollie offered it to him." Fumbluff stepped forward, to the edge of the Writer's Block. "I told John Summers to bring Georgie here. Flint's recent attacks and their proximity to Scatterplot made me uneasy." Fumbluff sighed again, this time closing his eyes. "I thought we had more time." He tapped his throat three times.

"Let's go right now!" Fenton grumbled loudly. "We'll find Rollie D, and we'll take the Aetherquill from her by force! We'll be back before the coronation!"

"By force?" Blaze Nelson shouted. "You and what army?"

"He's right!" Scribe Hambrey cried. "The Altercockers are armed!"

"One of them had a gun," Apurva exclaimed. "He pointed it at Roscoe's head!"

Georgie looked past the edge of the Writer's Block at all the Scribes who were now nervously looking amongst themselves. In his mind's eye, he saw Roscoe's mother crying and he remembered the promise he'd made to her. In his mind's ear, he heard Rollie D's last words to him back in the forest: *There's never just one way to solve a problem. Come find me before you decide to do something stupid.*

Georgie put his hands on Blaze's desk and hoisted himself up. He took one step around the side of the Writer's Block and fell off the platform. Apurva screamed as he landed on his back, and had just enough time to glimpse the seven pillars of light rising hundreds of feet into the Cathedral's ceiling before he passed out.

Chapter 17

Georgie and Apurva Jump

Pain.

Everywhere.

Georgie's back ached and his neck felt stiff as rock. But his right hand hurt the most. With his eyes still closed, he tried wiggling his fingers, then groaned. Had someone whacked his hand with a hammer while he'd been out?

He stirred. He was in a bed. On a mattress. Whoa, a really soft mattress. What time was it? How long had he been out?

"Georgie?"

He cracked his eyes open and saw Apurva's face swimming above his own. Judging by the nightstand and the second bed beside it, Georgie figured they were in some sort of bedroom.

A healthy fire crackled in a fireplace on the opposite wall. Apurva was sitting beside Georgie, and his first thought was: *I've never been alone in a bedroom with a girl in my entire life.* Then, out loud, he wondered, "What the heck happened?"

After making sure Georgie was really okay, Apurva brought him up to speed. "We're back at Corrigendum. Fenton carried you the whole way." She pointed to a package wrapped in elephant leaves on the night table. "Before he left, Fenton gave me those. Six sandwiches. I don't know what we need sandwiches for—we just had dinner you know—but that's beside the point. Are you *sure* you're okay?"

Georgie swung his legs over the side of the bed. "Rollie D. We gotta go find—"

"Fumbluff said not to go *anywhere*," Apurva interrupted, "at least not until after the Coronation Ceremony."

Georgie rubbed his eyes and sighed.

"Sorry," Apurva said, "your head's probably pounding."

It was.

Apurva stood up and plunked down on the second bed, facing Georgie. "I think we *both* need to slu-slu-slu-sleeeep," Apurva said with a great big yawn, then unbuttoned her shirt and pulled it over her head. She was wearing a white tank top with spaghetti straps underneath.

Georgie looked away, all of a sudden finding the blank wall above his bed very interesting.

Apurva grabbed a pair of folded pajamas on the foot of the bed—velvet smocks and pants trimmed with woven bands of copper—and stepped behind a screen with four panels in the corner of the room. In the firelight, Georgie could see Apurva's silhouette behind the artwork on the bamboo panels: paintings of Pocket Horsemen, of warriors, of mountains and rivers and on the last panel, a large circular building—like a colosseum.

"Hey, Georgie," Apurva called, startling Georgie.

"Huh?"

"Can you believe we were talking about Miss Ellipsis's essay assignment outside school this afternoon?"

It *had* been a really long day. And something told Georgie the day wasn't nearly over yet. He thought about Roscoe. Then he thought about Mrs. Harris again, the tears and rain rolling off her face and the promise he made to her.

Apurva came out from behind the screen, her clothes bunched in her arms. She smiled at Georgie and he returned it.

He had to tell Apurva about being inside her memory, didn't he? Wasn't that, like, the right thing to do? He felt a little embarrassed having seen the inside of her bedroom.

A Scribe sees with his heart and writes with his mind. It didn't say anything about a Scribe doing the right thing, but Georgie figured it was sort of implied.

"What're you thinking about?" Apurva regarded Georgie

carefully. "Don't tell me it's nothing, because I can *tell* it's something."

"I need my space," Georgie blurted. "The neon sign above your bed surrounded by the planets."

Apurva's eyes went wide, and Georgie wished he'd led with something else. Out of all the things he could have said, that was maybe one of the stupidest.

"I . . . I think it's really funny," Georgie quickly added, although that didn't help matters at all.

"*Wait—wha—huh—*" Apurva stammered. "How do *you* know about that!?"

Georgie started over from the beginning. Apurva said nothing while Georgie spoke, busying herself with folding and refolding her clothing at least three times until her jeans and school shirt were equal-sized squares on the night table.

"I think Fumbluff *wanted* me to see that memory because he wanted me to understand that I'm not the only one with an important mission." Georgie looked up at Apurva. "You have an important mission, too."

Apurva stared down at the floor.

"I'm sorry," Georgie whispered. "I wanted to tell you earlier, but I wasn't really sure what to—"

"It's okay," Apurva whispered back. "At least now you understand what's been going on with my mother. It's been really hard." Tears were forming in Apurva's eyes. "Remember what Fumbluff said about the Department of Reclamation and Recovery? Do you think they can help my mom?"

Georgie nodded vigorously. "Yeah, I bet they can. And we're gonna—"

Apurva shook her head. "My mother's memories are all messed up now *because* of Flint, but if Flint gets to the Aetherquill before you do, so many more people will be hurt. My mother can wait."

Georgie gulped. Apurva was carrying so much pain inside her. He wondered if *he'd* be as selfless if their situations were reversed. He wasn't so sure. "You really mean it?"

Apurva smiled and hawked a gob of spit onto her open palm. She stuck her hand out. "Sincerely."

Georgie laughed and pumped Apurva's hand three times. Firmly. Then let go.

They sat there for a moment, taking it all in, until Apurva broke the silence. "That was pretty cool back there in the Cathedral, Georgie. The way your hand was moving like lightning. You had it in you, Georgie. You had this cool power locked inside you all along!"

"You really think so?" Georgie asked. "That it's cool?"

"It's the coolest thing I've ever seen in my life."

Georgie's cheeks flushed. He was a writer of memories. Maybe not the coolest thing ever, maybe Apurva was *exagga-the-ratings* as Roscoe would have said, but it was definitely pretty neat.

"Thanks," Georgie said. "And thanks for coming . . . here. To Scatterplot." Then he smiled at Apurva. "*Sincerely.*"

That got them talking about Roscoe, wondering where he was and how he was doing and how the Altercockers were treating him. He told her what he could remember about the sensation of recording memories inside the Scribes' Orb, and about the promise he made to Roscoe's mom.

A cool breeze blew through a set of double doors opened to a small balcony.

Georgie stood shakily, pins and needles tingling all up and down his legs. They walked out onto the balcony— Apurva keeping a hand hovering near Georgie's arm just in case—and peered over the stone banister. At least twenty feet below them, a brick pathway separated the gardens from the mansion. A wagon filled with hay was parked on the brick pathway directly below. Beyond the pathway a vast landscape unfolded, lightless save for the patches of mist highlighted by moonlight. Torchlight from the Seminary, more than a mile away, twinkled through the fog.

"Rollie said that she believed there was never just *one* way to solve a problem," Georgie began. Something about the cool night air on Georgie's face gave him a second wind. "But what if Rollie doesn't have a better plan to defeat Eldritch?" He looked over at Apurva. "What then?"

Apurva leaned against the stone banister and looked at Georgie. "You're not actually considering Fumbluff's . . . well, *are* you?"

"What if my father *can't* be saved?" Georgie asked. "But, at the same time, I could defeat Eldritch and save everyone back home? All our friends. Our family." Georgie didn't actually *have* any family back home, but Apurva got the point. "Do I kill Eldritch even though that means hurting my own dad, or do I leave Eldritch alone, even if that means putting everyone we know at risk?"

"Oh, Georgie," Apurva sighed. "That's a moral conundrum of significant complexity."

Apurva split her pony in two equal halves and pulled it tight. "A conundrum is like a puzzle or problem that isn't easy to solve because all the choices have downsides and—"

"Apurva," Georgie smiled. "I know what a conundrum is."

Even though he didn't.

They were silent for a minute, allowing the wind to curl around them, allowing the world to turn.

Then, at the exact same time, Georgie and Apurva said, "We need to find Rollie D."

"Jinx!" they both giggled in unison.

"Georgie," Apurva said, getting serious again. "Even if we *wanted* to go find Rollie, we can't. Fumbluff had Dullwick Ratriot—remember Dullwick, the butler with the rip on his robe sleeve?—place guards all over Corrigendum." She lowered her voice to a whisper. "Even right outside our bedroom door!" She looked over her shoulder through the balcony doors.

"Besides," Apurva continued, "we have no idea how to even *find* Rollie D."

Georgie already worked that one out. "Edie and Ore would know. But we don't know where—"

Apurva grabbed Georgie's wrist. "The blacksmith's store with the colorful roof! Third house from the top of the hill. Ore *told* us!"

Georgie had completely forgotten. "You're a genius!" He hurried back into the bedroom. There was a waxed-canvas rucksack with leather straps next to the fireplace. Georgie put the six sandwiches from Fenton inside the pack then handed it to Apurva. "For your clothes. No time to change out of your pajamas now."

Apurva took the pack but stared blankly at Georgie. "Georgie, did you hear what I said? We can't just walk out our bedroom door. There are guards—"

Georgie smiled. "We're not walking out the bedroom door."

✧ ✧ ✧

A minute later, they were back on the balcony, Georgie wearing the rucksack like a backpack, peering over the edge of the banister.

"Georgie, no way," Apurva said definitively.

"We have to."

"We'll break our legs! We don't know how deep the hay is!"

"I'll go first."

"No!"

"Hold my hand."

"Also no!"

"We have to find Rollie D before the Coronation Ceremony!"

Apurva squeezed her eyes shut. Then she nodded.

They slung their legs over the railing and stood with their backs and butts against the balustrades.

It was a far drop.

"Georgie . . . this is a *really* bad idea."

"It might be."

"I'm going to scream."

"Please don't."

"I'll try not to. But I really think I will."

"On the count of three . . . One."

"Georgie!"

"Two . . ."

"Georgie!"

"Three!"

They jumped.

Chapter 18

Definitely Dark Magic

ay.

In his hair, in his ears, poking at his cheeks and stuck up his sleeves and tickling his nose.

Apurva tugged at his arm.

"Apurva? You okay?"

Georgie was on his back, and only just realized the weight on top of him was Apurva. His ear throbbed. Apurva's face swam into focus—why did her face keep doing that?

"I think I landed on top of you," Apurva groaned, rolling over and giving Georgie a hand off the wagon.

◇ ◇ ◇

They crouched along Corrigendum's outer wall, the only sounds the distant clangs of guards' armor somewhere unseen. The night was still and chill as they cut silently through the garden, careful to crouch the entire way until they reached the fields of feather grass, where they were able to stand at full height and still remain completely hidden. They found the Great Road sometime later, keeping in the shadows as they hurried the winding way to the roundabout.

The steep staircase carved into the ridge was slippery with nighttime mist, which made the descent slow and steady.

Once they reached the city, the houses and buildings became more crowded together until they were all connected with one another in a winding, sloping, seemingly random pattern of alleyways and cobblestone roads. Here and there, candlelight flickered from behind a shuttered window.

"This is it," Apurva whispered a short time later when they reached Stone's Blacksmiths, Bladesmiths, and Problem Solvers, with its crazy-quilt roof of colorful porcelain shingles. As they climbed the steep hill, the view of the sleeping city stretched out before them. They could see the giant ridge and the stone staircases looming in the distance. The third house from the top of the hill looked like it was leaning to one side or had sunk into the earth. A pack mule tied with a rope to an iron peg was asleep in the front yard.

Georgie opened the gate.

"Everyone's asleep," Apurva said.

Georgie grabbed his slingshot from the rucksack and loaded it with a wood chip from the walkway. He aimed at the second-floor window and released.

THUNK!

They waited. There was a breeze. The mule opened one eye and then went back to sleep.

Nothing.

On his third try, the wood chip sailed straight into the house because the window had opened. There was Ore, pulling back the curtains all crusty-eyed and sleepy-looking.

"Stop shooting!" Ore whispered.

"We need your help," Georgie called back.

Georgie heard boots coming from up the hill, just around the bend. Then the loud voice of a night guard, "Who's there!?"

Ore shut the window and disappeared.

Georgie was looking frantically for somewhere to hide when the front door creaked open.

"Inside!" Ore stood there, fumbling with his robe. "And quiet! You're better off getting caught by a night guard than waking up my mom."

◇ ◇ ◇

The Obey's kitchen was unlike any Georgie had ever seen. No refrigerator or microwave, just stacks of copper bowls exposed on unvarnished wood shelves and an assortment of buckets, ropes, and pulleys. Ore had seated Georgie and

Apurva at the kitchen table, in the middle of which was a small wooden plate of nuts and seeds.

Edie came tiptoeing down the stairs now, all bleary-eyed. "What . . . what . . . *what!?*"

Ore rolled his eyes. "Here she comes."

"It's like, the middle of the night," Edie whispered.

"But wait'll you hear what Georgie and Apurva are up to," Ore said.

Edie stopped halfway between the kitchen table and the staircase. "What?"

"Eh, forget it," Ore said. "It's only about Georgie becoming a fully coronated Scribe tomorrow. And a treacherous mission to find Rollie D and the most dangerous artifact to ever exist. You're probably not that interested."

Edie grabbed a jug of milk from the counter and handed out clay cups. "Tell me everything," she said, pouring milk for Apurva first.

"Is it fresh?" Apurva asked, trying to sound as polite as possible.

"Milked yesterday, princess," Ore replied.

"From an *actual* cow?"

"No, from a pigeon," Ore replied. "Yes, from an actual cow! Where does *your* milk come from?"

Apurva hesitated, then took a sip. "Cows."

◇ ◇ ◇

Georgie recounted everything that had happened since they'd last seen the twins. About the Aetherquill, how Flint

Eldritch was actually the missing half of Georgie's father, about the writing test in the Cathedral, and finally, how they'd jumped from Corrigendum's third-floor balcony.

When he was done, Edie poured herself another cup of milk, but now her hands were shaking.

"Butter my butt and call me a biscuit," Ore whispered, looking at Georgie with great admiration. "He put you two in the same room!?"

Edie rolled her eyes at her brother. "It's very impressive, Georgie. Congratulations. Reading *and* writing! I can hardly believe it."

The floorboards above their head creaked, then settled. Edie and Ore stared at the ceiling.

"Shhhh," Ore whispered desperately, "keep it down, pal."

"We need your help finding Rollie D," Georgie whispered, looking from Edie to Ore, then back at Edie. Even though Ore acted like he was in charge, Edie most certainly called the shots in the Obey household—Georgie didn't need to be a Scribe to have figured *that* out.

"And Roscoe," Edie added. "Your friend, remember?" She looked at Georgie coldly. "Rollie D kidnapped him, so you might want to add 'and seeing if Roscoe is alive' to your list of errands."

Georgie didn't blame Edie—she'd grown up believing Rollie D was a dangerous villain. She hadn't seen Rollie D and his dad talking in the garage like they were old friends.

Either way, Edie was right. Of course he wanted to check on Roscoe.

"Yes," Georgie agreed, doing everything he could to remain on Team Edie. "Of course."

Georgie smiled at Edie, but he never knew how to smile when he didn't mean it, and was probably showing too much teeth.

Edie grimaced and looked away.

Ore grabbed a fistful of nuts from the bowl in the center of the kitchen table. "Rollie D and the Altercockers move around. We have no idea where they are."

"Is there a river?" Apurva asked. "Rollie said Roscoe would 'sleep at the bottom of the river' if you attacked her with the Pocket Horsemen. *Remember?*"

Ore swallowed hard. "There *is* a river! Supposedly, at least. Far, far into the forest."

"Will we get back before the Coronation Ceremony?" Georgie asked.

"Get back?" Edie asked. "We're not *going*. Not anywhere. Especially into the forest, especially *far* into the forest. It's so entirely out of the question that I shouldn't even have to state it."

"This'll nearly kill me to say," Ore said, "but I agree with Edie. Going into the forest is a bad idea. The first thing you learn as kids is not to go into the forest. Not for anything. Especially at night."

"You two came into the forest to get us," Apurva challenged. "Didn't you?"

Ore looked down sheepishly. "Well yeah, I'm sorta known as an expert. That's why Fumbluff pointed me for the mission."

"Ah-pointed," Edie corrected matter-of-factly.

"Whatever. You just need to stay super quiet, avoid the main paths, and not get lost. I'm good at all three."

"Ore?" Edie said, her voice low and slow. "Don't. Even. Think about it."

"How will you get there?" Ore prodded.

Georgie cleared his throat. "Pocket Horsemen?"

"Ha! Dummy, you don't know how to call them, you don't even know how to whistle!"

"So *you* call them for us!"

"And weapons? Supplies? *Snacks!?*"

"I have my slingshot. And we've got six sandwiches. And also, this isn't a hostile rescue mission. Rollie D isn't going to hurt us . . . I don't think so, at least "

"You blew two fingers off one of her men!" Ore exclaimed. "Did you forget that little fact?"

Georgie had not forgotten. The man's name was Yooker Tenderfoot. And he had been pointing a gun at his best friend's head. He did what he had to do, but Georgie still made a note to offer Yooker Tenderfoot a sincere apology if they ever crossed paths again.

"Okay, okay," Edie said, in her best I'm-clearly-the-only-adult-in-the-room voice, "here's the plan"—she eyed her brother—"the *only* plan. We'll go, but not in the dead of night. We'll leave before dawn, before Mom is up. She'll think we went up to the Seminary to help set up the Coronation Ceremony."

Ore was nodding enthusiastically now, unable to conceal his admiration for his sister.

"If we move quickly, and if things go well—*big* ifs— then we'll be back in Scatterplot before the Coronation Ceremony begins in the afternoon. Hopefully we'll find Rollie D. Hopefully we'll find Roscoe."

"Big hopefullies!" Ore added with a huge smile on his face.

Georgie wished they'd just leave now, but his father once told him that compromise was like picking a movie to watch with friends: You might not get to watch your top choice, but at least you won't be watching alone.

◇ ◇ ◇

A few minutes later, Georgie was lying on the Obey's living room floor under a quilt (one he was unfortunately sharing with Ore) staring into the small fire burning in the fireplace. Apurva and Edie were bundled under spare blankets on the sagging living room sofa.

Ore shifted with a moan and a yawn. "Pssst, Georgie, you asleep or what?"

"Yes," Georgie whispered back. He was wide awake. "You?"

"Nope. Whatcha thinkin' about?"

"Nothing." But Georgie was thinking about everything. He was thinking about his father; how Georgie had snapped at him when his dad brought up his mother on the way home from school. He wished he could take that back. He was thinking about memories of utter and complete defeat. Even though he hoped Rollie D was going to have answers, he was feeling rather defeated himself.

"You think you'll stay here forever?" Ore asked.

CHHHHAAA–*SHOOOO*, Edie snored.

Ore threw a sock at her head and she bolted upright, looked around, then dropped her head back to the pillow.

"I don't know," Georgie responded finally.

"You should."

"He can't," Apurva said. She had just powered her iPhone on, and her face was awash in its bluish glow. "He has school. Then high school. Then college. We can't just stay here forever."

"Paradiddle Pete!" Ore cried, throwing the quilt off both him and Georgie and skittering beside Apurva. "What *is* that thing?"

Apurva giggled. "It's a phone."

"A phone?" Edie asked, rubbing her eyes. "An artifact from your world? Is it magic?"

"It's not magic," Apurva said, "it's technology. I guess it's a little like magic."

Edie sat up and clumsily squished her body next to Apurva's.

Ore leaned his face closer. "Is it *dark* magic?"

Apurva laughed again. "Edie, move over. No, it's not dark magic. It's just a phone . . . for calling people. Although no one uses it for that anymore. Mostly just texting."

"Sounds like dark magic to me," Ore said.

"It's not, but my battery is about to die."

Edie gasped. "I'm so sorry to hear that!"

"Huh? It's not sad! I can recharge the battery. It's okay. There's no service here anyway."

"Service?" Edie asked. "Like Dullwick? Like a butler?"

"No, no. Like, we pay a company every month to make the phones work . . . so we can connect with friends and family and look things up online and stuff."

"You have to pay to connect with family in your world?" Ore asked. "With friends?"

"Forget it," Apurva said.

"Can I hold it?"

Apurva put the phone in Ore's hand. He sucked air in as if he'd touched a lump of burning coal. He turned the phone over slowly, inspecting its glossy surface. "I . . . Phone," Ore said, mostly to himself, reading the words under the logo. "Oh, I get it. You named it I Phone."

"Cute!" Edie said. "Love that."

"Everyone's phone is named iPhone."

Ore stared at Apurva for a minute, his face contorted into something confused, like he wasn't sure if she was joking or not. Then he laughed. "Everyone names their phone the same thing!? That's gotta be the stupidest thing I've ever heard in my life! If I had one of these I'd name it . . ." Ore looked up at the ceiling for a moment. "I'd name it . . . well, I'd have to think about it! You can't rush genius, you know."

"Right," Apurva laughed, rolling her eyes. She took the phone back and tapped the photo icon. Ore and Edie both gasped, this time for real, when Apurva's camera roll opened. "These are all my photos," Apurva said.

Edie clapped a hand over her mouth. Ore tried stifling his laughter.

"What?" Apurva asked. "What's so funny?"

"A foe-toe is what we call a man whose wife ran off with a gaffer," Ore said. "Poor *foe-toe!*"

Ore used his index finger to reach toward the iPhone screen. "Can I try?"

"Knock yourself out," Apurva said. Ore looked at her apprehensively, then quickly tapped the screen as if he was expecting an electric shock. Ore tapped again, and all of a sudden, Roscoe Harris's voice blared from the speakers, shattering the midnight silence in Edie and Ore's living room.

"*And he's doooowwwn!* Ladies and Gentlemen, Georgie Summers has fallen! The crowd is going *absolutely WILD!*"

Georgie rolled to the sofa, reached up, and paused the video. The silence was astounding.

"*Definitely* dark magic," Edie whispered.

Georgie laid back down and stared into the fire, still awake long after Edie, Ore, and Apurva fell asleep. His thoughts eventually turned back to the Aetherquill. He wondered if what Fumbluff said was really true about the cracked eggs beneath a stack of heavy bricks. That it was too late to make things right again. To make his father *whole* again. At some point in the dead of night, he drifted into a restless slumber, where he dreamt troubled dreams of three-legged monsters, long black scarves wrapped around pale white skulls, . . . and beetles.

﷽ ﷽ ﷽

Chapter 19

An Early Morning Mission

eorgie rubbed his eyes, stretched, and propped himself up on his elbows. He felt refreshed.

Edie and Ore were already in the kitchen, tiptoeing silently about, each of them with matching rucksacks strapped to their backs. Georgie and Apurva took turns splashing cold water on their faces from the washbasin. No time for a shower, and come to think of it, Georgie wasn't sure if Scatterplot even *had* showers.

Ore climbed up onto the counter and opened the window above the washbasin. The predawn air felt somehow *joyful*, and while Georgie had no idea how air could feel joyful, Edie and Ore would have explained it's exactly how Coronation Ceremony mornings have dawned in Scatterplot for centuries.

Ore stuck his head out of the window and whistled. Like a song. Two notes.

Upstairs, the bed creaked. They heard a cough.

Then, quiet.

Phiz and Bugle appeared out of nowhere, giant blocks of shadow in the early morning light just beginning to rim the mountains in the distance.

◇ ◇ ◇

They entered the forest just as the day was warming up in earnest. Edie and Apurva rode atop Bugle, while Ore and Georgie rode Phiz. A thousand slender rays of creamy sun slanted through the trees. Birch trees with their weathered white trunks, steep hills and shallow ravines, felled logs and timber. Everywhere covered in moss and pine and vines and roots.

The Pocket Horsemen walked delicately, careful to step around fallen branches and slowing to a crawl when the terrain dipped or climbed.

Georgie replayed Fumbluff's words in his head: *The only way to defeat Eldritch, to save everyone you love, is to give Eldritch a memory of utter and complete defeat. Making him believe that he'd failed. It will destroy him.*

And Rollie's command: *Don't do anything stupid.*

Oh, Georgie missed his dad. His dad wasn't much of

a problem solver, and Georgie couldn't remember a single time his dad had ever given him a piece of advice, but sometimes, when his dad would smile and rub his ear, it was just as good. Maybe even better.

The four of them got to talking about the Aetherquill. Ore speculated about what *other* powers it may have, Edie wanted to know who used the Aetherquill on Georgie's father all those years ago, and Apurva, astute as ever, wondered why Rollie D wanted Georgie's father to take the Aetherquill in the first place . . . and give it to Georgie.

Georgie thought about that first conversation he'd overheard in his garage, when Rollie urged his father to take the pen. Why? Did Rollie's plan involve the Aetherquill? Was there something else she wanted him to do with it?

Eventually, and thankfully, Ore changed the subject. He wanted to know what school was like in New York. Pretty girls, obnoxious bullies, idiot teachers . . . all the good stuff.

They had been climbing uphill for about an hour and now they broke from the trees. They were near the summit of this particular mountain, the air thinner and much colder.

"Hold on tight!" Ore cried, then kicked Phiz hard and they took off in a wild gallop.

Georgie grabbed hold of Ore and clenched his legs against Phiz's back muscles. The Pocket Horsemen ran like wildfire, their knuckles pounding the ground like a hurricane. They ran even faster as they crested the summit and faster still as they descended the other side, toward the tree cover below. The rush of cold air pulled frozen tears from Georgie's eyes. The ground on this side of the mountain was marshy and wet, and the Pocket Horsemen's knuckles sank into the boggy wetland.

"I think Rollie D and my dad were, like, friends," Georgie said once the Pocket Horsemen slowed their pace. "But the Altercockers *hate* the Scatterplotters, don't they?"

Edie was concentrating on the terrain, her eyes scanning left and right as she steered Bugle around brambles and hidden boulders. "We hate the Altercockers, too. Don't forget that."

Georgie unwrapped Fenton's package of sandwiches— pastrami! He handed the sandwiches out, nearly falling off Phiz's back stretching out to Edie and Apurva.

"Why?" Georgie asked, licking mustard off his fingertips. "Why do Scribes hate Altercockers?"

"They're thieves and kidnappers," Ore said. "And they're dirty. Disgusting."

"Why do they hate *us* then? The Scribes . . . Scatterplot?"

"Rollie blames the Scribes for everything that happened to her," Edie said. "They kicked her out. Fumbluff and the Scribes. They kicked her out of Scatterplot. But she deserved it."

"Wait, Rollie is from Scatterplot?" Georgie asked.

"Oh, yeah," Ore answered. "Rollie was one of us. Now, she's what my mother calls *persona non grata*."

"What does that mean?"

"An unwelcome person." Ore unwrapped a second sandwich. "She was caught breaking into the Library and altering the books."

"*Altering* the books?"

"Oh, yeah," Ore said. "Not *destroying* the books, but *altering* them. She'd pick out specific pages or lines and overwrite them."

"Why?" Apurva asked.

"No idea," Ore answered sharply. "I'd ask her, but I'm not yet ready to die with one of her arrows impaling my heart. Anyway, that's how they got their name. The *Alter*cockers. Get it?"

"Whoa," Georgie said, perplexed. "What happened to her?"

"Rollie was kicked out when she was sixteen," Ore said. "Eventually, she formed a tribe. All the exiled wanderers from other baronies and cities. She fed them. Led them. Gave them a family. That sort of thing. Dig it?"

"She was messing with people's memories," Edie said. "*Your* memories. The memories of the people in your world. Something bad happened, but we don't know the whole story."

Georgie wondered if his father knew about Rollie D's being a criminal outcast for altering the Great Books.

Georgie sighed. "I need to pee."

"Here!?" Ore blurted.

Georgie looked around at the trees and boulders and shrubs in every direction. "Where else should I go?" One of Roscoe's favorite refrains came to him just then: Out in the open, let it flow, where it lands, nobody will know.

Ore brought Bugle to a stop.

"How are you going to wash your hands?" Edie asked.

Georgie's cheeks burned red. God, *girls!*

Phiz bent down low, allowing Georgie to slide smoothly off his back. "I'll wipe them on some leaves. Promise."

He walked twenty feet up ahead and relieved himself behind the largest tree he could find. As he finished up, he heard something rustle behind him.

"GEORGIE!" Ore screamed. "Get *BACK!*"

But it was too late.

SNAP! CRACK! GRRRRABIM!

Two meaty arms shot from the prickly shrubs and grabbed Georgie around the neck.

One of the hands had only three fingers.

Chapter 20

You . . . Got . . . CAUGHT?

Georgie's entire face stung from the thorns that had torn through his cheeks, lips, and ears. Blood trickled from the cuts.

He was on his back, lying on a patch of wet moss, and staring into Yooker Tenderfoot's happy face.

"GOTCHOO!" Yooker cried, grinding his knee into Georgie's chest.

Georgie bit his arm. So much for a sincere apology.

"OWWWW!" Yooker shrieked and punched Georgie in the face.

Georgie's vision shuddered and he felt one or two of his teeth loosen. He spit out a clot of blood and saliva.

Yooker hoisted him to his feet and dragged him around the blackberry bramble.

They should have stayed at Edie and Ore's house, drinking fresh milk. From an *actual* cow!

"NO! PLEASE!" It was Edie, she was shrieking. *"PLEASE!"*

A second Altercocker had a knife against Ore's neck. She was an enormous woman, pimples, a mustache, the works. Her hair was braided in messy ropes and she wore a vest made of fur and leather ties. Her calves looked like fire hydrants. Both Yooker and the woman wore open-toe sandals with canvas straps wrapping around their feet and ankles.

"PLEASE!" Edie shrieked again, raising her hands. "Please don't hurt my brother!"

The Altercocker waved her knife at Edie and Apurva. "You two miss pretties! Get off the beast, and do it nice and slow. Keep your hands where I can see 'em!"

Bugle and Phiz were growling angrily, but with a knife to Ore's neck, they held their place.

Edie, still sobbing, slipped off Bugle's back and put her hands back up. Apurva followed, staring at Georgie, her hands in the air.

Yooker shoved Georgie in the back and sent him stumbling over a root toward Ore. Bugle and Phiz reared up, punching the ground and baring their teeth.

"Back 'em down, boy," Yooker said, pointing his knife at Ore, "if you know what's good fer you."

Ore put his hands up slowly and looked at the mountainous woman behind him. "May I?"

She nodded. "No sudden movements."

"Yes, ma'am." Ore approached Phiz and Bugle and patted the fur between their eyes. He hugged them, kissed them, and whispered into their ears. Georgie couldn't quite make out what he was saying, but it didn't sound like English.

The Pocket Horsemen whined, licked Ore's face, and then turned. Ore smacked each of them on their behinds and the Pocket Horsemen took off. The entire forest shook as they pounded back in the direction they'd come, until suddenly the pounding stopped, and there was just a receding shaking of the trees from high above.

Yooker Tenderfoot and the enormous lady exchanged looks and burst out laughing. "Four of 'em, Toots!" Yooker cried, showing off his yellowing teeth with a crooked grin. "Four Scribe kids! Jus' can't believe our luck. Rollie'll give us double portions. For a fortnight, Toots! A fortnight at least!"

"It ain't luck!" the gigantic lady named Toots cried. "We have an aptitude for the ambush! We are savvy on the sneak and slick with stealth and—"

Yooker interrupted by grabbing Georgie and putting his knife against his back. "I should slice this one open right now, Toots. For what he did to me fingers."

Apurva shrieked. "Don't hurt him!"

The Altercockers turned to Apurva. "And why shouldn't we?" Yooker asked.

"Yeah?" Toots asked, grabbing Ore once more by the shoulders. "Why shouldn't we?"

Apurva was trembling. "Because . . . because then Rollie would be angry, wouldn't she? Rollie D doesn't let you hurt kids from Scatterplot. Not without her permission."

Yooker's face contorted into something so confused and rageful that it was nearly funny.

"She's right," Toots said with a scowl. "Stow it."

Yooker pulled the knife away from Georgie's back with a grunt and shoved him forward.

They marched slowly through the boggy marshland, their soaking wet feet the least of their problems. Yooker and Toots walked an arm's length behind them, their knives drawn, and smelling awful. Edie was still sniveling and every few minutes she'd break down in great, heaving sobs until Toots shoved her hard in the back, at which point Ore would invariably shout, "Hands off!," at which point Yooker would invariably shove *him* hard in the back.

And so it went for what felt like an hour of sloppy, wet cold. Burning legs and screaming toe blisters. Georgie was hoping they were making good time, but at least they were *definitely* going to see Rollie D now.

A short while later, Georgie heard the sound of rushing water.

The river!

The trees were thinning considerably and late-morning sun poured into a clearing up ahead. Georgie saw something, fifty feet away or less, near the clearing, behind a tree.

A man with the sun at his back, his face in shadow.

But his boots. Georgie recognized those shiny black knee-high boots with the pointy toes and silver snaps along the side. Those were Flint Eldritch's boots.

Georgie ran.

"GET HIM!" Yooker screamed.

"GET HIM!" Toots screamed.

"YOU GET HIM!" Yooker and Toots both screamed at the same time. They stuck fingers in each other's faces.

Georgie ran as fast as his tired legs would carry him, nearly slipping on a patch of moss, pinwheeling his arms for balance before catching himself against the tree he'd seen Flint Eldritch standing behind.

But Eldritch was gone.

Dad! Georgie thought, his own voice echoing inside his head. *Dad! Where are you?* He circled the tree once more. Was his mind playing tricks on him? Was he sleep deprived? He called for his father once more—this time aloud—but the only response was the loud cry of a woman's voice.

"LAUNDRY TIME!"

Georgie knew that voice.

Rollie D.

Georgie ran across the clearing (checking back over his shoulder for Yooker and Toots, who couldn't be far behind), and found himself standing at the top of a steep ravine running down to the riverbank.

There were Altercockers everywhere.

Girls and boys were skipping stones in the water. Across the river and up another steep ravine, Georgie couldn't believe his eyes: floating tents, hovering between the trees, at least ten feet off the ground. Some large, some small, all of them the same faded beige fabric. The tents dipped and shook in midair as men and women jumped effortlessly in and out of them, some dressed in furs, others with their arms exposed to the cold. Down below on the forest floor, fires burned in stone pits, where more Altercockers sat roasting small animals over makeshift spits.

Rollie D poked her head out of the largest floating tent in the camp. She jumped to the ground and landed gracefully, as if the drop wasn't ten feet but ten inches. Her fur cloak was open. A gold object hung from a necklace around her neck, partially hidden beneath her chemise. Her hair was untied, a burning red river over her shoulders and down her back. Her bow was still holstered against her hip and her quiver was still slung against her back.

"LAUNDRY TIME!" Rollie shouted again, hoisting an enormous basket off the ground. "COME ON, YOU SMELLY, IMPUDENT, FREELOADIN' SCALLAWAGS!"

The Altercockers stopped what they were doing—smoking, eating, roasting, stone-skipping, playing a strange game of cards and dice—to fill Rollie's laundry basket. Moored to boulders along the opposite side of the river were a collection of boats and river transports.

A young girl dressed in a dirty smock skipped up the ravine to where Rollie stood and dropped an armful of laundry into Rollie's basket. Rollie smiled at the girl. "Tell your old man if he doesn't surrender his filthy garb, the next time he'll deal a hand of Gotcha you'll be a grown lady."

The girl giggled and skipped off.

Rollie cupped her hands to her mouth. "Be fleet! Be swift! Be rapid! I said *LAUNDRY TIME*, you ragamuffin good for nuthins!"

Georgie scanned the riverbank, the tents, and the forest for any signs of Flint Eldritch. He looked at everyone's feet and saw loads of clogs, sandals, and dirty toes—but no polished black boots. On his second go-round, just as he was catching his breath, he saw Roscoe.

Roscoe! Alive and well!

He was sitting across the river on a large flat rock, his feet dangling into the water. He held a wooden stick that ran straight through three of the largest sausages Georgie had ever seen. There was a group of Altercocker children sitting around him. Roscoe took a bite of sausage and juice dripped down his chin. He said something just then that must have been pretty funny because all the boys and girls burst out laughing.

"*Roscoe!*" Georgie called as loud as he dared. "*Roscoe!*"

A moment later, he had his slingshot drawn, a pebble in its leather pouch.

This would not be an easy shot.

Roscoe brought the sausage shish kabob to his face again . . . and Georgie released.

WHOOOOOSH!

The tiny pebble flew across the river and knocked the bottom quarter of the sausage clean off the skewer.

Roscoe bit down on nothing.

The Altercocker girls and boys giggled and clapped. They thought it was a trick!

But Roscoe looked up, the color draining from his face. Georgie stepped out from behind the tree and waved frantically.

Roscoe's eyes went wide.

Georgie put a finger to his lips. *Quiet, Roscoe.*

Roscoe dropped his skewer and jumped up on the rock. He drew a deep breath.

Oh God, Georgie thought.

"SUMMERS!" Roscoe shouted at the top of his lungs. "You CAME! GEORGIE! Cheez-Its, Mary, and Joseph Stalin! You CAME for me! HA! I can't believe it! I KNEW it! Look at you! You wet rag! HE CAME FOR ME! I *told* you he'd come for me!"

Roscoe was pointing and hopping up and down, but, except for him, the entire river bank was silent as every single Altercocker—man, woman, boy, and girl—*and* Rollie D stopped what they were doing and stared straight at Georgie.

Then Yooker was behind him, like Georgie knew he would be at any moment, and he rammed Georgie in the back with both hands, sending Georgie tumbling headfirst down the ravine. He somersaulted in the mud and moss and—

Splash!

—came to a stop on his back in the freezing cold river water. Yooker lifted him up by the neck and twisted his arms behind his back. Georgie looked at Roscoe, whose face was now molded in a tragic frown of shock and dismay.

"Caught?" Roscoe whispered. "*Caught!?* Georgie! You . . . got . . . *CAUGHT!?* This is why you struggle socially! Oh, Georgie, girls don't like *caught!* Girls like daring escapes and wild adventures! They don't like—"

"I like him!" Apurva shouted, struggling in Toots's grip. "GET YOUR HANDS OFF ME!"

Toots gave her a push down the ravine, and she stumbled next to Georgie.

Apurva looked at Georgie's mud-streaked face. "I like him," she said.

Georgie's feet were blistering. His cheeks stung. His clothes were soaked.

But he'd never felt so warm.

CRITICAL

Chapter 21

Inside Rollie D's Tent

Yooker Tenderfoot marched Georgie across the ice-cold river. The water rose to Georgie's thighs and . . . never mind. He was soaked.

Rollie was standing on the other side, waiting.

"They came for me, Rollie!" Roscoe exclaimed. "I told you they would!" He started to climb down off the rock.

Without taking her eyes off Georgie, Rollie drew her bow and arrow in a blur and aimed it at Roscoe.

"SID'DOWN!" she bellowed, and Roscoe dropped like a suitcase filled with bricks.

Now Yooker and Toots had Georgie, Apurva, Edie, and

Ore corralled on the riverbank in front of Rollie. A group of Altercockers formed around her.

Rollie fingered her gold necklace chain, and now Georgie could see the shape of the object attached to it, mostly hidden beneath her chemise. Could Rollie D actually be wearing the Aetherquill around her neck?

"You told me to come find you after I saw Fumbluff," Georgie said, looking over at Apurva. "Well, I saw Fumbluff." He glanced over his shoulder at Edie and Ore, and beyond them, the growing group of Altercockers.

"I beg your forgiveness," Ore muttered in Rollie's direction, tapping his throat three times and not making anything close to eye contact with her. "Our Coronation Ceremony starts in a few hours and it's my first one ever and I *really* can't be late. So . . ." Ore shuffled in place. "Can you let us go? Please and thank you, ma'am?"

Rollie shot a look at Ore. "Are you mocking me?"

Ore shook his head from side to side violently. "No, ma'am." Ore bowed his head and Georgie almost burst out laughing at how insanely terrified Ore looked in that instant.

Rollie rubbed her eyes and sighed. "I should just kill you all," she said, mainly to herself, sounding like a defeated mother of one too many idiot children.

"We *should* kill 'em, Rollie," Yooker Tenderfoot yelled. "They're Scribe kids! Scatterplotters!"

"Scatterplotters!" Toots shouted, as if she was a horror-shop toy programmed to repeat Yooker's last word every time he spoke. "And we got four of 'em, Rollie! We gonna get somethin' from you, Rollie? We gonna get somethin' good?"

"Shut up, Toots," Rollie said.

But Toots Tenderfoot did not shut up—she did the opposite of shutting up, her calls to at *least* put the kids from Scatterplot to hard labor getting louder and louder.

Rollie's eyes narrowed to angry slits and she marched toward Toots. Suddenly Toots had nothing at all left to say. A moment later Rollie was back, dragging Toots Tenderfoot by the ear.

"*Ow! Rollie! Ow! Ow! My ear!*" Toots yipped, her tippy toes hardly touching the ground. "*My ear! You gonna rip it clean off, Rollie!*"

Rollie deposited Toots on the ground, in the mud. "Unfortunately," Rollie said, "the ear is not an easy thing to detach from the head."

"I'm sorry, Rollie," Toots whimpered.

"She's sorry!" Yooker shouted, but stayed where he was, making no real effort to help his . . . wife? Sister? Who knew.

"What are ears for, you little wastrel?" Rollie shouted at Toots.

"For lis'nin', Rollie, for *lis'nin'!*"

"For listening, that's right. So, when I say be quiet, you—"

"Be quiet—I be quiet!"

"Stand up."

Toots stood, her head bowed, eyes on Rollie's feet.

"Triple duty!" Rollie shouted. "The barge, *all* the

pontoons, and the food rafts. Oiled, sponged, and mopped. Thrice daily!"

"Oh no, not triple duty!" Toots cried. "Anything but triple duty!"

Rollie raised her arm and Toots flinched. "For a fortnight."

"Too long!" Toots whimpered. "Not fair! I hate cleaning boats!"

"Don't we all," Rollie said. "Get out of my sight."

This time, Toots listened, and Georgie watched as she headed for the boats, Yooker trailing sheepishly behind her.

When they were gone, Rollie turned back to Georgie, wiping her hands on her cloak. "So . . . you met Fumbluff."

Georgie nodded.

"And?"

"He's a Scribe," Ore said, making a real habit of speaking when not being spoken to. "Reading *and* writing!"

Rollie stepped closer to Georgie, her face now inches from his own. "Is it true?"

Georgie nodded.

"Impressive." Rollie lowered her voice so only Georgie could hear. "Do you understand who Flint Eldritch is now?"

Georgie nodded again. "He's my father. But also not my father." Georgie paused, not entirely sure how to say it. Rollie looked up at the perfectly blue and cloudless sky. "There's a storm coming," Rollie muttered. "I can feel it." She looked back at Georgie. "Fumbluff's plan is a bad plan. No child should be asked to choose what Fumbluff expects you to choose. No child should be asked to *do* what Fumbluff expects you to do."

A great flood of hope coursed through Georgie just then. Exiled criminal outcast or not, this woman was actually making sense. "That's why we came to *find* you—"

Rollie snapped her fingers. "Not here, where the air is open and the breeze carries words." She turned. "My tent. Follow me."

She stopped on a patch of dirt below her tent, which hovered at least fifteen feet above their heads.

"Jump," Rollie said, looking at Georgie.

Georgie cleared his throat. "I'm sorry, Rollie? I'm not sure what you mean?"

Rollie rolled her eyes, grabbed Georgie under the armpits, and threw him up into the air.

And up Georgie went.

He glided upward, like some magical force was pulling him against the natural laws of gravity, and landed softly inside Rollie's tent. It took him a second to feel his legs again on solid ground (even though Rollie's tent floor sagged beneath his weight). Looking through the open flaps, he could see the river and tree branches and the tops of the tallest Altercockers' heads and—

Oomph!

Georgie dropped to the tent floor to avoid Roscoe and Apurva, who both floated into the tent just then and landed on wobbly legs beside him. Rollie landed a moment later and sat the three of them down on a tree stump in the center of the tent. "You need to be back in time for the

Coronation Ceremony," Rollie began, fingering the chain around her neck. "The Aetherquill's power will only work for an *ordained* Scribe."

"Yeah," Georgie sighed. "Fumbluff said the Coronation Ceremony is like getting a license to write in Whisperloom. Without it, the writing won't . . . *stick*."

Rollie nodded. "Your father is trapped inside Eldritch. *Beneath* Eldritch. Fumbluff believes there is no way to—"

"Hey, Rollie?" Roscoe interrupted politely. "Can you repeat that? Because it sounded like you said Georgie's dad is trapped *inside* Flint Eldritch, haha, I was lis'nin', Rollie, I was, but I must've misunderstanded—"

Misunderstood, Georgie thought. *Not misunderstanded.* It had only been a day and Roscoe was already talking like an Altercocker.

"You heard me right," Rollie said, then told Roscoe everything Fumbluff had already told Apurva and Georgie about the Aetherquill and how Flint Eldritch came to be.

Roscoe's eyes went wider and wider as Rollie spoke, just like they did when Georgie told Roscoe about his father's kidnapping—a conversation that felt like it took place ages ago.

When Rollie was finished, Roscoe looked like he could use a cold drink of water.

"Rollie," Georgie began, feeling antsy. "Is there another way? Is there *any* way I can save my father?" He exhaled, then added, "Tell me the truth."

"Boy," Rollie said, her eyes narrowing, "I wouldn't tell you anything *but* the truth. What do you take me for?"

"The disrespect from this one!" Roscoe exclaimed, and gave Georgie a whack on the back of the head. "Please excuse my dear friend, Rollie, he means no—"

"Roscoe," Rollie snapped. "Shut up."

"After the coronation," Rollie continued, addressing Georgie, "Fumbluff will bring you to Quillethra, the realm from which the Aetherquill originated. They'll only let coronated Scribes in . . . or out."

"Who's *they*?" Roscoe asked.

"Quillethrans," Rollie said, as if Roscoe should have understood this. "The custodians of all Libraries and the guardians of the Librarian. They're not exactly *people*, like us, they're more like . . ." Rollie paused, searching for the word.

"Angels?" Apurva asked tentatively.

"Something like that."

Rollie looked back at Georgie. "And when you get there, Fumbluff wants you to use the Aetherquill to destroy Eldritch and kill your father."

"Holy moly, macaroni," Roscoe exclaimed.

This wasn't news to Georgie, but hearing it stated so plainly still made Georgie's face burn.

"But here's where Fumbluff and I disagree mightily," Rollie continued, blowing an errant rope of red hair out of her eyes. "I *knew* John Summers. When he was *whole*. He was a fighter. You might even say he was part Altercocker before the Altercockers existed. And *I* think John Summers still has some fight left in him. Might have a *lot*."

The hair on the back of Georgie's neck stood ramrod straight.

"The Aetherquill can make someone believe a memory that isn't true," Rollie continued. "It—"

"*Sick!*" Roscoe cried. "Use it on me, Rollie! Make me believe *Roscoe's Rag* has, like, a *million* YouTube subscribers! Do I care if it's actually true? No, I do not! Lie to me, baby. Lie to me!"

Apurva and Georgie and Rollie *all* told Roscoe to shut up at the same time, and Roscoe did, casting his eyes down at the floor of Rollie's tent. When Georgie turned back to Rollie, she was holding a slender arrow and stroking its smooth feathers. "If I killed a child accidentally with my bow and arrow, I'd never shoot the same again. Whether I'd *actually* killed the child, or not, wouldn't matter. What matters is belief. My *aim* would be forever weakened. My *grip* would be forever compromised."

She stowed the arrow in her quiver in a blur. "If you use the Aetherquill not to *destroy* Eldritch, but to cause him to weaken his *grip* on your dad . . . maybe, just maybe . . . *reintegration.*" Rollie made two fists and put them one on top of the other. "A reversal of light and shadow. Good and evil." Her two fists changed positions. "Put your dad back on top. John Summers *whole* again . . . do you understand, Georgie?"

Yes, Georgie thought he understood. And with that understanding came an uncomfortable tightening in his stomach, a premonition that things were about to start moving fast, that some catastrophic event was hovering just around some near-future bend.

Rollie pulled the chain around her neck, and emerging

from beneath her chemise came what looked like a long golden bullet, with tiny grooves running down the barrel. The Aetherquill. Georgie was sure of it. "It's a far more dangerous and risky plan," Rollie said, "but a dangerous *good* plan beats a safe *bad* plan by a mile, wouldn't you agree?"

Georgie nodded. He agreed with that wholeheartedly.

Rollie held up the Aetherquill, the delicate chain running through an eyehole in its cap. "But you have to ask yourself this, Georgie, son of John."

Rollie unclipped the Aetherquill from the chain.

"What are you willing to risk to save the man who raised you?"

Everything, Georgie thought, staring transfixed at the golden pen.

"How far are you willing to go to save your father?" Rollie opened her palm, and the Aetherquill laid there, perfectly balanced. She held her hand out to Georgie, beckoning him to touch it, to take it. To *claim* it.

"How?" Georgie whispered. "How do I get Eldritch to . . . weaken his hold on my dad?" He could feel the Aetherquill's power radiating from that golden, grooved barrel like an invisible current of electricity. "And what happens if he *does?*"

Rollie smiled, showing her smooth white teeth, like beach glass. "A Scribe sees with his heart and writes with his mind. Have you heard that yet?"

Georgie nodded, not taking his eyes from the Aetherquill.

"I can't tell you what you'll need to write when the time comes, kid. But I believe you *can* save your dad. More than save him—bring him *back*. And I believe you already have the answer inside you." Rollie stretched her open palm further. "Now take it."

Georgie's hand was steady when he lifted the Aetherquill from Rollie's palm, and when he closed his fist around it, the entire world seemed to come to a complete standstill. His breath didn't just slow, it *ceased*, as if inhaling and exhaling no longer mattered. The Aetherquill thrummed hotly in his fist, like it was alive.

Georgie unscrewed the cap. If the solid gold nib had once been shiny and polished, it was no longer. A patina of brown film covered the silver curlycue inlays around its edges.

He looked up and saw tears in Rollie's eyes. "She was the last one to use it."

Georgie looked closer at the Aetherquill's nib.

Engraved in its center, in tiny script letters, was: *PENELOPE S.*

𝍃𝍏𝍊   𝍓𝍏𝍑𝍐𝍕   𝍆𝍑𝍊𝍒𝍐𝍔𝍒𝍑𝍐𝍖𝍑

Chapter 22

Coronation Day in Scatterplot

By the time Georgie, Apurva, Edie, and Ore approached Scatterplot, it was late afternoon, and even from a distance, Georgie could see the cobblestone streets were packed with happy Scatterplotters of all ages. The sense of coronation joy in the air was palpable.

What Georgie sensed even more was the Aetherquill in his pocket, thrumming warmly against his thigh.

Hours earlier, as Rollie was sending them on their way, the Altercockers had whooped and hollered when

Roscoe'd announced he wanted to stay with them. That was right after Rollie had wished Georgie luck, because, in her opinion, Flint Eldritch wasn't likely to leave any survivors. That's what did it for Roscoe, who was eager to declare that he'd choose hanging out with the Altercockers and eating roasted sausage kabobs over Flint Eldritch and *"not likely to leave any survivors"* any day of the week.

But then Roscoe had gotten serious—something Roscoe Harris had only done once or twice in his entire life—and pulled Georgie and Apurva close. *I'm learning how to fight here,* he whispered, low enough so the Altercockers couldn't hear. *And we may still need to fight. Go get coronated, Georgie. Protect the Aetherquill. We're going to see each other again soon. I can feel it.*

Georgie'd tried talking Roscoe into coming back to Scatterplot, but one thing everyone knew about Roscoe Harris was that he was as stubborn as a boulder.

Now, as they slowed to a crawl because the city was teeming with bustling passersby, Georgie *did* feel it. He would see Roscoe again soon. Things were moving fast now, and there was more adventuring ahead. He couldn't stop thinking about what Rollie had said about reintegration. That there was a chance he could not only save his dad, but make him *whole* again. The idea itself sent swarms of mad butterflies swirling in Georgie's belly.

They passed a florist, a fish shop, and a few stalls sell-ing handmade toys that spun, flipped, and danced along the shopkeeper's wooden countertops. Georgie put his hand over his pants pocket, feeling the Aetherquill's shape beneath his hand. It thrummed against his thigh. It was powerful, alright, he could tell that much.

She was the last one to use it, Rollie had said. Yesterday, before dinner at Corrigendum, Fumbluff had said that the last time the Aetherquill was used, it was used on his father. Did that mean Georgie's mother used the Aetherquill against his father? And if so, *why?* What had his mother been trying to accomplish? What had his mother been *thinking?*

"Did you hear what I said?" Ore asked, bumping Georgie in the shoulder.

"Huh? Sorry. Spacing out."

"You do that a lot," Ore said, bringing the Pocket Horseman to a stop and sliding off its back. The streets were too clogged now to keep riding. "I said, we made great time! Coronation doesn't start for another hour!"

Another knot tightened in Georgie's stomach. Once he was coronated, once he was an officially ordained Scribe . . . there would be no turning back.

They passed Gammer's Glasswerx on their left. Across the street, a pair of banjo players strummed and tapped their feet to the rhythm of their music. WE PLAY FOR FREE, BUT WILL STOP FOR MONEY! read a handwritten sign propped against an open instrument case.

Georgie kept thinking about that one word: *Reintegration.* Rollie had said his father was a fighter. Georgie never saw his father lift a finger to hurt a fly. He desperately wanted to meet this version of his dad Rollie had described. A *fighter* . . . fighters are courageous. Daring. Bold.

But . . . how? Rollie said the answer was already inside

him. *A Scribe sees with his heart and writes with his mind.* But Georgie was drawing blanks. And with the coronation just an hour away, that made Georgie feel very worried.

Further up the cobbled street, the door to Stone's Blacksmiths, Bladesmiths, and Problem Solvers swung open violently, and taking up most of the empty doorway, looking like he was on the verge of a heart attack, was Charlie Fenton. His mane of black hair was messier than usual, sticking out in clumps every which way. "GEORGIE! APURVA! YOU'RE IN BIG BIG TROUBLE, EDIE AND ORE OBEY!"

Ore laughed and ran over to Fenton, who wrapped Ore in a bear hug. Edie followed next.

Fenton, wiping sweat from his considerable forehead, was *very* happy to have found them. He and Scribe Hambrey had been looking for them all day. Fumbluff and the Scribes were scared half to death about what might have happened to Georgie!

Fenton walked with them now, not letting them out of his sight or beyond arm's length because that's what he'd promised Fumbluff. The crowd of Scatterplotters was now a sea of men, women, and children, all making their way merrily toward the ridge like a slow-rolling wave. Flower wreaths crowned the girls and a man standing behind a booth beside the blacksmith's shop saluted Georgie and Ore, then handed them each a laurel garland. It smelled like fresh pine and rosemary.

Somehow, Edie convinced Charlie Fenton to let Apurva and her go home to change—they couldn't *possibly* show up to their first Coronation Ceremony looking like this! Charlie agreed apprehensively, and made them promise to meet them on the Great Lawn in thirty minutes. As long as Georgie was with him, Fenton figured, Fumbluff couldn't be *too* upset. Edie and Apurva pinky-promised and hurried up the hill and out of sight.

◇ ◇ ◇

"I can't *wait* for the fireworks!" Ore said when they were near the top of the ridge overlooking the city. "Mom says they light up the entire sky for an hour at least!"

Georgie remembered how his father had brought him every July 4th to the bleachers overlooking Dotty Pond. They'd bring a blanket and peanut butter sandwiches. Those were his best memories.

When they reached the Seminary, Georgie and Ore followed the crowd to the Great Lawn, which was as long and wide as three football fields. Georgie could hear music coming from beyond the tent.

And the SMELLS!

Kettle corn and funnel cake!

"Come on!" Ore shouted, leading Georgie around the other side of the main tent, Fenton huffing as he followed close behind. Game booths and food stalls dotted the enormous lawn, and children ran between them, darting in every direction.

Ore pumped his fist in the air. "This is better than I'd dreamed it would be! Come on!"

The boys took off, heading deeper into the fairgrounds. The grass was firm beneath their feet and the afternoon sun was crisp and delicious on their faces. For a magical minute, Georgie nearly forgot about his dad, the Aetherquill, and Flint Eldritch.

Ore took a small handful of coins from his pocket. "It's not a lot," Ore said, trying to keep his smile. But Georgie knew what it was like not to have enough spending money. "The food's free at the coronation fair, but the games . . . gotta pay to play."

Ore offered another weak smile. "We have enough for one game. Pick wisely."

Just then, three kids about their age came around the Ring Toss booth. "Ore Obey!" a boy with long blond hair shouted. "Play anything yet?" His outfit was fresh and ironed. One of the two girls in the group had a giant stuffed dragon coiled around her waist.

"Nothing yet!" Ore said, slipping his meager pile of coins back into his pocket.

"Maybe your mom'll start saving her money," the new boy said, "and in fourteen years you can play more games."

The boy laughed and ran off with the girls, but not before giving Ore a hard shove in the shoulder.

"Hey!" Fenton roared, "get back here you little dimwit!"

Ore stared at the ground, unable to look up at Georgie. "Edie'll bring more money," he said quietly.

"Hey, man. It's okay," Georgie said. He thought about the bully with the pigtail in Miss Ellipsis's class. He thought about the peanut butter sandwich stuck to his butt. They may have been in a different world, but when it came to bullying, it was all the same.

"Yeah, it's okay." Ore slapped at a tear. Ore had been so excited for the Coronation Ceremony, and Georgie didn't want his day ruined over one stupid bully and one mean comment.

Georgie smiled. "That kid couldn't pour water out of his own shoe if the instructions were written on the heel."

Fenton roared with laughter.

Ore smiled back. "You really think so?"

"You're way smarter than those idiots," Georgie said, and put an arm around Ore's shoulders. "I *know* so. And you're gonna make a *very* good Scribe. Sooner than you think, I'd bet."

Ore laughed, the joy returning to his face. "Thanks, *parceiro*. Means 'partner.'"

"In which language?" Georgie asked, smiling.

"Portuguese, obviously!"

They continued on together, past the Music Hall Ball Guzzler game, where you had to throw a rubber ball through a mouth in a wooden portrait of a smiling Fumbluff.

They passed the Hoopla game. "Only one winner in six," Ore said as they moved on. "*That* game is basically Great Road robbery."

They finally stopped at a booth with hardly any line at all and an old man leaning against the counter. *TRY THE OLD TYME COCONUT SHY!* was painted in colorful letters on a banner. "What a BEAUTIFUL day!" the pitchman sang, noticing Georgie and Ore standing there. "Hey, hey, hey, step right up and give the old-time coconut shy a try! Jus' six pinnies nearly *guarantees* ye a PRIZE!"

Ore went zero for three, but Georgie knocked his first two coconuts clean off their little saucers. Georgie hit the third coconut dead center. It wobbled, about to fall . . . but then it settled. The pitchman swept the gold coins into his apron.

Ore called the old man a slimy old cheat, then he and Georgie were off to find candy.

Finally, when the throngs of people made their way slowly to the main tent, Georgie, Ore, and Fenton stood by the Seminary stairs holding tins of kettle corn.

At first, Georgie thought it was a trick of the light, because the figure that caught Georgie's eyes coming up the Great Road looked like an angel. It *couldn't* be a girl . . . couldn't be Apurva. Surely nothing, even in *this* world, could possess such heart-stopping beauty.

But it *was* Apurva, in a cream-colored silk dress with a glittering gold belt tied high and snug around her waist. Her hair was pulled back in double Dutch braids, tied together in an updo, with loose curls falling softly below her chin.

Then she was there, stopping a few feet from Georgie to twirl in place, pinching the sides of her dress like it was a ballroom gown. Georgie did and said all that he could, which was nothing.

Apurva's smile gave way to a frown. "You don't like it?" Apurva asked, her cheeks flaring with color.

Georgie gulped. "It's fancy . . ."

"Oh, I *knew* it," Apurva said and looked at Edie. "It's too fancy! Let's go back and change."

"NO!" Georgie nearly shouted, his voice much louder than he intended. "It's perfect. It's really perfect. You look perfect."

Ore, with a mouthful of kettle corn, punched Georgie's shoulder. "Tell us, Georgie, how does Apurva look?"

"Perfect," Edie said, and all four of them laughed and linked arms and headed for the giant tent.

The coronation was about to begin.

Parents carried toddlers in their arms, children counted their candy, and teenagers whispered excitedly to one another. The happy crowd shuffled slowly through the open tent flaps, many of them embarking on the last half hour of their lives.

Chapter 23

Run!

It was a completely different world inside the tent.

Gaslit candles cradled in glass bowls hung from the ceiling, filling the enormous space with a warm orange glow. The tent beams, which seemed a mile high, were festooned with cords of white light and flowers of every color. The place was quickly filling up with hundreds of happy and smiling Scatterplotters.

"That's the dais," Ore said, pointing to a long empty table with sixteen chairs elevated on a platform. "The middle seat is Fumbluff's. The seven new Scribes sit on his left. The seven senior Scribes on his right."

Georgie didn't need to be a genius to realize there was an extra seat up there.

"The extra one's for you, partner!" Ore exclaimed, then turned to a dessert table and began assembling a precarious pyramid of chocolate strawberries, sugar-dusted truffles, and fudge cake on his plate.

Georgie's wasn't feeling very hungry. He grabbed a handful of what looked like pumpkin seeds, ate a few (they were *very* salty), then poured the rest into his robe's pocket. He was starting to feel a little nauseous.

He looked around at all the Scatterplotters—some were dancing with partners on the packed-dirt dance floor, but most people were just milling about, engaged in excited conversation.

He didn't want to sit up there on the dais with the Scribes and Fumbluff.

What if Rollie's plan didn't work? What if he couldn't make his dad whole again? He'd be risking the lives of everyone back home. On the other hand, Fumbluff's plan was equally terrible.

It's your decision to make, Fumbluff had said. *And yours alone.*

But what if he *didn't* have to decide? Maybe he'd just skip the coronation altogether. Then the Aetherquill's power wouldn't work, and Georgie wouldn't be on the hook. Roscoe would've called him a wimpy, whiny, wet noodle just for thinking like that. No, Georgie wasn't going to wuss out. Not when so much was at stake. He looked over at Apurva, who was overwhelming in that silk dress. She smiled, and Georgie smiled weakly back at her. He wasn't even sure if skipping the coronation was *possible*, come to think of it. Something about a specific time, once every fourteen years, when all the realms aligned. Maybe getting coronated . . . just *happened*.

Fenton appeared behind them and gave Ore's hair a hard tussle. Somehow, Fenton managed to balance four heaping plates of food in his other hand. "Glorious!" Fenton mumbled. "The food! Have you eaten yet? Don't let me hold you up! But don't leave my sight!"

Georgie's stomach twisted again. He wondered what Fenton would say if he knew the Aetherquill was in Georgie's pants pocket at this very moment. Would he tell Fumbluff? Georgie wasn't ready to let the Editor in Chief know that he now possessed the very artifact Fumbluff planned on convincing Rollie D to hand over.

Just then, the entire tent erupted in applause as Fumbluff entered the tent. The band that had been playing on the opposite end of the dance floor kicked up a notch. Georgie, Apurva, Edie, and Ore snaked their way through the hundreds of circular dinner tables—each one dressed in velvet purple linens with a puck-shaped candleholder made of stone in the center.

They found a table close enough to the dais to make Mrs. Obey happy, but not close enough to be mistaken for total coronation nerds. Apurva laid her napkin neatly across her lap. Georgie wanted to say something to her, something smart, maybe something about her mother, but before he could—

GONG! GONG! GONG!

The talking and laughing died down to excited whispers as everyone shifted their chairs to face the stage.

Fumbluff stood on the dais beside a small, hand-hammered gong. He put his hand against the ancient cymbal to steady its vibrations, and soon the great tent fell completely silent.

Ore slid into his seat beside Georgie with a fourth or fifth helping of seven-layer strawberry cake, edible chocolate books, and caramel candy apples.

"Stocking up for the speech," he whispered. "Otherwise it's death by boredom."

"*Shhh!*" Edie whispered.

Fumbluff looked out at the crowd before him. "There would be no coronation without the great Librarian, may her days be long and pleasant." He tapped his throat three times—and a thousand or more people in attendance did the same.

A few tables over, a little girl with bright blue eyes waved at Georgie and smiled. Georgie waved back, but that knot in his stomach tightened again.

"But today," Fumbluff continued, smiling now, "we look *forward*. Today, we CELEBRATE OUR WORK!"

The crowd erupted.

"For the young ones here today, yes? This is your first coronation. May it be the first of many!"

Another gush of applause and cheers.

"And now, join me in welcoming our seven new Scribes to the Scribehood!"

The crowd went wild.

"Apprentices who've risen to Scribehood on the tides of both skill and character." The Editor in Chief presented his hands as if he held skill in one and character in the other. "We are preservers of memory and the recorders of truth. *Many* baronies serve the Librarian, but *our* Library . . . *our* Scribes, yes? Scatterplot has always been a jewel amongst its neighbors. We cover New York after all . . . yes, a slice of New Jersey, a wedge of Connecticut, just past Greenwich. Our Scribes are the cream of the crop, the crème de la crème, the best of the best!"

The crowd whooped and whistled.

"There is much pain and suffering in the world. People lie, people cheat, people hurt."

Fumbluff paused for a moment.

"We do not envy our neighbors over in Tokayah. At least *we* don't have to cover Washington, DC!"

The crowd laughed, and Fumbluff laughed along with them.

"*Memory* must be preserved. To distort the past would be *worse* than a lie. It would be a life of *unknowing*. But there are forces who wish to destroy our work—to create a world of darkness, emptied of all the good we work so hard to protect. And today, there is a very special individual I'd like to call up to take a seat at this fine table . . ."

Georgie's stomach did another somersault. He felt hot fudge in his throat. He stood up.

"Georgie, are you okay?" Apurva whispered. "You look pale."

"Need some fresh air."

Georgie couldn't go up there. Nope. No way.

"Now?" Ore whispered. "Fumbluff is about to call you up!"

But Georgie was already snaking through the dinner tables. He heard Fumbluff say his name and felt Fumbluff's eyes on his back as he stepped from the tent and onto the Great Lawn, nearly colliding with a waiter. He made it through the Seminary's outer archways, where it was cool and shady, just before hugging a pillar and puking into a corner.

He felt better, and better still when he vomited a second and then a third time. When there was nothing left, he wiped his mouth on his sleeve. With the Aetherquill thrumming warmly against his thigh, Georgie continued down the Seminary's stone walkway, past the quad and the domed study hall. The walkway opened on a terrace with a balcony. From there, Georgie could see the hilly landscape stretching out to the horizon.

It was quiet here. Peaceful. He tried to think about what he would write with the Aetherquill when the time came. *To weaken Flint's grip,* as Rollie put it. He grabbed a few pumpkin seeds from his pocket and tossed them over the railing. He watched them rise, arc, and fall out of sight far below. He remembered his father tossing those Jolly Ranchers that Georgie had stored in his Xbox disc tray. His father had said something to him then . . . what was it?

Great marksmen can hit moving targets.

Yes, that's what it was. Georgie remembered telling his dad that he sucked at hitting moving targets, which was true.

And then his father had given him advice: *Don't aim at where the target* is. *Aim at where the target is* going.

Georgie reached into his other pocket and palmed his slingshot. *Aim at where the target is going.*

Something nagged at the back of Georgie's mind, just out of reach, he could *feel* it, just like having a word at the tip of your tongue or a sneeze that never comes . . . his dad *never* gave him advice, not like that . . . and wasn't there something else his father had said then, something that Georgie thought sounded totally random? But before Georgie could remember what it was—

ZZZHT. ZZZHHHHT. BRRRUMMM.

Way out in the distance beyond the terrace, just above the crown of the first hill, a black line appeared in the air. A floating black line—just like the one Georgie had seen in his driveway. The air curved inward on either side of it, and a moment later two flaps of sky peeled back.

Flint Eldritch stood on the other side.

Georgie blinked hard. He smacked himself in the face.

Eldritch was still there, and now he was climbing through the portal, one leg at a time.

The silver snaps on his black boots flicked sun into Georgie's eyes.

To the left and right of where Flint Eldritch stood, a hundred more black lines appeared. Their flaps peeled back like batwing doors in midair, and from each tear climbed a stream of men dressed in all black. They held spears and other makeshift blades and daggers. They kept coming until what looked like an army of at least four hundred men had gathered behind Eldritch.

With a single, tallow-like finger, Flint Eldritch pointed straight at Georgie. Straight at the Seminary.

Flint's men began to march.

Within seconds, the steady beating of boots was very loud. The banister vibrated under Georgie's hands as Eldritch's army descended toward the Seminary.

What Georgie saw next would have made him puke again if his stomach had not been empty. Two more black lines appeared above the hill, wider and higher than the other lines Georgie had seen. The flaps peeled back, and Georgie saw them—the three-legged creatures he'd seen through the portal in his driveway ambling along that desolate beach. Their long, hairy legs twitched through the portals and found solid ground, and then their bodies scrambled into Scatterplot with frightening agility. The monsters stood tall, five times the height of Flint's men, with round, bulging bellies covered in a mat of black hair. Their eyes spun in their sockets, attached to floppy stalks jutting from their hairless heads.

One of the creatures reared up on two legs, its third leg wiggling into the sky like a finger. The creature's underbelly was a hundred pulsing eggs inside a sack made of crisscrossing bands of thick, white mucus.

The ground was really throbbing now, and Georgie could only see the heads of the monsters behind the dust wall Flint and his men had kicked up.

Georgie's legs did not freeze and his voice did not go dry. His body and mind were in fine order, in fine *terror*, as he stumbled away from the banister and ran for his life down the arched walkway along the quad.

As he broke from the outer Seminary arches into the sunlight, he heard Fumbluff's booming voice.

" . . . may we have ANOTHER fourteen years of PEACE!"

"Aye!" Came the deafening roar of a thousand Scatterplotters.

"And may we be granted enough paper to avoid a paper SHORTAGE!"

"AYE!"

"And may we—"

Georgie flung himself through the tent flaps and skidded to a halt in the center of the dance floor.

"RUN!"

Silence as Fumbluff's mouth snapped shut and everyone stared at Georgie.

Then, whether it was one of the three-legged creatures or one of Flint's men, Georgie had no idea, but a wild, inhuman cry warbled through the open tent flaps.

People jumped to their feet, knocking their chairs and copper silverware to the floor.

"*RUN!*" Georgie screamed again. "*FLINT ELDRITCH IS HERE!*"

𒀭𒊩𒌋𒊩 𒀭𒊩𒌋

Chapter 24

Total Pandemonium

Fumbluff ran to Georgie and shook him by the shoulders.

"How far? Georgie, how FAR!?"

Georgie could *smell* him; the rotten meat and decaying fish. He and Fumbluff turned to see Flint Eldritch strolling onto the short strip of lawn separating the Seminary from the coronation tent.

Behind him, the Dregs of Mishap pumped their spears over their heads.

And Flint Eldritch was leaving *boot*prints. Georgie was frozen in place, trying to catch a glimpse of his father—just a sign of life would be enough—but all he could see was Flint's grotesquely pale skin stretched tightly around his bones.

Flint stopped, smiled, the Dregs of Mishap streaming past him like rushing water around a rock.

"*CHARLES!*" Fumbluff roared. "*BLAZE!* CLOSE THE TENT!"

Charlie Fenton and Blaze Nelson flew past screaming Scatterplotters and began tying the great tent flaps shut. But before they could finish a wooden spear sailed straight through the opening.

"WATCH OUT!" Georgie cried.

Fenton dove and knocked a woman out of the way, catching the spear with his chest. He crashed to the floor, clutching at the spear that impaled him.

"CHARLIE!" Georgie screamed.

Blood bloomed like a flower across Fenton's tunic as the dance floor filled with frenzied Scatterplotters. Georgie could no longer see him. "SOMEONE HELP FENTON!" Georgie yelled. "HE'S HURT!"

Bu-*BAM!* Bu-*BAM!* Bu-*BAM!*

The Dregs of Mishap were slamming their bodies against the tent. Georgie turned just in time to see two brilliant beams of white light shoot from Fumbluff's out-stretched palms—just like the light that had spilled from his father's hands.

The beams of light splashed against the canvas walls like water from a firehose. Fumbluff slowly moved his hands left and right and up and down and the tent fabric seemed to thicken and strengthen everywhere the white light touched.

Inside the tent was total pandemonium. A thousand trapped Scatterplotters shrieked, shoved, and searched for their families. Georgie jumped atop a nearby table, accidentally kicking the stone candleholder to the floor.

"APURVA! APUR—"

There she was!

With Edie and Ore, being jostled by a wave of hysterical Scatterplotters. He had a fleeting moment to think about Roscoe and his stupid training with the Altercockers. All the good it was doing now.

"APURVA!"

But Georgie's voice was swallowed by Blaze Nelson's, thundering above the chaos. "EVERYONE OUT THE BACK!"

Blaze and another group of Scribes and Scatterplotters were at the back of the tent now, behind the dais, cutting through the canvas with a knife.

"TO CORRIGENDUM!" Blaze bellowed.

But now a terrifying silence had descended like a fog, and no one moved. The Dregs of Mishap had stopped slamming against the tent. In their place, a giant, hulking shadow appeared just outside, rising high along the wall.

SCRATCH. SCRATCH.

The canvas indented against the weight of one of the monster's hairy legs, as tall and hard as a telephone pole. Fumbluff directed his beams of white light at the monster's shadow, but his light was waning . . .

The creature scratched once more. *SCRAAAAATCH.*

Then it began to climb. The shadow slithered up the tent

wall, up and up it went, using the seams between the panels as footholds.

The tent sagged and moaned as the monster clambered overhead.

"Everyone OUT!" Fumbluff roared, sweat dripping off his forehead, his beams of light hardly even reaching the roof.

The monster squealed and began to jump, its shadow disappearing for a sickening moment before pummeling back down. The tent beams creaked and bowed dangerously.

Only a few Scatterplotters managed to make it out before—

RRRRIIIIIIP!

With a mighty crash, the three-legged monster tore through the roof and smashed through three trestle tables. It landed on its back in a mess of buttercream cupcakes, whipped cream scones, berry tarts, and pie pops.

It wiggled its hairy, beanpole legs, and then, in one freakishly fast maneuver, flipped itself upright and rose above the crowd. Its eyeballs spun in their sockets, and thick greenish-gray liquid dripped from its open beak. A stiff, black tongue jutted out from behind a row of razor-sharp teeth like a blade.

"APURVA!" Georgie screamed. "EDIE! ORE! APURVA!" He could barely hear his own voice above the bedlam.

The monster whipped its head as it swooped down upon the crowd. At least twenty Scatterplotters went flying across the tent, some somersaulting in midair and slamming limply against splintered tent beams. Now, as the monster swooped its head back the other way, it opened its beak wide. Saliva dripped from the monster's teeth onto the upturned faces of the frozen Scatterplotters below it. The monster chomped with ferocious strength and—

Georgie screamed and closed his eyes, but the shrieks of pain and terror rang loudly in his ears. They had to get out of here. They had to *do* something, before the monster killed every last one of them. He looked around frantically for his friends, but it was Blaze Nelson he saw, leaping clean over a pile of unconscious men and women and hurtling toward the creature with his knife drawn. The monster turned to face the Scribe, spraying a mixture of blood and mucus. Blaze cocked his arm, and this time, the monster didn't rear up on two legs—it hunkered down.

It's protecting its belly! Georgie realized.

"*GRAAAAAUMPH!*" Blaze cried, and threw his blade.

The monster ducked even lower, but the knife sliced one of its eyestalks cleanly off its head. The blade clattered to the dance floor and skidded to a stop by Georgie's feet.

Now the monster reared up, pistoning its third leg into Blaze's chest.

"*OOOMPH!*"

Blaze went flying backward. Blood so dark it was nearly black oozed from the stumpy wound in the creature's lozenge-shaped head, but that didn't stop it from advancing.

Georgie grabbed Blaze's knife from the floor. He looked up just in time to see Fumbluff launch himself over a table with one hand and land in a feet-first slide. Fumbluff thrust his palms forward, but only a trickle of white light came out.

The monster reared up over Blaze Nelson.

"FUMBLUFF!" Georgie cried. "CATCH!"

Fumbluff looked up.

Georgie threw.

It was a bad throw.

The monster looked away from the Scribe—leaving him for dessert, perhaps—its remaining eyeball jiggling like a magic eight ball as it tracked the knife's arc.

Fumbluff dove headfirst . . . . and caught the knife by the handle!

The monster lunged at Fumbluff, but he rolled onto his back and—

SCHLLOOOP-SMACK-POP!

Fumbluff drove the blade into the monster's underbelly sack. Its pulsing eggs exploded in a syrupy fountain of green puss.

The monster flung its head back with the most awful, hair-raising sounds of agony. It teetered and buckled and swayed, giving Fumbluff time to avoid being crushed to death, just before it thudded to the floor with one final, impotent cry.

It was dead!

Behind the dais, Scribes ferried Scatterplotters through the tear in the tent. Georgie could see the game booths and the food stalls, now empty and abandoned. But—

Oh. No.

The Dregs of Mishap had set up a perimeter. Scatterplotters were stampeding from the tent and running straight into their arms.

Georgie craned his neck to see above the mountainous creature lying dead on the floor, and there she was. Apurva! She had the blond-haired girl who had waved to Georgie earlier cradled in her arms like a baby.

And there was Ore! And Edie!

Ore had his arm around the boy they'd met earlier, the one Charlie Fenton called a little dimwit.

"GUYS!" Georgie screamed. "HEY! APURVA! EDI—"

BOOM! BOOM! BOOM!

Three giant tent beams came crashing down, sending chunks of splintered wood flying like projectiles. Georgie covered his head as he turned—

The entrance to the tent was gone, the fabric torn to shreds.

Now, roaring with victory, the Dregs of Mishap charged forward.

A few brave Scatterplotters turned to meet them, but they were unarmed and outnumbered and no match for Flint's army.

Above their screams, Georgie heard Flint Eldritch cackling, and from the corner of his eye, he saw Fumbluff pushing against the tide of fleeing Scatterplotters, toward the front of the tent, toward the sound of that horrible laughter.

"Apurva," Georgie groaned, but then went very quiet, not even a breath, as the second monstrosity stomped into the tent, knocking Dregs and Scatterplotters alike out of its path.

It stopped in the center of the dance floor to survey the scene.

It was even bigger than the first one.

Apurva!

Georgie found her easily, now that most of the tent was cleared out . . . or dead. She was staring up at the monster, her eyes wide with terror. The creature stared back, its eyeballs spinning wildly.

"HELP ME!" Apurva shrieked as she turned her back on the creature, trying to protect the little girl who was sobbing into her shoulder.

The monster gave its own ferocious screech in return.

Georgie grabbed his slingshot from his pocket and rapid-fired the last of his marbles. His shots landed, bouncing off the creature's beak and eyeballs, but the creature didn't even notice. Georgie screamed and waved his arms and threw silverware . . . but the creature couldn't be bothered.

The monster's crazy eyeballs had gone steady.

Locked on Apurva's smooth, slender back.

Chapter 25

A Weapon and a Strategy

great and mysterious calm descended upon
Georgie.

He lunged at the nearest table and swept the
plates to the floor. Just the stone candleholder at the center remained. Georgie gathered the tablecloth around it to
make a pouch, grabbed a twisted fistful of tablecloth, and
began to spin it around his head like a helicopter blade.

He'd only have one shot.

The monster was one gigantic step away from Apurva.

Georgie spun his hips in one last rotation . . . and

released. The puck soared high above the dance floor in a parabola, like a comet streaking across the sky.

CRUNCH!

The stone puck shattered the top of the monster's open beak into something unrecognizable. It stumbled drunkenly to the side, caught itself, and then lurched at Georgie, blood falling thickly from its broken mouth.

Georgie ducked, just in time, and watched the monster's leg whoosh within inches of his face. He saw that the black hair matted thickly around its bones was not hair, but a million slimy worms, slithering up and down.

Georgie backpedaled as the monster stumbled after him, its lower jaw pumping up and down like a broken nutcracker.

The creature shrieked, spraying hot mucus all over the dance floor.

Without taking his eyes from the monster, Georgie bent his knees and picked up one of the chunks of wood that had splintered off the fallen tent beams. He flipped it in his hand so the sharp end was pointing forward.

Georgie baited the monster deeper into the tent, all the way to the far wall, and when there was nowhere else to go, Georgie swung—not at the creature, but in a low sweep under the tent wall—and chopped straight through one of the ropes securing the tent wall to the stakes buried in the Seminary lawn.

TWING-SNAP!

The rope snapped against Georgie's spear.

The tent wall sagged.

Georgie cut the next two ropes . . . and that was all he

needed. The giant tent wall deflated like a parachute. Georgie dove out of the way in a somersault while tent fabric draped over the monster like a tremendous bedsheet. The monster thrashed and squealed.

"*AGGHHHHH!*" Georgie buried the tent stake straight into the thrashing monster. Georgie had no clue where in the monster's body the sharp point landed, but it didn't really matter because the tent fabric went dark with blood and the monster's thrashing slowed to a sputter and its screeches of agony were now only a choked garble.

Apurva was there a moment later, her chest rising and falling mightily.

"Apurva!" Georgie threw his arms around her.

"The tent's gonna collapse!" Apurva gasped.

They ran together back toward the dais table, jumping over chairs and dead bodies, and made it halfway across the dance floor when—

"HAHA! HAHAHA!"

Georgie froze. That cackling laughter turned his intestines into icicles.

Georgie turned . . .

Sweat glistened on Flint's pale forehead beneath his black hood. His long, bony fingers began uncoiling the black scarf around his neck. An instant later, Fumbluff jumped between Flint Eldritch and Georgie. His robe and face were covered in blood and slime.

"GO!" Fumbluff roared, shoving Blaze Nelson's dagger back into Georgie's hands. "RAPIDLY! To Corrigendum! I'll hold him off as long as I can."

Fumbluff shut his eyes and clenched his fists. White light spilled from the cracks in his fingers.

Georgie, Apurva, Edie, and Ore ran from the tent, stumbled onto the Great Lawn, and then stopped, squinting as their eyes adjusted to the blinding sunlight. The Dregs of Mishap were closing in. They had created a wide semicircle, stationed not more than six or eight feet apart. Scatterplotters were running pell-mell every which way. Georgie watched in horror as Flint's men tossed a woman onto a pile of bound and gagged Scatterplotters.

Apurva turned to Georgie. Her updo had come apart in the commotion, and color burned high in her cheeks.

"I have a plan," she said, grabbing something out of Edie's purse. "Follow me!"

Apurva kicked off her heels and started to run.

"Apurva, wait!" Georgie shouted as he, Edie, and Ore started to run after her.

Up ahead, two of Flint's men smiled widely, revealing a crooked set of silver teeth. They licked their lips, bent their knees, and opened their arms.

"APURVA! STOP!" Georgie screamed.

Apurva kept running, tapping whatever it was she had grabbed from Edie's purse.

Is that her iPhone? Georgie thought. *But there's no reception here!*

They were close enough now to Flint's men for Georgie to see the gaps between their rotten teeth.

Ten yards.

Apurva howled—

"AAAAHHH-AYYOOO!"

—and threw her iPhone into the air.

It landed face up on the grass between the two Dregs of Mishap, who looked curiously at the bluish-white light glowing from its screen, their eyes growing wider . . . then Roscoe Harris's voice blared from the iPhone's speakers.

For my new subscribers, welcome to episode seventeen of Roscoe's Rag!

The Dregs of Mishap, their arms as thick as their necks, each stepped toward Apurva's iPhone in a trance, as if they both feared and desired the object on the ground very much.

"It's magic!" Apurva shouted. "DARK magic!"

"Magic!" The two Dregs of Mishap grunted and lunged for the phone in a headfirst dive, each trying to snatch it before the other—

KLUNK!

Their heads collided like pool balls with a hollow thud, knocking both of them unconscious at the exact same time. They landed limply on top of the iPhone like slugs.

Without breaking stride, Apurva jumped over the Dregs followed by Georgie, Edie, and Ore. They hurdled across the Great Lawn, away from the tent and the rest of Flint's men.

"FASTER!" Apurva cried, and all four of them, more or less shoulder to shoulder now, ran even harder, flying past the abandoned game booths and away from Flint's men.

❖ ❖ ❖

When they finally reached Corrigendum's gates twenty minutes later, their clothing pasted to their skin with sweat, they paused, catching their breath and listening to the occasional scream drifting across the landscape from the Seminary.

"All our friends . . ." Ore said, on the verge of tears.

Edie put an arm around her brother. "It'll be okay."

"Did you . . . did you see Mommy anywhere?"

Edie shook her head solemnly, now looking on the verge of tears herself.

The mansion itself seemed to frown as they hurried across Corrigendum's plaza. Halfway to the double doors, Georgie stopped short and stared up at the darkening sky. Beyond the clouds, faintly outlined, he could see a criss-crossing network of the most intricate patterns and shapes. The lighted network of nodes and connector lines seemed to follow an invisible dome-like shape stretching far and wide in every direction. The multicolored patterns rotated slowly, until each color overlaid on top of one another, making a single, unified pattern that seemed to contain every color of the rainbow. There was a brilliant flash of light—and at the same moment, Georgie felt all the muscles in his body *ripple,* as if someone had injected him with a head-to-toe jolt of electricity—and then the light and the patterns in the sky were gone.

"Guys!" Georgie whispered. "Did you see that!?"

Edie, Ore, and Apurva were already at Corrigendum's front doors. "See *what!?*" they whispered back in unison, all three of them looking terrified.

The Coronation Ceremony is very serious business, Fumbluff had said. *It happens at just the precise time, when all the realms are aligned, once every fourteen years.*

Georgie was a Scribe now. He was sure of it. He remembered how he'd considered skipping the Coronation Ceremony, but based on what he'd just seen—and *felt*—skipping his coronation had never really been an option.

"Never mind," Georgie said, hurrying to catch up with them. "But I think I just got coronated."

◇ ◇ ◇

Georgie led the way down a long, torchlit corridor that ended at a set of wide-open wooden double doors. The room they found themselves in was dimly lit, with a tall wardrobe against the far wall. Cracked leather sofas flanked the fireplace. Georgie scanned the room for signs of trouble, but then he did a double-take, his eyes landing on one of the many portraits lining the walls.

It was a portrait of his mother.

Penelope Summers.

Georgie stared back, his mother's eyes a dazzling hazel color flecked with bronze. Her golden-brown skin swelled softly above a square-cut bodice, where brushstrokes as thick as honey pulled paint up her long neck. Her lips were full but strong and twin patches of color rose high on her cheekbones.

The Aetherquill burned against his thigh, and then a terrible ache washed over him; the ache of a lonely heart.

He heard her voice just then, like a soft breeze and the fluffing of crisp cotton bed sheets. And when she spoke from inside his head, he felt her warm lips kissing his face. She spoke quietly, like a breath, like the end of a song, and then she was gone.

I love you, she said.

◇ ◇ ◇

They were about to head back down the long corridor when Georgie, Apurva, Edie, and Ore stopped short.

Click. Click.

Scratch.

"Did you hear tha—" Ore began.

"*Shhhh!*" Georgie hissed, spinning around and facing the tall wardrobe on the far wall.

Scratch. Scratch. Click clack.

Someone—or something—was inside the wardrobe.

BAM!

The chest doors blew off their hinges in a crash of splintering wood. Georgie, Apurva, Edie, and Ore all froze in horror. What stood in the chest's broken frame, eight-feet-tall and shiny as black chrome, was more horrible than anything in Georgie's worst nightmares. At first, Georgie thought it was a man because the hulking form was standing on two legs, but then he realized that it wasn't even human.

It was an eight-foot-tall beetle.

The clicking noise had come from its giant black pincers, curved like horns, opening and clicking shut over a small, toothless mouth surrounded by leathery skin. The beetle ducked and shuffled sideways out of the wardrobe, its bulbous black eyes bulging and its antennae bobbing like fishing rods.

A long black scarf was coiled around its neck.

Flint Eldritch, Georgie realized. If a shadow could ever fully come to life, this is what it would become. He thought of that horrible shadow Fumbluff had made on the wall when he shook and rattled the torch he'd been holding. *Is my father in there somewhere?*

The beetle screeched and lunged forward. Georgie pushed Apurva into Edie, and all three of them stumbled and fell into Ore. The giant beetle snapped its pincers, missing Georgie's face by inches and instead tearing clean through the back of Fumbluff's leather armchair. It spun back around, smacking its black lips with its baby tongue.

"THERE! OVER THERE!"

It was Scribe Hambrey!

Then came Blaze Nelson's voice, roaring like a hurricane from right behind them. "*DOOOOWN!*"

They dropped to the floor as Blaze and Scribe Hambrey leaped over their heads, landing between them and the beetle. They were each wielding a wooden tent stake, the sharp ends alight with raging fires. The beetle stumbled away, waving its antennae frantically.

Blaze and Scribe Hambrey moved to flank the beetle, left and right. "Back!" Blaze roared.

The beetle screeched and flapped its massive, leathern wings, and rose into the air. Then it crashed through the wall, obliterating the portrait of Penelope Summers, and disappeared in a series of crashes and booms.

Scribe Hambrey, whose plastic glasses were smudged and cracked, turned to Georgie. "The four of you, get out of here fast. Meet Fumbluff behind the Timbernotch Tavern. He's rounding up as many survivors as he can."

Then Scribe Hambrey spread her palms wide, blasting two beams of white light into the floor. She and Blaze lifted into the air and disappeared through the broken wall, giving chase to Flint Eldritch.

◇ ◇ ◇

"Follow me!" Apurva shouted, running back down the corridor, across Corrigendum's entry hall, and into the dining room. They rounded the long table and stopped in front of the rectangular cutout in the dining room wall, where the Great Books had first appeared last night.

"We can climb," Apurva said, ducking into the compartment.

"*That's* your plan?" Ore asked. "What about the front door!?"

CRASH! "YEEEEE!" "GET THEM!" SMASH!

Flint's men were in Corrigendum now, and there would be no going out the front door.

Apurva jumped and managed to wedge herself inside the pipe with her back and knees. Then she wiggled up and out of sight.

Edie followed. Then Ore.

Georgie climbed into the dusty space and looked up into total blackness.

"Jump!" Ore whispered from above his head. Georgie couldn't see Ore, not even the shape of him, but he jumped, wedged himself, but . . .

"I'm slipping!"

Then he felt Ore's arm loop under his armpit. "I got you, partner."

Georgie readjusted and locked himself against the curved walls of the tube. "Apurva?"

For a moment there was nothing, and then Apurva spoke from high above. "All good!"

"Edic?"

"All good," she replied.

"Ore?" Georgie asked.

"Not present," Ore said.

The four of them began to climb.

Chapter 26

The Brain Catches Fire

They climbed, and climbed, and climbed some more, through Corrigendum's roof, still climbing, until the pipe leveled out very high up in the air, even higher than the highest ridge of Corrigendum's roof.

Georgie could see the ground below and the shapes of the trees like he was looking through a pair of dirty yellow glasses. They squeezed on in single file, suspended a hundred feet in the air. Just as they passed one of the wooden supports, Georgie heard a sudden explosion of glass.

He turned and could see Corrigendum in the distance, slightly warped through the curved walls of the pipe.

Flint Eldritch, still in beetle form, came crashing through one of Corrigendum's third-story balcony doors. Was it the room he and Apurva were in last night?

Beetle/Flint stumbled backward and tripped over the railing. Before the bug could right itself, Emma Hambrey rushed forward and jabbed her torch into its belly.

"*OOOOHHH-EEEEE!*"

Even from this distance, Georgie could hear Flint's agonized scream as he fell three stories and crashed to the ground, smoking like a jet engine.

"THEY DID IT!" he screamed, his voice echoing inside the pipe.

But the beetle stood, a plume of black smoke rising from the tips of its antennae.

Flint disappeared beneath the tree cover, leaping over boulders and smashing headfirst into small trees . . . heading in their direction.

"Oh no," Georgie whispered.

BAM!

The monstrous beetle stumbled from the trees below and rammed its flaming head into the wooden support directly behind Georgie. The entire pipe rocked back and forth like an earthquake.

"WE'RE GONNA DIE!" Ore screamed.

But Georgie realized with rising horror that it wouldn't be the fall that killed them. Because now the trestle support was on fire.

The flames licked upward toward the pipe rapidly. The dry old wood gave the thirsty fire all the fuel it needed, and seconds later, Georgie felt the tube beneath his palms heating up until it burned the skin on his knees through his pants.

Black smoke seeped through the gaps in the panels.

"*MOVE!*" Georgie shouted, before going into a coughing fit. The tube was filling up with smoke and he could hardly see Ore, who was only a few feet in front of him. Up ahead, Apurva was wheezing.

They were all going to die up here.

The smoke was pouring in too fast. Georgie's palms blistered against the pipe's surface, which was as hot as a stovetop. Georgie crawled, eyes watering, burning, covering his mouth and nose with his coronation robe. He was alone now, the smoke so thick he could barely see his own hands. He crawled another two feet toward Apurva through the yellowish-black haze and then, when his lungs couldn't handle it anymore, he collapsed.

"Apurva!" Georgie choked.

Edie and Ore were gone. He hoped Edie and Ore had escaped the smoke and fire. He hoped they'd survive.

Georgie's eyes closed . . . and just then the pipes rocked back and forth so violently that Georgie and Apurva were slammed from side to side. The hundred-foot-tall trestle support beams creaked and crumbled in a tremendous mess of flames and smoke and splintered wood.

CREEE-AAAACK!

Behind them, where the trestle support had been, the pipe broke in two.

Then Georgie was moving. Sliding backward . . . downward . . . and before he knew what was happening, he realized he could breathe again. He took a heaving gulp of fresh, precious air. Then another . . . and another.

Georgie and Apurva tumbled backward, skidding toward the opening.

Georgie slid feet-first from the pipe's jagged and broken mouth on his stomach, but instead of free-falling into the bonfire a hundred feet below, Apurva caught him, her hands locked like handcuffs around his wrists.

"*GEORGIE!*" she screamed. "*I'M SLIPPING!*" Her bare feet slipped slowly along the smooth curves of the inner pipe, and Georgie dropped another six inches. His stomach leaped into his mouth. Now, Apurva's head and shoulders protruded from the broken pipe.

"*GEORGIE!*" Apurva sobbed. "*I CAN'T HOLD ON! OH GOD, OH GOD, OH GOD!*"

One of Georgie's hands slipped from Apurva's grip.

Georgie closed his eyes. He tried to remember how Ore whistled for the Pocket Horsemen. Was it two notes? Three? Was it like Morse code? He put two fingers in his mouth. He blew.

Nothing.

Georgie looked down, and there was Flint Eldritch, back in human form, staring up and smiling. His face was black and sooty, and his scarf was coiled around his neck.

Georgie adjusted his tongue. The last thing Georgie heard before blowing the air out of his lungs was Charlie Fenton's voice: *A Scribe does not write with his hand; a Scribe writes with his mind.*

Georgie blew again.

His father would have been proud. As would Penelope Summers, who could whistle better than anyone. Beginner whistles are often raspy or husky. But the whistle Georgie blew was clean and unwavering, the sort of whistle a good wind could carry for miles.

An instant later, the trees shivered in a speeding ripple.

"GEORG-*EEEE!*" Apurva screeched.

They fell.

And they both shrieked as they plummeted toward the fire below.

Georgie's world spun. Sky then trees then fire then Apurva then sky then trees then fire then Flint then sky—picking up speed, faster and faster, the bonfire closer and larger and hotter with every rotation.

Then, two things—two *forms*—sprang from the trees. As they sprang they grew and transformed and became giants. Out of the corner of his eye, Georgie saw Apurva crash into one of them . . .

OOMPH!

Then Georgie slammed face-first onto the other black furry thing. Before he could think of anything else, he was grabbing that deep carpet of fur with both hands, twisting his fists into it, searching for the familiar knob of bone, wrapping his legs tight around its muscular form.

Bugle landed in the burning remains of the trestle support like a thunderquake, sending beams flying every which way. Georgie was distantly aware of singeing heat against his feet, legs, and thighs. Then Bugle leaped out of the bonfire and landed on solid ground.

The Pocket Horseman roared viciously, rearing up on its hind legs and punching the ground. The earth shook.

Georgie lifted his head, sure he'd see Apurva engulfed in flames—

"GEORGIE!"

Georgie whipped around, and there she was. Alive! She was mounted on Phiz's back, surrounded by trees and boulders and craggy rock formations.

Phiz and Bugle grumbled and pounded the earth again, kicking up clouds of dust and pebbles.

Then Georgie heard laughter from behind him.

Eldritch.

Bugle lowered his head as he turned to charge at Flint, but before taking a single lunge, Flint shot his arms out, the baggy cuffs of his torn black robe flying out like loose sacks from his withered wrists.

Georgie felt a warm blast, then he was thrown from Bugle's back. He landed on his ribs and slid backward until he collided with a boulder. A cool trickle of blood ran down the back of his neck.

GRRRROOOOAAR! Bugle bared his teeth at Flint, but Flint only stood there, his hand outstretched, and blasted the Pocket Horseman onto his stomach with a spear of purple light. The humongous gorilla-horse was sent sliding backward as if he were just a puppy.

Apurva screamed for Georgie, but then Flint blasted her clean off of Phiz's back. Apurva flipped like a rag doll, her limbs limp. She landed on her side, then crawled to Georgie and put an arm around him.

They were backed up against a boulder. Phiz and Bugle struggled to their feet but Flint slammed them back down. Georgie heard their jaws breaking against the hardpack.

Flint laughed harder, advancing on Georgie and Apurva. The Dregs of Mishap were coming through the trees behind him now—tall and wide and ferocious. They readied their spears as they approached.

"Georgie Summers!" Eldritch laughed. The first beetle poked its head out of the hole in Flint's neck, antennae twitching before scampering beneath his shirt. "I should have killed you in New York." He strolled casually toward where Georgie and Apurva lay. "But maybe this was better. You saved me the trouble of retrieving the Aetherquill from Rollie D. She's a tricky one—oh, indeed—but she gave it to you, didn't she?" Flint cackled madly. "Give it to me, boy. Now."

Georgie struggled to his knees in front of Apurva. "Get away from us!" Georgie choked. Two more beetles flopped and scurried out of the hole in Flint's neck.

"Alternatively," Flint continued, a lunatic grin stretching the skin on his face into something half-human, "I take it off your dead body."

Flint smiled as he stretched his arms out.

Georgie hugged Apurva as tight as he could.

And waited for Flint's magic to shatter his head against the boulder.

Chapter 27

Roscoe Learned to Shoot

At first, Georgie thought the fiery mass soaring over his head was a burning chunk of debris. The sun blinked in and out as the form flew in front of it, a shadow of horse and woman and bow and quiver.

But what Georgie mistook for a conflagration was a billowing wave of red hair.

Flint stopped in his tracks as the humongous horse soared over Georgie's head and landed between him and Flint Eldritch in a thunderous cloud of dirt.

It was Rollie D!

Perched behind her, clutching her waist like it was a

basket full of YouTube subscribers, was Roscoe Harris. Beneath Roscoe's eyes were streaks of blue paint, and while Georgie would never admit it, he looked like a proper warrior.

"*Run,*" Rollie commanded.

"Do as she says!" Roscoe shouted, then smiled crazily at Georgie and Apurva. "We got your back. *You wet noodles!*"

But Georgie couldn't move. His back felt like it had been pierced by an iron stake, something which you might find in that blacksmith's shop.

From her quiver, Rollie drew four arrows, a slender shaft of wood between each finger. She laid them against her bow's horizontal plane like rake tines, pulled back, and fired. The arrows sliced across the clearing and struck four of Flint's men between their eyes. They dropped to the ground with a thud.

A second later, a fifth man dropped to the ground, an arrow sticking out of his stomach.

"I got one, Rollie!" Roscoe shouted. "Jus' like you told me! Kept both eyes open the whole time, and kept my head steady!"

Flint Eldritch screamed. "*Get away, you meddlesome—*"

Rollie already had another arrow drawn against her bow. She fired at Flint just as he stretched his palm in her direction. Rollie's arrow splintered in midair, colliding with Flint's blast of dark energy, but sharp shards of wood impaled his palm. Flint screamed in pain and flung his other hand out.

But Rollie was faster. Her next arrow flew straight through Flint's hand. He howled and stared at the arrow running through his bloody hand like a pole through a carousel horse.

As Flint pulled Rollie's arrow out of his hand, more Dregs of Mishap came through the trees, braying their ugly battle cries. Rollie holstered her bow against her hip, and with a cry of her own, tossed Roscoe off the horse just before whipping it in the butt with the reigns. The horse took off. Rollie shot up, backflipped, and landed on the ground in a squat, her green cloak fanning out on the ground.

The horse sped into the group of Dregs, kicking three of them in the chest. They flew backward like cannons and their spines broke like dry kindling when they connected with tree trunks. Rollie dove headfirst into Georgie and—

BAM!

A blast of Flint's purple force shattered the boulder, right where Georgie's head had been a second ago. He felt chips of smoking rock against his legs and arms.

Rollie doubled back, firing off three more arrows at Flint before pulling Apurva to her feet and rushing her around the boulder.

"*Do you still have it!?*" She was breathing heavily.

Georgie put his hand on his pocket, feeling the Aetherquill's shape, and nodded.

Rollie exhaled nervously, and Georgie watched in amazement over her shoulder as Roscoe drew arrows across his bow—not as fast as Rollie but faster than Georgie would have ever believed—and fired off shot after shot at Flint's men.

"Roscoe and I will hold them," Rollie D said. "And I was

never here. Do you understand me? I'll kill you myself if you say otherwise. I was never here. GO! NOW!"

With Apurva holding Georgie around the waist, they stumbled away from the boulder and into the forest, Georgie pausing once to look back for his best friend from across the street. He heard the *thwang* and *whoosh* of his and Rollie's bow and arrows and more Dregs thumping to the ground.

Phiz and Bugle looked hurt, but they were alive. Georgie's back blazed with pain as he mounted Bugle. Apurva quickly mounted Phiz, and the Pocket Horsemen hobbled away.

Thirty minutes later, they reached a wide dirt road. To their left, the road snaked out of sight toward the distant mountains.

Georgie's mind, which had been in survival mode since the moment Flint appeared in the middle of Fumbluff's speech, now slowed down. Edie and Ore! Where were *they*? Had they made it out of the burning pipe alive? All the dead bodies. The innocent people of Scatterplot who'd never see another Coronation Ceremony.

And Fenton . . . he'd had an arrow sticking out of his blood-stained tunic the last time Georgie'd seen him.

The day had grown chillier and darker, the sun nearing the end of its descent behind the mountains. They went right, and a few minutes later, a sharp curve in the road led them into a long straightaway. Up ahead, two figures were running like mad. Georgie couldn't tell if they were Scatterplot survivors . . . or Dregs of Mishap.

He and Apurva tried to turn Bugle and Phiz off the road and into the tree cover, but the Pocket Horsemen wheezed and brayed, then started after the two running figures in a hobbled, injured gallop.

The figures up ahead must have heard the giant beasts thundering down the road behind them because they turned. The two figures jumped up and down, waving their hands in the air frantically.

They were . . . *kids.*

"Is that . . . ?" Georgie shouted to Apurva.

"EDIE!" Apurva shrieked.

"It is! It is! It's Edie and Ore!"

The Pocket Horsemen barely had time to come to a complete stop before the Obeys dragged Georgie and Apurva off their backs and into bear hugs. Georgie's ribs and back screamed in pain as Ore squeezed him tight, but still, it felt good. *So* good.

"You're alive!" Ore said, pulling away from Georgie and slapping him on the shoulders.

"You too," Georgie replied and gave Edie a hug, who flung her arms around him like he was her brother. "We didn't know what happened to you! The smoke, it was everywhere! We . . . we couldn't breathe. We kept going."

"All the way to the Library," Ore said.

Edie looked from Georgie to Apurva. "We thought . . . we thought you *died*!"

"How *did* you get away!?" Ore asked.

"We need to get to the city," Georgie said. "To Fumbluff. South of the Notch. We'll tell you on the way."

❖ ❖ ❖

Night had fallen and it had started to rain by the time they reached the Notch, leaving an unpleasant chill that crept into Georgie's bones. The winding and hilly city streets, which had just this afternoon been clogged with the optimistic sounds of happy Scatterplotters hurrying to the Coronation Ceremony, were now desolate and slippery. Georgie wondered how much longer they had before the entire city was crawling with the Dregs of Mishap.

Crawling like beetles.

◇ ◇ ◇

"Do you hear anything?" Edie whispered loudly when they reached the end of the dark street.

"Not with you screaming in my ear," Ore whispered back.

Georgie heard faint footsteps, mixed with the whistling wind. He looked around the corner and saw someone standing at the forest's edge, waving a long line of survivors across a grassy hill sloping up from the road.

Georgie, Apurva, Edie, and Ore ran to the group of bruised and bloodied Scatterplotters. The few who looked up at them said nothing. Women, men, and children all shuffled along hopelessly. Many cried silently.

Some cried not so silently.

Halfway up the grassy slope, Georgie and Apurva almost collided with . . .

Charlie Fenton!

The strips of tent fabric wrapped around his chest where the arrow had struck him made him look like the world's largest and clumsiest mummy. He groaned in pain as Edie and Ore flung themselves into his arms. Georgie hugged Fenton too, but gently. "Blaze came back for me," Fenton choked through his tears. "Saved my life. But so many others . . ." Fenton shook. He couldn't finish.

He didn't need to.

Fenton was alive, and a billowy flicker of hope, like a struck match in the wind, flared within Georgie.

But what now? Georgie wondered. *What are we going to do? Can I still travel up to Quillethra and write with the Aetherquill?*

A hand fell on his shoulder. Georgie turned, staring up into Blaze Nelson's stony face. Blaze just pointed further up the slope where Fumbluff stood, shrouded in shadow, hidden from moonlight.

"Go to him," Blaze whispered.

Chapter 28

The Caravan of Survivors

Fumbluff's robes were torn. His face was smudged with dried blood. The sparkle in his eyes was gone.

He's gone dim, Georgie thought.

"Georgie," Fumbluff said weakly. He stared into Georgie's eyes. "Yes?"

It wasn't a question. It was a statement of gloomy finality. Of loss, defeat, and regret.

Georgie nodded. He felt like screaming. Rollie *said* Flint was getting closer . . . getting stronger! Why wasn't there more protection around the Coronation Ceremony?

Why wasn't Fumbluff more prepared? Why couldn't the Coronation Ceremony have come a day earlier?

Fumbluff shook his head. "Every fourteen years, Georgie. At just the right time, yes? A cosmic window, if you will. Did you see it? I'm sure you *felt* it. It's how it always was. It's how it will always be. You're an official Scribe now."

The last of the survivors crossed into the forest, with Blaze and Fenton bringing up the rear.

"Oh, Georgie, I have failed you," Fumbluff whispered. "I have failed Scatterplot. I have failed the Librarian. I have failed your mother and your father."

Fumbluff scratched his head and rubbed his eyes.

"It's not over yet," Georgie said, "is it?"

"Passage to Quillethra is possible only from Scatterplot's Cathedral," Fumbluff whispered, his voice as tired as he looked. He stared into Georgie's eyes, then dropped his gaze to Georgie's right pants pocket. "You have the Aetherquill now, but it's too late . . ."

Fumbluff *knew*, he'd known all along. Georgie's heart hammered as Fumbluff spoke. "Flint Eldritch will station his men . . . we have no army . . . the city is lost . . . the plan is ruin—"

"*What plan?*" Georgie asked aloud, a bitter anger simmering inside him, one that must have begun to boil when Fumbluff first laid out his plan.

Fumbluff closed his eyes and breathed out shakily. "The plan to stop Flint Eldritch and—"

"And *what*!?" Georgie interrupted. "And *kill my FATHER*!?" The last of the survivors passing by stopped and looked over at Georgie and Fumbluff.

Fumbluff exhaled shakily. "It was the best plan we had, Georgie." Fumbluff's voice was such complete sorrow and grief that for the first time, Georgie's heart hurt for Scatterplot's Editor in Chief.

"I would never have done it," Georgie said. "*Never*."

"Maybe so."

"Rollie D said there was another way, that—"

Fumbluff shook his head and held Georgie by the shoulders. "The Aetherquill *must* not be used in a lower realm. It's an exceedingly dangerous proposition. Catastrophe. Unpredictable danger." Fumbluff closed his eyes again. "I know. Because I've seen it before."

There was only one time the Aetherquill was used in a lower realm, as far as Georgie knew. "My mother?"

Fumbluff opened his eyes, and Georgie watched a single tear track down the deep wrinkles in his ageless face. He nodded.

Now Georgie *really* wanted to know what happened all those years ago. Why his mother used the Aetherquill under such dangerous circumstances.

But that wasn't a question for now. "We need another plan, Fumbluff. I'm not giving up."

Georgie thought Fumbluff would ask him to hand the Aetherquill over, maybe even take it from him by force, but instead, he smiled and patted Georgie on the head. "I didn't expect you to."

Georgie looked behind him at the dark and lifeless city. From this distance, the ridge beyond the city was just a dark ribbon running horizontally across the nightscape.

Blaze Nelson doubled back from the edge of the forest. "The Dregs of Mishap," he grunted, pointing to a cluster of bobbing yellow lights moving slowly down the ridge. "They're coming. We should go."

Fumbluff nodded and put his battered top hat back on. How in the world that silly velvet hat survived, Georgie had no idea.

"Where are we taking everyone?" Georgie whispered to Fumbluff, though he had a pretty good idea.

"Rollie D told us very clearly *not* to come back," Apurva added. Apparently, she had the same idea as Georgie. "And she seemed quite serious about it."

Fumbluff smiled weakly. "That doesn't surprise me."

They were at the forest's edge now, out of the moonlight. Total darkness. Georgie knew the figures on either side of him now were Edie and Ore just by their outlines.

"What about everyone else?" Apurva asked. "Everyone Flint captured? What will happen to them?"

"Mommy!" Ore whimpered.

"Eldritch will detain the Scribes," Fumbluff whispered. "He'll forbid them from recording memories, the beginning of terrible confusion and chaos for innocent people back in your world. He'll still be looking for the Aetherquill, so we must keep moving and moving quickly."

Edie sobbed silently, and this time, it was Ore's turn to comfort her.

More flickering lamplights appeared on the ridge.

Apurva put an arm around Georgie's shoulder and they walked with Edie and Ore into the forest.

Georgie did not look back.

❖ ❖ ❖

The caravan of survivors slogged slowly through the cold forest. Georgie figured there were about two hundred men, women, and children. Fumbluff led, while Blaze Nelson and Emma Hambrey hurried up and down the line handing out warmkins to the children. Charlie Fenton stayed at the back, hobbling along with a walking stick fashioned from a dead branch.

The temperature dropped as the night drew on, and before long, they were walking through a thick layer of snow. Bugle and Phiz walked beside them, carrying the children too tired and weak to carry themselves. The only sounds were snow crunching under two hundred pairs of feet and chilly breath exhaling into the wilderness.

At some unknown hour, Fumbluff held up a hand and the survivors made camp. They did not make a fire. Fenton unpacked wrapped meats from his rucksack.

No one spoke.

They were too tired, and there was nothing to say.

❖ ❖ ❖

The survivors got moving again after what felt like an hour or two of fitful sleep. They walked quietly, breaking from the tree cover around midday, then scaling the craggy and open mountain summit and descending back into tree cover as the sun began to set.

Georgie's face was frostbitten. He kept touching the shape of the Aetherquill in his pants pocket, maybe to make sure it was still there, maybe because the solid thing was a touchstone to a time before Flint Eldritch conquered Scatterplot, a time when Georgie felt there was actually a shot at saving his dad.

◊ ◊ ◊

By sunrise of the second day, Georgie's muscles screamed in pain. Apurva hadn't spoken a word to him since the previous night. Even Edie and Ore had been silent as the dead. Some of the weaker survivors could no longer walk through the forest without help. Others stumbled, tripping over stumps and roots. Some fell to the floor and refused to stand again until a fellow survivor pulled them to their feet.

Georgie was nearly delirious with fatigue. He was losing the details of everything and wondered if this was what the people back home were feeling now that the Scribes were no longer recording their memories. What would happen to them? And hey, where was Roscoe? Had he and Rollie survived?

He thought about Apurva's mother and knew Apurva

must be worrying about her now more than ever. He hugged Apurva and touched her cheek. Her skin was rubbery and frigid and pale; dark circles of exhaustion ringed her eyes.

◇ ◇ ◇

It was late afternoon of the second day when Georgie heard rushing water. His heart jumped—just barely. Fumbluff brought the caravan to a stop. All around, survivors slumped against trees. Others lay down on the ground in a heap, hugging family and friends.

Georgie went to Fumbluff, who was looking straight ahead, to where the tree cover ended. To where the wide river cut through this endless forest like the Great Road in Scatterplot cut through the fields of feather grass all the way to Corrigendum. He followed Fumbluff's gaze, and standing at the edge of the clearing, at the lip of the ravine, was Rollie D.

Chapter 29

The Scatterplotters in Enemy Territory

Rollie's cheek was bruised, and there was a small cut where her neck met her collarbone, but other than that she looked pretty much okay.

She snapped her fingers and a hundred or more Altercockers appeared, coming out from behind trees and bushes, forming a wide circle around the Scatterplotters.

"We come with no ill intentions, Rollie," Fumbluff began in a cracked whisper. "We come to you for shelter. For protection. Many of our people are dead. The rest have been captured." Fumbluff swept his arm around. "We're all that's left of Scatterplot."

Rollie ignored Fumbluff and stared straight at Georgie and Apurva instead. "I told you not to come back."

"We need your help," Fumbluff continued softly. "To whom else can I turn?"

"YOU AND YOUR KIN ARE NOT WELCOME HERE!" Rollie thundered. "You *betrayed* me. Yes, it was many years ago, but looking at your face still makes me sick."

Holy smokes, Georgie thought. *What in the world happened between* those *two!?*

Then, from behind Rollie, beyond the edge of the ravine, Georgie heard Roscoe's voice. "Rollie!? Where'd everyone go? *Hello?*"

Relief crashed over Georgie. A moment later Roscoe appeared, dressed in leather moccasins and a thick potato sack shawl wrapped around his shoulders. He stared at Georgie for a moment, then broke into a run.

"GEORGIE! You miserable rag!" Roscoe shouted. "You made it! You look like you came out of the giveaway hamper, but you *made* it, you reeky onion-eyed foot licker!" He flung his arms around Georgie.

Apurva was there a moment later, and Roscoe wrapped an arm around her too. Georgie wished their three-way hug would last longer than it did, but then Rollie was dragging Roscoe away, looking angry enough for steam to come pouring out of her ears.

But Rollie was more than just an angry warrior.

Georgie remembered the tears in Rollie's eyes when she gave him the Aetherquill. And she *did* save his and Apurva's lives back in Scatterplot, even though she said she'd kill them if they said anything about that.

"Rollie," Georgie began, his voice rusty with thirst. "Help us—"

"I did not solicit your opinion," Rollie shot back. "Coming here in the first place was both selfish and reckless. How do you know Flint's men weren't following you?"

And as if right on cue, a splashing came from the river.

Rollie and Fumbluff hurried to the edge of the ravine. Georgie, Apurva, and Roscoe followed. Two men leaped from a small raft to the shore. Georgie recognized the daggers looped around their belts from the blacksmith's shop. Flint's men, dressed in black leather, with cavernous foreheads that stuck out far enough to keep their noses dry in a downpour, scurried up the sloping ravine—one of them pulling a dagger and the other pulling a piece of paper from his vest.

They were still fifty yards away when Rollie shot them through their chests. She didn't even take her eyes off Fumbluff as she aimed and released. The Dregs of Mishaps' eyes flew open. They fell to their knees and bowed, not to Flint Eldritch, their master, but to the hard ground, crunching their foreheads against a rock with enough force to have killed them each a second time.

The paper one of the men had been holding fluttered and landed nearby.

"Get it, Toots," Rollie said, and Toots Tenderfoot, who had been standing beside Yooker near the edge of the ravine this entire time, did as she was told, handing the paper to Rollie obediently. Georgie, peering around Rollie's arm, saw that the paper was a detailed map of what looked like a tangled web of rivers, waterways, and tributaries. "Eldritch knows we never camp too far from a river," Rollie spat angrily to Fumbluff, roughly folding the paper and tucking it inside her cloak.

Georgie wasn't certain, but he thought steam was *actually* coming out of Rollie's ears now. "Bringing the Aetherquill back here, the most powerful artifact in the known universes—puts my people in grave danger."

Either Rollie didn't realize Toots Tenderfoot was still in earshot, or she just didn't care. Toots turned and whispered something to Yooker, whose eyebrows arched so high up they became part of his actual hair. Yooker in turn whispered something to the group of five Altercockers standing beside him, and within seconds, the Altercockers were all muttering excitedly to each other.

Georgie only caught bits and pieces, but it was obvious what the Altercockers were all so excited about. The Aetherquill. They probably had no idea what it was or what it could do, but it didn't matter. They knew it was powerful.

The Altercockers shuffled forward restlessly.

Georgie stepped back, looking to Rollie for help, but from the look on her face, she wasn't about to offer any. The Altercockers grunted and stamped their feet and cracked their knuckles. They came closer and closer. They were all staring at Georgie.

"Rollie!" Charlie Fenton roared. He was leaning against a nearby tree, the bandages around his chest coming undone. "Control your people!"

Two Altercockers broke from the ring and rushed at Georgie. Apurva shrieked. Roscoe threw up his fists, stupidly preparing to fight. The particularly dumpy and potbellied one swung his hips into the other, and they both tripped and landed in a tangled mess. Another Altercocker leaped over them, seizing the opportunity to grab Georgie.

All the noise—Apurva's screams, the rushing river, the Altercockers' stampeding feet—faded, and all that was left in Georgie's mind was something his father once told him: That most bullies weren't *really* bad kids. They were just lonely and sad kids. And the biggest bullies were the loneliest and saddest of them all.

Georgie drew a deep breath. "DO NOT MOVE ANOTHER INCH TOWARD ME OR MY FRIENDS!"

His voice boomed throughout the clearing, and any of Scatterplot's survivors who had fallen asleep were awakened with a start. The Altercockers who were rushing at Georgie stopped in their tracks, dumbfounded at the boy who screamed with such frightening authority.

Everyone stared at Georgie, waiting for him to speak.

"Don't you SEE!?" Georgie thundered, addressing not just the Altercockers and Rollie D, but Fumbluff as well. "Don't you see what your hatred for each other has caused!?"

He turned to Fumbluff, his heart beating a mile a minute. "Flint killed innocent people. *Your* people! They didn't deserve to die! You *NEEDED* Rollie D! You *NEEDED* the Altercockers! Rollie *knew* Flint was coming, and even if you *did* believe it, you didn't believe it enough! We could have fought! We could *still* fight!"

Now Georgie faced Rollie D. "But we need YOU!" He

addressed the Altercockers next. "*AND* you! Don't turn your backs on us!"

Georgie climbed atop a nearby tree stump. He scanned the crowd of Scatterplotters and Altercockers.

To Georgie, everyone looked the same now.

"People are dead. Come on! WAKE UP!"

One Altercocker took a shuffling step forward. Then another. "But . . . I want the Aetherquill!" the Altercocker grumbled, then resumed his waddling run at Georgie, now with both hands outstretched like he was coming in for the world's most painful embrace.

He didn't make it very far.

Yooker Tenderfoot took one swift step sideways and swept his three-fingered fist into the Altercocker's chest, sending him to the ground hard enough to make the forest floor shake.

"The boy makes a point," Yooker Tenderfoot said, turning clumsily in place, addressing his people. "Flint Eldritch is our enemy, too! The Scatterplotters are snobby and smart-alecky. They are snooty and snippy. They are arrogant and bossy. But they are not our enemy!"

Yooker took Toots by the hand. They made the most unattractive couple on the face of *any* planet, but the gesture was romantic anyway.

"We're *fighters*," Yooker grumbled on. "Are we not!? Is this not a fight worth fighting?"

A few of the Altercockers nodded their heads.

The rest of them turned to Rollie D.

"Thank you, Yooker," Rollie said. "Now shut up and stand back."

Yooker did as he was told (not letting go of Toots). Rollie stepped onto the tree stump and stood next to Georgie.

"All in favor of fighting for Scatterplot, say *aye!*"

"I!" Roscoe shouted, throwing his arm up and wiggling his fingers like he wanted to be called on.

Rollie shot a glance at him and Roscoe quickly lowered his hand.

"Whether we like it or not," Rollie said after a long pause, "the battle has already found us." She motioned to the two lifeless Dregs of Mishap lying face down on the forest floor, then turned to Fumbluff.

Dark patches puffed beneath the Editor in Chief's eyes. He hadn't slept in days, but even so, the blue twinkle of hope had resurfaced. He reached up and put a hand on Rollie's arm but she shook it off.

"You and me?" Rollie spat at Fumbluff. "We're not good, okay? Let me be very clear about that."

"Okay, Rollie," Fumbluff said, withdrawing his hand. "I understand."

Rollie looked out again into the crowd of Altercockers and Scatterplotters. "I ask again, one last time. All in favor of joining Scatterplot in a battle against Flint Eldritch, SAY AYE, AND SAY IT NOW!"

Two Altercockers near the back of the crowd raised their hands and yelled, "*Aye!*"

Yooker and Toots stepped forward together, their free hands raised in the air. "*AYE!*"

It was infectious. Or maybe the Altercockers had been waiting for this moment for a long time. Soon, the entire forest shook with the Altercockers' *aye*s and stamping feet.

Those with weapons waved them high in the air. The rest grabbed hands and hugged whoever was standing next to them. The Scatterplot survivors were mostly on their feet now. A few even approached the nearest Altercocker and kissed them on the cheek.

Georgie, his chest heaving and feeling wide awake, looked up at Rollie D and saw something he didn't expect to see.

A real smile.

PART THREE

Shadow
and Light.
Light and
Shadow.

Chapter 30

Two Tribes United

Rollie D liked to say that great warriors weren't just fast and accurate with a bow, but always thought two steps ahead, like the best *Gotcha* players. So while the Altercockers helped the Scatterplotters across the river, Rollie was busy dragging the dead bodies of the Dregs of Mishap onto one of the pontoons moored to the riverbank. She instructed a pair of Altercockers to captain the boat a few miles upriver, hoping to throw Flint's men off their trail.

The Altercockers, having a lot of practice, were quick and efficient in dismantling their camp—packing up their makeshift spits, shoveling the fire embers into the river—and before long, there was hardly any sign of them having been in this particular spot along this particular stretch of river.

Soon the entire group, Scatterplotters and Altercockers alike, was on the move, heading deeper into the forest, the tents cradling the wounded and weakest Scatterplotters floating peacefully through the trees. By the time Rollie's bobbing oil lantern came to a stop, night had nearly fallen and they were deep into the forest, where the trees and shrubs and brambles grew in a tangle.

Rollie dispatched a group of Altercockers to hunt for dinner . . . *quietly.* Another group was in charge of clothing—the Scatterplotters' jackets and socks were not made for living in the wilderness. Another group used the giant canvas rolls from the narrowboats and pontoons they left behind to make mattresses.

One of the Scatterplot survivors, a junior blacksmith named Shepherd from Stone's Blacksmiths, Bladesmiths, and Problem Solvers, rounded up his own crew, constructing a small workshop in the woods. *If* they were going to fight, they'd need more weapons and armor. He rubbed his thick auburn mustache and nodded when Apurva and Edie volunteered to collect rocks for the forge's walls.

Georgie and Roscoe paired up to collect branches of deadwood for the dinner fires.

Fumbluff, as it turned out, was not very resourceful when it came to making camp in the woods, but he *did* know the waterways and rivers from here back to Scatterplot better than anyone, even Rollie herself, a fact Rollie was not pleased to have to admit. Rollie handed Fumbluff the map Flint's men had been carrying. She told him to mark any routes back to Scatterplot Flint and his men didn't know about . . . if there were any.

◇ ◇ ◇

By the time Georgie and Roscoe set off to collect firewood, the moon shone through gaps in the tree cover, lighting their way just enough so that they didn't need a lantern.

"I was scared you wouldn't make it out," Roscoe said to Georgie, all the humor gone from his voice. He sounded sincere now, as if all his growing up had been sandwiched into the past few days.

"*Fartbag.*"

Well, maybe not *all* his growing up.

"You're calling *me* a fartbag?" Georgie smiled. "You better lay off the stew tonight. We're not training for chemical warfare."

Roscoe laughed. "Remember that time in third grade when the plants in Mr. Johnson's class started to wilt and you called my farts a new and deadly form of greenhouse gas?"

Georgie started giggling, which in turn caused Roscoe to giggle, and soon they were both cracking up. "One time you farted so loud Mr. Johnson screamed that you'd be the first person to achieve flight without a plane!"

That made the two of them laugh so hard they nearly cried.

It had been a while since either of them laughed like

that, and it felt good. But as they continued on into the dead of night through the thickets, the mood got somber again.

"That *was* nuts, back in Scatterplot," Georgie said quietly. "You and Rollie literally *flew* over our heads."

"You bet we did," Roscoe agreed. "I'm a pretty good shot now myself, eh?"

"You're no Georgie Summers with a slingshot," Georgie said, nudging Roscoe. "But still . . . pretty impressive." They dropped a branch onto their pile of firewood. "You and Rollie saved our lives."

"Don't mention it." Roscoe smiled. "Actually, on second thought, *mention* it."

As they took trips carrying their firewood back to camp, Georgie told Roscoe everything that had happened after Rollie'd given him the Aetherquill. The Coronation Ceremony fairgrounds, Flint's attack, how they'd climbed through the pipes, ending with how now, according to Fumbluff, the Scribes would be forbidden from recording any new memories.

"Cheez-Its, Mary, and Joseph Stalin," Roscoe exhaled when Georgie was finished. "So what's the plan now? I mean, *Fumbluff's* plan is dead, isn't it? We can't go up to . . . what was it called?"

"Quillethra."

"Right."

"And even if you *did* use the Aetherquill," Roscoe said, lowering his voice to a whisper, "like, on *this* realm, it would only work on a page of whisperleaf. Rollie told me that."

That sounded about right to Georgie. "And Rollie doesn't have any whisperleaf?"

"Negative. Said so herself."

Georgie sighed and grabbed one end of a log.

Roscoe lifted from the other side. "Hey, Georgie, you're not giving up, right?"

Georgie shook his head.

"So then get rid of that sad sound in your voice, you wet noodle. Just spank it right into oblivion. You're making *me* depressed now!"

Georgie smiled again, and on the count of three, they lifted.

◊ ◊ ◊

The camp was bustling now. Georgie and Roscoe helped Rollie kindle the fires, while Roscoe told Georgie all about life with the Altercockers. Georgie only caught bits and pieces of it. His mind was thinking about Rollie's plan, to somehow use the Aetherquill to make his dad whole again. But what would *Rollie* say about using the Aetherquill on a lower realm . . . ?

" . . . I coughed my guts out the first time," Roscoe said.

"Coughed from what?"

"Am I talking to a doorknob? The cigars! That's what I'm saying, man. Toots let me try a cigar one night. Coughed my guts out. But then she gave me some beer to wash it down with."

Roscoe showed Georgie how to stoke flames delicately, with a slender branch.

"And you know the craziest thing?" Roscoe continued, "I haven't even thought about my parents since we got here. Not once. I *love* it here."

◇ ◇ ◇

Dinner that night was roasted meats over an open fire and it was just as delicious as anything Scatterplot served up. Rollie even made sausage skewers for the children as a special treat. The bonfire's flames cast long, dancing shadows throughout the campground, warming all the cold, tired people huddled around it.

Georgie sat between Roscoe and Apurva, legs crossed, watching the flames. A few Altercockers began to play their ancient instruments. The percussionists played softly, the stringed notes were like raindrops, and the hand-carved wooden flutes breathed like a beating heart. The Altercockers didn't play their instruments perfectly, but they played with all their soul.

It was a sad tune—a song full of grief and longing.

Rollie D, who'd been sitting nearby, stood up and began to sing. Her voice quivered at first, her second note trembled, then she settled into something sweet and mournful.

> *See and hear our destinies,*
> *In pages marked with memories.*
> *Make your marks, stand so still,*
> *By magic ink and valiant quill.*

Fumbluff stood up and began to sing with Rollie.

Even pain and loss and tears of death,
Are kept by us as life to breath.
Let's laugh and dance for destiny now,
To make the future full.
On Scatterplot's hills, let's dance until,
Great Books are filled with memories good.

Rollie ended on a high note, her eyes squeezed shut, and when she opened them, all that could be heard were the knots popping softly in the fire. Apurva snuggled close to him and rested her head on Georgie's shoulder, and that was how they were when Rollie tapped them on the shoulder a few short minutes later. "Both of you come with me." Firelight danced in her reddish-green eyes.

❖ ❖ ❖

Georgie thought the combined weight of all the people in Rollie's tent would surely cause the floor to rip, but even under Rollie D, Fumbluff, Shepherd the blacksmith, Charlie Fenton, Scribe Hambrey, Blaze Nelson, Georgie, Roscoe, and Apurva, the tent floor hardly sagged at all.

Fumbluff sat on the tree stump, marking the map with a charcoal stick. "There *is* a way back home unnoticed by Eldritch's map," Fumbluff said softly. "If my memory serves me correctly." He chuckled in rusty, anxious hiccups. "It's a circuitous route, narrow in some parts, but a small pontoon will do."

Rollie seemed satisfied enough with that.

Charlie Fenton was in a corner, fiddling with his bandages, which once again had become undone.

"Let me help you with that, old bear," Rollie said, then wrapped Fenton's bandages snugly around his chest with surprising gentleness.

"Thank ya, Rollie," Charlie whispered, tapping his throat three times and more than a little red in the face.

Rollie addressed everyone assembled in her tent. "We're outnumbered. If we go to war with Flint, without a plan to destroy him . . . without the Aetherquill . . . we'll lose. Flint and his army are too powerful. Oh, we'll kill a few of his men. Even *more* than a few, but in the end, we'll lose."

"We can't use the Aetherquill on this realm," Fumbluff sighed. "It's too—"

"Stop, please," Rollie snapped, closing her eyes and shaking her head. "I'm trying not to get angry at you, Fumbluff, but you're making it very, *very* difficult. What happened with Penelope and John was bad, I admit that, but it doesn't mean it'll happen again. This may be our only chance to *reverse* that damage."

"It's too dangerous," Fumbluff repeated. "Last time, using the Aetherquill on a lower realm caused great damage to its recipient, yes? To John Summers. What if this time, it causes irreparable damage to the *writer?*"

Georgie felt the butterflies again. That was a scary thought.

"It should be *Georgie's* call to make," Roscoe said assuredly. "And as far as the Aetherquill goes . . . me and Georgie?

You all have no idea of the crazy stuff we got up to as kids. We don't quit because of *danger.*" He said "danger" like it was a word that made him queasy. "Mr. Summers is in a real pickle, caught in a jam without the bread, and when it comes down to it, it's Georgie's call to make."

Everyone in the tent was looking at the host of *Roscoe's Rag*, home to fourteen YouTube subscribers in another world. Georgie loved Roscoe for what he'd just said.

"None of this even *matters*," Georgie exhaled, rubbing his eyes. "Flint has Corrigendum on lockdown. He's taken over the Cathedral and the Seminary. Even if I *wanted* to use the Aetherquill, there's no whisperleaf to write on."

The group swayed gently amongst the trees.

Finally, Fumbluff stood up (which only brought him to Rollie's shoulders) and smoothed out his topcoat. "There *is* whisperleaf," Fumbluff said softly, then closed his eyes, as if he regretted saying it. "A single page."

"Where?" Rollie asked.

"I never thought it would come to this, yes?" Fumbluff said. "But that doesn't mean I didn't make a backup plan. I'm not as square as you make me out to be, Rollie." Fumbluff looked sullenly around the tent. "Underground. In the ruins of Scatterplot's original Library." Fumbluff turned to Shepherd the blacksmith. "There's a secret door beneath the forge in Stone's workshop."

Was that *admiration* Georgie saw in Rollie's eyes as she regarded Fumbluff? "Well," Rollie breathed. "That's good to hear, old man." She tied her hair up with a leather strap hanging from a peg above her bed and began to pace around the tent. Even if there *was* whisperleaf hidden underground in Scatterplot, they still needed to get to it. Rollie scrunched her brow, mumbled something to Scribe Hambrey, nodded her head, then resumed her pacing.

Until suddenly, she stood still. "We're going through the portal. We're going to New York. We're going . . ." Rollie paused, seeming to search for the right word. " . . . shopping."

Fumbluff sighed, as if he was expecting Rollie to say something preposterous like that.

Rollie put one leg up on the tree stump. "Gather around and listen closely."

Chapter 31

Rollie D Tells a Love Story

Georgie, Apurva, and Roscoe fell asleep that night in the Tenderfoots' tent under a thick burlap blanket, and when Rollie shook them awake before dawn, the rest of the camp was still fast asleep.

Roscoe was staying behind (once again, *his* decision) to help Scribe Hambrey with her part of the plan. He had one of Yooker's shawls draped around his shoulders, and Georgie couldn't help but notice the healthy muscle that seemed to have magically appeared these last few days along Roscoe's arms.

"You think my father aged like forty years?" Roscoe asked,

rubbing the sleep from his eyes. "Like, now he's ninety years old and thinks he's a pigeon?"

"I don't think so," Apurva said seriously.

"Shucks," Roscoe yawned.

A shadow passed over their small group. Georgie turned around to see Rollie D standing over them.

"It's time." She dropped a rucksack with leather straps at Georgie's feet. "Food and supplies. Strap it on." Then she handed Georgie a leaf of parchment with three lines of charcoal writing on it. "Your shopping list."

❖ ❖ ❖

With the early morning sun to light their way, getting back to the river took half the time than it did last night. The Altercockers' boats were still there, moored to the riverbank, and a few minutes later they were aboard the narrowboat, cutting through the gray water.

Georgie sat down and rested his back against the bulkhead. "Rollie?"

"Yeah, kid?"

"What happened between my mom and my dad?"

The water was calm, and a thin layer of fog shattered by the morning sun curled off its surface.

Rollie sighed. "It's an old story. Not one I'm fond of retelling . . . because I'm a part of it. Besides, it's about love. You're too young for stuff like that."

A soft wind blew a loose ribbon of Apurva's hair against Georgie's cheek. It smelled like sea salt and wild berries.

It was weird, sitting on this rickety boat with Apurva Aluwhalia. It was *more* than weird. It was mysterious and exciting.

"We know what love is, Rollie," Apurva said.

Rollie laughed. "I guess you do. There's something pure about love at your age. Grown-ups are the *real* monsters. Fashioned from bruises and broken hearts left unmended. Time doesn't heal all wounds, you know. Time just *wounds*."

The water gurgled and whooshed around Rollie's oar.

"It was your father," she began. "John Summers broke my heart."

As she spoke, she paddled harder or softer, with the current of her story.

"I was five when my parents died. I grew up in the Seminary under the great Sanka Siskroll, Scatterplot's last Editor in Chief, and all I ever wanted to be was a Scribe. Your dad was two years older than me, but we were best friends just the same. We did *everything* together. We joined the apprenticeship together. We were study partners. Whisperloom came easy to us . . . the reading, the writing . . . *seeing*. We loved it.

"But second year, I started getting antsy. I wanted to see the world *beyond* Scatterplot. I decided to sneak through the portal between realms—just once. Just to see what it was like. I could have gotten in *serious* trouble. Only officers of the Librarian and each barony's Editor in Chief are allowed to travel through the portal. Back then, your garage was just an abandoned shed on abandoned land. I came through, roamed around a bit, then took a bus to New York City."

Rollie smiled, like she was remembering an inside joke. "I didn't know you had to sacrifice tokens or procure a tick-it to ride the bus! The driver stopped me, but then he saw my apprentice's robes, mumbled something about the homeless, and let me through."

Rollie let out a great, rattling breath. "I saw this young girl uptown that day. Must've been about seven years old. Her clothes were filthy. She was alone. She looked like she needed a friend. I followed her around all that day, until late in the afternoon, when she was sitting on her apartment stairs. I wanted to say something to her . . . introduce myself, but I didn't. I was scared. Meddling with lower-realmers can mess with their memories. So I watched her sit there, eating a cylindrical sandwich wrapped in foldable metal."

Burrito, Georgie thought. *A burrito wrapped in tinfoil.*

"A group of nasty boys came up the street and ripped that sandwich straight out of her hands. They laughed and took turns taking bites until the little girl started to cry. I was so angry that night back in Scatterplot. I wanted to do something to *help* that little girl."

Rollie sighed. "I told your dad what happened. At first, he was upset at me for going to New York in the first place, but then we started talking. You know what? Your dad wanted to help that little girl, too. Or maybe he just wanted to help *me.* He told me about memory deletion—something I hadn't heard about until then. A Scribe—if they were *really* good—can overwrite a specific memory.

"It took some convincing, but your dad agreed to help me break into Scatterplot's Great Library that night. We found the little girl's book easily enough because the Great Books are cataloged in chronological *and* alphabetical order and I knew her last name from her mailbox. We found the memory, and I wiped that memory clean—which, by the way, is just about the worst crime you can commit, at least according to the Scribes.

"But I knew what I was doing."

Rollie sighed again.

"At least I thought so. The next day I went back to New York. I watched the little girl playing in a sprinkler, just being happy. I remember *feeling* happy. I remember feeling like maybe I was the friend that she needed.

"But then those nasty boys came back.

"The girl didn't recognize them. She had no *memory* of them. She waved them over, inviting them to play.

"They played, alright. They pulled her ponytail and shoved her to the cement. She begged the boys to stop hurting her, but one of them grabbed her delicate fingers and bent them so far back they snapped. She shrieked for help, but the boys just shoved her back and forth, laughing.

"I can still see what happened next in slow motion, clear as a memory in the Great Books. A city bus turned up the block. Horns blared. The bus swerved to avoid a car coming the other way. At that same moment, one of the boys shoved the little girl in the back. She tripped on the curb and stumbled into the street. The bus swerved again, violently, and I heard a soft thump just before the bus crashed head-on into a storefront. I still remember the sign above the shattered glass: KATZ'S PHARMACY.

"The boys ran away, but I stood there, hidden, frozen with terror. People started to scream. Then I heard the sirens. A medical potions chariot with flashing, cosmic lights sped past me."

An ambulance, Georgie thought with horror.

"I pushed my way through the crowd," Rollie D continued. "Then I saw her. The little girl's head was rolled to the side, her body twisted. She was dead. But her eyes were still open, and they stared right at me. I ran."

Rollie lifted her oar, letting the boat drift, staring out into the wilderness on either side of the river.

"And it dawned on me, Georgie, in a horrible instant I'll never forget. *I was her murderer.*

"I had erased her bad memory, but I had also erased some of her *knowledge.* If she had known those boys were bad news, she would never have waved them over. She would never have stumbled in front of that bus."

Georgie could see the look of pain on Rollie's face, even all these years later. He felt bad for Rollie. She had been trying to *help* that little girl. And besides, it wasn't *totally* her fault; his father was a part of this too.

"I told your father what happened. We were sitting on the ridge overlooking Scatterplot, and I was crying. He didn't say anything. Not a word. What happened to that little girl was eating him up inside. He blamed himself as much as I blamed *my*self.

"I showed up to our study sessions less and less after that. I would go exploring, sometimes for days at a time, deep into the forest beyond Scatterplot's borders. Meanwhile, your father started to study more and more with Penelope, a new apprentice, beautiful as all hell, and *smart*. Smart as a whip."

Rollie exhaled slowly, untied her rucksack, and handed out meat sandwiches wrapped in elephant leaves.

"Time passed. Your father's grades started to slip. He was falling behind the other apprentices, especially Penelope, who loved your father more than anything. Penelope tried helping him, but it was no use. *A Scribe sees with his heart and writes with his mind*, and John's heart was clogged with regret over helping me break into the Library that night, and his mind was filled with sadness over that little girl's death."

Rollie pulled the boat onto the mossy riverbank. They would have to go the rest of the way to the portal by foot now.

"I found the Aetherquill on one of my expeditions," Rollie continued, leading the way through the trees. "*How* I found it is a tale for another time, but I knew what magic it contained. I couldn't bring that girl back from the dead, but I thought the Aetherquill might be a way to make things right with John Summers again."

Georgie felt goosebumps tingle up his arms and neck.

"Your father wanted no part of it. He said he'd rather give up the Scribehood completely than risk using the Aetherquill in a lower realm. I think that was *partly* true, but mostly, I think he *wanted* all that guilt and shame. That changing his reality through the Aetherquill would be . . . like *cheating*. Do you see what I mean?"

Georgie and Apurva nodded.

"I gave the Aetherquill to Penelope. She loved your dad so much, maybe *she'd* be able to convince him. To use the Aetherquill to implant a belief so potent that it would change John's reality forever. A belief that the little girl I killed—*we* killed—was alive and happy and well. Might that open his heart and mind again?"

A thick layer of snow now blanketed the forest bed, and Georgie felt a chill deep in his bones.

"Your mother didn't use the Aetherquill right away—she knew it was a dangerous artifact with unpredictable consequences. She waited *years*. She married your father, hoping that would help. But his guilt was too strong."

It must have been close to midday, but Georgie had lost all sense of time the moment Rollie'd started talking.

"Your mother was scared. Terrified of bringing you into a world without a father you could look up to. She had no one else to turn to. She had no other options. All she had was the Aetherquill."

Rollie slashed at a thicket. "And she used it."

Rollie walked slower now, looking around for something. "You both know what happened next."

"Flint Eldritch," Georgie said weakly.

Rollie nodded. "For days, we thought your dad was going to die. He was unconscious . . . he must have been fighting the splintering of his own mind. Fighting the Aetherquill's false story your mother wrote him. He'd be lying there in bed, still as stone, until without notice, he'd begin to shake and scream. It was me and Fenton and Penelope who had to hold him down." Rollie ducked beneath a low-hanging branch and motioned for Apurva and Georgie to follow. "We saw Flint Eldritch *come out*," Rollie said, her voice wavering. "That's the best way I can put it. Black smoke pouring from your father's mouth and nose, like the expulsion of some horrible, living infection. It was a shadow, alright, and it was *alive*."

Georgie thought once again about that shadow-monster on Corrigendum's dining room wall. Those tentacles licking up to the ceiling. Georgie shivered.

"We watched the shadow-thing slink like an oil spill out of the open window," Rollie said. "By the time it reached the edge of the forest, the thing had *legs*. I know I sound like a crazy lady, like I have a few loose screws, but it's the truth. I doubt Fenton wants to talk about it, but if you ask him, he'll say the same thing. Your father woke up after that. But he was . . ."

"Diminished?" Georgie asked.

"*Blank*," Rollie said. "He wasn't the John Summers I knew. He wasn't the John Summers *any* of us knew. Penelope was distraught. Two nights later, she left you with Fumbluff and Fenton and came to me. She threw the Aetherquill at me with disgust. Told me to destroy it. Or to keep it. She didn't care. Said she was going after Flint, which was the name we all gave the shadow-thing by then . . . we had to call it *something*. I tried to convince her not to—that it was a death sentence, but she was a stubborn woman, your mother, and she ran off before I could stop her.

"I never saw her again after that night."

Rollie closed her eyes, but not before Georgie saw tears

glistening there. "I searched for her." Rollie bunched up a handful of fabric from her thick woolen cloak. "All I found was her cloak, covered in blood. Eldritch had killed her." She smoothed out the cloak fabric. "I've never gone a day without wearing it."

Georgie put his hand on a tree trunk. For a moment his vision swam. All his life he'd thought his mother died in a car crash. Apurva stepped over a patch of vines and put a hand on Georgie's back.

"*I* was the one who started this entire chain of terrible events," Rollie continued. "Fumbluff reported me to the Librarian. There was a meeting, a hearing, and a judgment. I was exiled from Scatterplot. If John had still been . . . *John,* he'd have convinced Fumbluff to let me stay. I'm sure of it. Your father was a fighter, like I told you. But exiled I was, and even after all these years, as bitter as I am about Fumbluff reporting me, I know he did what he had to do. I didn't go to another barony. I vowed never to live as a reject, and that was the promise I made to the very first outcasts I took in. The Altercockers are my family now."

Rollie had her knife out, and she was poking at the air in the center of a small clearing.

"And that's basically it," Rollie said quietly. "That's the story."

Lots of different emotions battled for attention inside Georgie's head. His mother had done something terrible, but she'd been trying to help his father. His father had done something terrible, too, but *he'd* just been trying to help Rollie. He thought of his own friends, Roscoe and Apurva, and wondered how far he'd go to help *them*. His parents had been brave, and Rollie'd been brave, even if things hadn't turned out the way they'd planned.

Georgie looked up and saw a shimmer in midair, a curve, like the pages of an open book meeting at the binding. Rollie sheathed her knife and took a small gold object from her rucksack.

"Stand back, kids."

Chapter 32

Georgie and Apurva Go Shopping

Rollie rolled her arm up and down, and just as it had when Flint Eldritch first appeared in Georgie's driveway, a black line appeared in midair, an inch or two thick and the height of a door. The line hovered a foot off the snowy ground.

Rollie shoved her hand through the slit, through the *tear*, and pulled open a giant elastic flap. This wasn't Georgie's first time seeing between worlds, but still, he wasn't prepared for the pure *strangeness* of it all. He stared past Rollie and into his garage. The naked bulb hanging from the ceiling was still on. The window was sealed with yellow police tape.

Georgie felt the same dizzying sensation of being whirled through a vortex of color, but a moment later he landed on both feet in his garage. It was stiflingly hot, and beads of sweat formed on his forehead and the tip of his nose.

Apurva climbed through next, followed by Rollie, who landed in a battle-ready position, knees bent and one hand behind her head ready to pull an arrow from her quiver. The portal snapped almost entirely shut behind her, leaving only a thin black line marking its center. Rollie stood tall, unbuttoning the top three buttons of her cloak. *My mom's cloak*, as Georgie had come to think of it.

"Lead the way, Georgie," she said.

Georgie opened the garage door and midday sun flooded in. Georgie shielded his eyes as he stepped out onto the concrete landing. Nothing had changed, and why would it have? They'd been gone for five *days*, not five *years*. But it *was* unusually quiet. The cars, the occasional dog bark, even the distant jingle of the neighborhood ice cream truck, which was usually a sure bet on hot summer afternoons like this one. Georgie couldn't hear any of it.

Georgie felt for the Aetherquill in his right pocket. In his left pocket, his slingshot. He asked Rollie if he could run inside to restock his ammunition. Rollie nodded and told him to be quick.

Georgie took the garage stairs by threes.

Two soup bowls still sat in the kitchen sink, unwashed. Upstairs, his bedroom door was slightly ajar, and he had a terrible suspicion that Flint Eldritch would be on the other side . . . maybe lying down in his bed. And even if Georgie screamed, there would be no one to hear him.

But his bedroom was empty, exactly as he'd left it five days ago.

A single sock and a pair of tighty-whities lay on the floor halfway between his closet and his bed. He dumped the copper cup of marbles sitting on his desk into his pocket and turned to go, but the card his father had given him on his seventh birthday, when his father was still able to write and drive, caught his eye. There had been a five-dollar bill and a photograph of the Grand Canyon tucked neatly inside the card. It was one of those long-exposure shots, where the night sky arced for a million miles, lit up by a billion sparkling stars and colorful streaks of galaxy.

Georgie took the card down and, even though he knew it by heart, read it again.

> *Happy Birthday, kiddo.*
> *Seven!*
> *You're a world-class kid, Georgie. And you're my best friend, in this world and every world.*
> *See the picture? How about a road trip? Out West! Me and you. End of summer . . . pretty neat, huh?*
> *Look at that sky, hey? Trying to count those stars would be like trying to understand just how much I love you. It would be impossible.*
> *Happy Birthday.*
> *Love, Dad.*
> *PS: Don't spend the five bones all at once!*

Georgie pinned the card back on the corkboard, careful to push the thumbtack all the way in. Then he heard a voice right behind him.

"So . . . this is your room?"

Georgie spun around. Apurva was standing in the doorway. He looked around frantically . . . his eyes landing on his underwear on the floor. He prayed Apurva wouldn't see them. "Hey," Georgie said. "Yeah."

Apurva stepped into the room. "You okay, Georgie? You look sad—"

"Me? No . . . I'm not. I'm just tired." Georgie rubbed at his eyes and faked a yawn. He'd never been less tired in his life.

Apurva sat down and bounced gently on Georgie's bed, making the worn and tired springs creak. "It's cute. Your bedroom."

"Thanks." Georgie felt his face burning.

"Do you miss it? Your room?"

Georgie looked around. Not really. "Yeah, I miss it."

"Me too! Don't you miss sleeping in your own bed?"

Definitely not. Falling asleep in the Tenderfoot's tent last night was probably the best night's sleep he'd ever had.

Georgie shrugged and took a step toward the door, hoping Apurva would follow.

"Georgie," Apurva said, looking down at her lap. "Now that we're here, I want to visit my mom."

Georgie didn't blame her, not one bit. But Rollie was in a rush to get back to Scatterplot, and he didn't think she'd want Apurva making a detour. Georgie was anxious to get back, too. He didn't like how *quiet* everything was. He was about to tell Apurva he'd go with her to visit her mom if Rollie agreed, but just then, Rollie swung open the bedroom door.

"Does everyone in your world grow up in huge houses with staircases and all?" Rollie asked.

No one *ever* referred to Georgie's house as *huge* before. It was the smallest house in a town *full* of small houses.

"Got your ammunition?" Rollie asked, not waiting for Georgie to reply. "It's time to go shopping."

❖ ❖ ❖

The police barricades and news vans Georgie had seen in the Writer's Orb were gone. A single police car idled just beyond Georgie's driveway, but both cops inside it were fast asleep when he, Apurva, and Rollie crossed in front of it.

Rollie walked briskly, her cloak trailing out behind her, her bow slung around her back, and her arrows poking out of the quiver strapped to her hip. Georgie wondered what someone would think or do or say if they saw him walking around with someone dressed like a warrior princess from the Middle Ages, but the streets were deserted.

They turned onto Main Street fifteen minutes later. They passed the bank and the drive-through ATM lanes. Halfway up the next block, they passed the Bridget Deli. An old woman with frizzy white hair stood on the sidewalk, staring blankly at a poster advertising Boar's Head American cheese.

"He's coming," the old woman whispered as Georgie walked past her.

Georgie stopped and turned. The woman looked at him and put a finger to her lips. Her eyes were red and vacant, like she didn't know who or where she was. She smiled, and it was the smile of a lunatic. "He's coming."

"What's happening?" Apurva whispered, frightened beyond telling.

"It's Eldritch," Rollie said matter-of-factly. "People haven't had a new memory in *days*. It's driving them insane, and it's only going to get worse."

Georgie couldn't look away from the old woman.

"Everything will be alright, won't it?" the old woman asked, and if a voice could be *dead*, this is what it would sound like.

"We hope so, ma'am," Rollie responded, and then Georgie saw something change in the old lady's eyes. They flashed back to life for a moment, and he saw in them a look of paralyzing fear. She reached one trembling, veiny hand toward Georgie's face and rubbed her shaking fingertips across his cheek.

"I once had a son," she said in a whisper. "Like you . . . but . . . I think—*I don't remember anymore*." Then she withdrew her hand, as if Georgie's cheek was a stovetop, and her eyes clouded over again. "Everything will be okay, won't it? Hunky-dory. Aces and spades. *Click click click*. He is coming . . ."

The old woman pulled the deli door open and disappeared inside.

❖ ❖ ❖

Georgie was relieved to find the hardware store open, even if it was completely empty except for a cashier in denim overalls behind the counter. When the door swung closed behind them, the cashier waved a hand at Rollie, who responded by pulling an arrow from her quiver and twirling it between her fingers.

The cashier didn't seem to care one way or another, which was odd. *Very* odd. He merely frowned, and Rollie frowned back.

Georgie and Apurva walked the aisles together, past the hammers and handsaws, until they found the fishing supplies at the back of the store. Georgie grabbed two spools of fishing wire. Apurva grabbed as many bags of fishing hooks she could carry in both her arms. "Fishing wire, fishing hooks—"

"And here's the lighter fluid," Georgie finished, grabbing a bottle of Ronsonol from the shelf. "That's everything on Rollie's list."

At the front of the store, the cashier scanned and bagged the items one by one. "Found everything okay?"

Georgie nodded. The cashier kept looking from the bags to the small computer monitor like he'd forgotten how to ring up a customer. "Going fishing, huh?"

"Sure," Georgie said.

"Total comes to $28.63. Would you like to round up . . . uh . . . uh . . . thirty-five, thirty-six, *thirty-seven* cents to donate to the Folded Daisy clothing drive for undressed children?"

"Sure," Georgie said, looking nervously at Apurva. He just wanted to get outta there.

Apurva pulled some cash from her wallet and handed it over to the cashier. The cashier looked down at the money like he had no idea how it got there, then looked up at Georgie and Apurva. His mouth had gone slack and his eyes had glazed over.

"Say, can I help you two?" His voice had changed. Now it was flat and emotionless, just like the old lady's had been.

Apurva gulped and pointed to the brown paper bags. "That's our stuff."

The cashier looked inside the bags.

"Going fishing, huh?"

"Yeah, sure!" Georgie said, getting anxious.

"Polaroid?" the cashier asked.

"*What?*" Now Georgie was genuinely creeped out. He imagined the cashier reaching over the counter with his knobby fingers and stroking his face while he stared over his shoulder with those emotionless eyes. Georgie shuddered.

"You asked for film? I've got 'em all right here. Model 660, did you say? Fifteen percent off our everyday low price."

The cashier slapped two packs of micro SD cards on the countertop, and Georgie nearly screamed.

"I didn't ask for SD cards," Georgie said shakily.

The cashier just stared over Georgie's shoulder with a look of eternal blankness. Then he blinked. He shook his head. He looked at Georgie and Apurva and smiled.

"Can I help you two?" he asked. "He's coming, you know. And things will be alright."

Then Rollie was there, reaching over the counter and grabbing the brown paper bags.

"Say, miss, did you pay—" the cashier started, but then he stopped, lost inside the fog of his own broken memory, and stared again over Georgie's shoulder like he was waiting for something spectacular to appear at the back of the store.

Rollie handed a bag to Apurva and a bag to Georgie and the three of them hurried from the General Store. They were halfway up the block by the time the door slammed shut behind them.

Chapter 33

Abandoned

purva didn't say anything the entire walk back to Georgie's house. She seemed sullen.

"Quickly now," Rollie said, rounding the back of Georgie's garage and taking the first two stairs. "No time to waste."

Georgie followed, but Apurva stood in place, next to her teal and purple bicycle, which was just where she had left it the morning she biked over to return Georgie's backpack. She cleared her throat. "Georgie?"

Georgie looked up. The brutal sun beat on his face.

"I'm . . . I'm not coming back to Scatterplot," Apurva said.

"What?" Georgie asked dumbly. He was sure he'd misunderstood. It'd *sounded* like Apurva had said she wasn't coming back to Scatterplot.

There were tears in Apurva's eyes. "I have to be with my mother. You see what's happening now that the Scribes aren't writing. I don't even know if my mother will know who I am *at all*. And if she does, even if she recognizes me one more time, I want to be there when it happens." Apurva pulled the hair that had fallen over her eyes away from her face. "Okay?"

Okay!?

Georgie wished Roscoe were here. Roscoe would be able to convince Apurva to come back. He looked at Rollie. "Rollie, can we stay for a day or two, then we'll all go back together? *Please?*"

"Don't even start with that," Rollie snapped. She put a hand on Georgie's arm and pulled him down one stair. "Let's go."

Apurva fidgeted with the tassels hanging from her handlebars.

Georgie thought about how Apurva and Edie had showed up arm in arm to the ceremony, Apurva in her beautiful silk dress. How they'd all giggled and walked into the tent together.

He turned back for one last goodbye, but Apurva had already gone. He heard the *tick tick tick tick* of her bicycle wheels on the other side of the garage. It felt like he'd just been punched in the stomach.

❖ ❖ ❖

Rollie pushed the garage door open, ushered Georgie inside, and approached the portal. "I'm sorry, kid." She pulled a giant flap open. It was snowing lightly in Scatterplot. "It hurts, I know."

Georgie landed face-first in the snow on the Scatterplot side, rolling over just in time to watch Rollie climb through.

The tear shut completely, and it was just Georgie, Rollie D, and the endless forest of birch trees.

Rollie helped him up, then wrapped Georgie in her arms.

❖ ❖ ❖

They walked in quiet silence through the snow and the cold and the night, until they reached the riverbank. The landscape seemed colorless . . . *lifeless.*

He wondered where Apurva was now. Was she asleep in her own bed? Was she with her mother? Had she seen that pair of dirty underwear on his bedroom floor? Is *that* why she hadn't wanted to come back?

No . . . Georgie knew that wasn't it. He remembered the golden-hued memory of Apurva giving her mother her medication. How she'd done it so patiently. Her neat and organized notes beside each scheduled doctor's appointment.

They were on the narrowboat now, cutting through the black water, the moon itself hidden behind a thick coat of cloud cover. They had what they needed from New York, and now they could put the second phase of Rollie's plan in motion. But even though they'd brought back important supplies, Georgie felt like he'd left the most important thing behind.

Georgie's eyes closed, and he nodded off to sleep.

◇ ◇ ◇

When he awoke, Rollie was lifting him off the narrowboat. Judging by the color of the sky, it was just a couple of hours until dawn. They had been gone for twenty-four hours.

Georgie stayed close behind Rollie, even though there were blisters on his toes now and his feet were killing him. They stopped just once for breakfast—more leftover meat wrapped in elephant leaves.

Georgie's hearing had gotten better (that's what spending this much time away from cars and sirens and smartphone speakers would do), and even though he couldn't see anyone, he thought he heard voices up ahead, somewhere through the trees.

They were getting close. Then, as Rollie picked up her pace, Georgie heard a wild shaking, as if a great wind had whipped up out of nowhere. When he and Rollie stepped into the clearing where the Altercockers and Scatterplotters had made camp, he saw them. Hundreds—no, *thousands*—of white birds fluttering their wings.

✧ ✧ ✧

"Let's see," Fenton said with excitement a few minutes later. He had given Georgie a long hug after Rollie'd told him about Apurva's decision. Now the original group, minus Apurva, was back in Rollie's tent. Rollie dumped the contents of the General Store bags onto her bed. Charlie Fenton tore open a package of fishing hooks and nodded with approval.

"Scribe Hambrey?" Rollie asked, like she was calling on someone in class.

Scribe Hambrey, whose gray hair was tied in a tight bun, stepped forward with two white birds in her hands and another three birds perched on her shoulders. A sixth bird stood atop her head. She placed one of them gently on Rollie's bed. It fluttered its wings but did not fly away.

Shepherd the blacksmith cut a length of fishing wire and tied it gently to the bird's tiny ankle. He tied the other end of the wire around one of the fishing hooks and jammed the pointy end of the hook into a small chunk of wood.

"Light it," Blaze Nelson said smoothly, then squirted the wood chunk with a fine layer of the lighter fluid Georgie and Rollie had brought back from New York. Scribe Hambrey held the bird above her head until the wood dangled just off the tent floor.

The bird uttered a short shriek when Rollie lit the chunk of wood with a timber match.

Scribe Hambrey released the bird and in a flutter it

flew from Rollie's tent, the flaming wood chunk soaring beneath it.

"It could work," Fenton said, turning to Scribe Hambrey. "How low can you train them to fly?"

"Nearly as low as a tall man on horseback, I suppose," Scribe Hambrey responded.

Rollie patted Scribe Hambrey on the shoulder, then turned to address the group. "Does everyone understand the plan?"

Everyone nodded, except for Georgie. "Georgie?"

"Yes," Georgie said flatly.

Roscoe, now dressed in a burlap smock with the sleeves cut off, cinched tightly around his waist with a belt made of worn leather rope, put a hand on Georgie's shoulder. "You gonna be alright?" He didn't wait for an answer. "Yeah, you're gonna be alright."

But Georgie didn't feel it *was* going to be alright. There was a pit in his stomach. He tried to concentrate on his father, and the mission, and Rollie's plan. He looked at Rollie, and she looked back at him. *Time just wounds.*

"You're going to have to sail back to Scatterplot alone, Georgie," Rollie said.

Georgie felt for the Aetherquill in his pocket. There was something comforting about its shape and weight. "I know."

"We'll create the diversion, drawing the Dregs of Mishap away from the city. You'll need to move quickly, use the darkness to your advantage, but you'll need to stay quiet, too. Flint will be looking for you."

Georgie's stomach twisted uncomfortably. "This is a

lower realm," he said. "I . . . I don't want to hurt anybody."
He thought about what the Scribes had originally told
him about using the Aetherquill on a lower realm. That the
atmosphere here couldn't handle the Aetherquill's energy.

It was Fumbluff who answered. "We have no safe strat-
egies or schemes left." He rubbed his forehead and sighed.
"If there's a chance to stop Eldritch . . ."

Rollie smiled at Fumbluff. "Now you're sounding like a
proper Altercocker."

Fumbluff's blue eyes twinkled. He tapped his throat
three times and bowed his head gently in Rollie's direction.

"When do we leave?" Georgie asked.

It was Charlie Fenton who answered. "Tomorrow
morning, before dawn. If our gait is good, we'll arrive at
Scatterplot's borders just after nightfall."

❖ ❖ ❖

Later, when the sun was out and it was warm enough for
sleeveless shawls, Roscoe found Georgie sitting alone on a
felled log at the edge of camp.

"Hey," Georgie said.

Roscoe sat down. "Hey yourself." He wore a belt of var-
ious swords and daggers. He even had a wooden bow and
a quiver of arrows strapped to his back. "Remember when
you gave me a couple of marbles? Back in your garage
when we thought we were ambushed? Jeez, we were sitting
ducks, weren't we? Now I'm armed up to my eyebrows, and
boy, I like the way it feels."

Roscoe adjusted his bow and quiver and shifted in place. "Sorry about Apurva."

"It's all good," Georgie said.

"No, it isn't. I'm not as dumb as you look."

Georgie shrugged.

"But you have me. That's just as good, right?"

"Very funny," Georgie said.

The two of them walked further into the forest, where Shepherd the blacksmith was running the forge in shifts. Edie and Ore were there, hard at work, hammering hot pieces of iron into swords and daggers. Ore looked up and waved at Georgie, his blond hair now blackened from soot and ash. Piles of weapons sat beside the forge, and the pile grew as the day and the work went on.

Meanwhile, Charlie Fenton and Blaze Nelson were busy making armor: chest plates, helmets, and wrist and ankle guards. Another station managed by Yooker and Toots Tenderfoot cut strips of leather and rope to make shoulder straps for the chest plates and chin straps for the helmets.

Georgie grabbed a hammer and stood by a tree-stump anvil next to Edie. An Altercocker brought him a piece of iron from the forge, and Georgie went to work.

CLANG! CLANG! CLANG!

He hammered the fiery end with all his might.

◊ ◊ ◊

After dinner, when the camp was going to sleep, Georgie laid down on a patch of grass just beyond the forge and stared up at the stars. He imagined himself with his father at the Grand Canyon.

Reintegration, Georgie thought. Something had been at the back of his mind, just out of reach, just before Flint Eldritch and the Dregs of Mishap attacked the Seminary. *Don't aim at where the target is*. *Aim at where the target is going*. It was the last conversation he had with his father, and something was telling Georgie that his dad was trying to teach him more than just marksmanship with a slingshot.

When he opened his eyes, Fumbluff was standing over him, silhouetted against the night sky.

"Sometimes the quiet has a lot to say." Fumbluff took off his top hat and sat down cross-legged beside Georgie. "If you listen closely to it, yes?"

"What if I can't get to the page of whisperleaf you hid?" Georgie asked. "What if I can't figure out what I'm supposed to *write*?" Then, because it was true, he added, "I'm scared."

"Oh," Fumbluff said softly, "I'd be worried if you weren't. A man without fear is dangerous. Bound to do something stupid sooner than later." Even in the dark, Fumbluff's eyes were alight. "You'll reach it. And as long as you *believe*, you'll know what you need to write when you do."

Georgie thought about how Fumbluff had exiled Rollie from Scatterplot when she'd been just a teenager.

He wondered if Fumbluff regretted it.

"I understand why Apurva didn't want to come back," Georgie whispered. "It's not like I blame her or anything. But I miss her, Fumbluff. Maybe I *am* a loser. I've only *really* known her for, like, seven days."

Fumbluff put a hand on Georgie's shoulder. "The heart doesn't count days, Georgie. And love doesn't keep time."

Georgie fell asleep alone under the stars that night.

Chapter 34
Final Goodbyes

The camp was in full swing by dawn.

Scribe Hambrey was busy with her flock of birds, which now looked to be at least two thousand strong. Roscoe, Edie, and Ore were put in charge of squirting a gigantic pile of wood chunks with lighter fluid. Then Scribe Hambrey would hammer a fishing hook into the wood chunk, tie a length of fishing wire to the hook and the other end delicately around a bird's ankle.

When that was done, Fenton and Blaze lined up all the Altercockers and Scatterplotters in rows, everyone with their rucksacks slung over their shoulders and helmets strapped around their waists. Everyone murmured anxiously (the Altercockers were complaining that their shoes were too tight), but the camp went utterly silent when Fumbluff and Fenton walked side by side through the crowd. Then Georgie and Rollie floated from Rollie's tent to the ground, and the four hundred men, women, and children erupted.

The cheers nearly sent Scribe Hambrey's flock of birds into a frenzy. Everyone roared their cries of love and luck and thanks and *yeehaw!* Those with swords threw their arms up to the sky.

"So, this is it, huh?" Roscoe said, walking over. He put a muscular arm around Georgie's shoulder.

"Yeah, Roscoe," Georgie said. "This is goodbye, I guess."

"Georgie Summers . . . just doing what he does. Saving the world. A regular buttsnorkeler."

"We're gonna give those Dregs of Mishap an ass-whoopin' that'll make them cry for their mommies. I'd sign on it in blood, but I know blood makes you *wooooozy.* You can count on me, Georgie. Six ways till Tuesday."

Edie and Ore came next, their matching sapphire necklaces twinkling in the morning light, hugging Georgie tight. Edie muttered something about being sorry for what happened with Apurva, but he couldn't quite make it out over the chants and the cheers. Ore gave Georgie his golden binoculars, muttering something about a parting gift.

Then came Fenton, his tunic loosely tied over his bandages. "You have your marbles?"

Georgie patted the small pile of slingshot ammunition in his jacket pocket.

"Yer a good boy, Georgie Summers. I'm proud of you. Your father is proud of you." And with that, he hugged Georgie hard enough to nearly crack his ribs.

Fumbluff stepped out of the early morning shadows. "Georgie, a long time ago—it feels like it anyway, yes? I told you something about adventures."

"That answers are best found at the end of an adventure."

"Yes, very much so. You're not at the end of yours yet, Georgie. But we're getting close."

Georgie didn't know what he was talking about, but at this point did it matter?

Rollie put her hands on her hips and cleared her throat. "LISTEN UP, YOU RAGAMUFFIN GOOD FOR NUTHINS," Rollie bellowed.

The camp went silent.

"DID EVERYONE PACK AN EXTRA JACKET?"

The camp stayed silent.

"JACKET! PARKA! COAT! ANORAKS! TUNIC! FROCK! AM I TALKING TO THE TREES?"

Slowly, people lowered their rucksacks to check for their jackets and shouted *yays* and *ayes* and *yeses*. Once Rollie was satisfied, she continued. "GOOD! IT'S GONNA GET COLD! DOES EVERYONE HAVE AN EXTRA SANDWICH? YOU'RE GONNA GET HUNGRY!"

This time everyone shouted affirmatives without having to be asked twice.

"VERY GOOD. NOW MARCH! WE'RE GOING TO SCATTERPLOT!"

Georgie was pounded on the chest, hugged, and even

kissed on the cheek as all the Scatterplotters and Altercockers streamed past him. Scribe Hambrey went last, surrounded by a cloud of birds as dense as the treetops flying in a low canopy above the marching troops.

◇ ◇ ◇

The large congregation of Scatterplotters and Altercockers reached the river a few hours later. Georgie and Rollie waited while the entire army splashed across the darkened water and up the ravine on the other side.

Georgie had an urge to scream for Roscoe . . . for Edie and Ore . . . for Fenton and Fumbluff . . . to come back, or to at least wait up for him. The pit in his stomach was like a twist of thorns.

But then they were gone, their footfalls receding until nothing was left but Rollie D unmooring the narrowboat from a boulder. The rope slapped to the boat's deck like a dead snake.

Rollie showed Georgie how to steer with the tiller attached to the rudder post. She used words like hull, bow, stern, and starboard—all gibberish to Georgie. He was about to sail off alone, unsure if he'd see *any* of his friends again.

Rollie gave Georgie a hand getting onto the narrow-boat's planked wooden deck.

"Will I ever see you again?" Georgie asked. He felt a dreadfulness seeping through him.

"Yes. When it's all over. But I have something to do first."

She handed Georgie his rucksack.

"There's extra meat in there. Some extra lighter fluid and fishing wire . . . just in case. And here's my lantern." She handed the lantern over to him. "You have your map?"

Georgie nodded.

"You remember the plan? All of it?"

Georgie nodded again. He remembered it all: the ladder, the signal, the shovel . . . and of course, the Aetherquill.

"Remember to wait for our signal." Rollie gave the narrowboat a gentle push away from the riverbank.

Georgie reached overboard and grabbed hold of a treetrunk jutting into the river, hugging it, keeping the boat from floating away. "Rollie?"

"Yeah, kid?"

The swarm of butterflies in Georgie's stomach had turned violent now. This must be what the very first astronauts felt like during the final countdown before launching to the moon.

"When I get there . . . *if* I reach the whisperleaf . . . I still don't know what I'm supposed to *write!* I don't know—"

"You're a Scribe now, Georgie Summers," Rollie interrupted, her voice gentle but firm. "See with your heart and write with your mind."

Rollie stepped into the shallow water and put a hand on Georgie's shoulder. "If Eldritch has one weakness, it is this: Now that he's conquered Scatterplot, he thinks it's over for the Scribes. He believes his victory is a sure thing. *Use that belief against him.*"

Georgie drew in breath to ask for more but before he

could, Rollie bent over and kissed him on the side of his mouth. "Now *go.*" She gave the boat one last shove.

Georgie let go of the tree trunk and began to drift away.

◇ ◇ ◇

The narrowboat rounded a bend, catching a current that thrust the small boat forward, and Rollie was gone.

Georgie unfolded Fumbluff's map and studied it for a while. Somewhere in the distance, an animal howled a lonely cry. Georgie got as comfortable as he could, with his back against a bulkhead.

According to Fumbluff, the water beneath him now was deep and cold and filled with strange life.

The narrowboat picked up speed.

Georgie followed Fumbluff's map closely, watching for the geographical features Fumbluff had described to him. The estuaries narrowed, and in some parts, he was drifting through marshland so narrow that he could run his hands through the salt meadow hay on either side of him.

By late afternoon Georgie was moving slowly through a brook. The mangled tree roots on either side twisted and plunged into the clear water.

He tried reviewing the plan. Rollie and Fumbluff thought it would work—that he'd make it to the hidden whisperleaf alive. But what if they were wrong . . . well, no point in thinking about what you cannot change.

But you can change it, Georgie.

It was the voice of Flint Eldritch, speaking from inside his head. *You can give up. You can give me the Aetherquill.*

Georgie wrapped his hand around the Aetherquill's ridged and ancient barrel. It thrummed warmly against his skin.

Georgie closed his eyes and exhaled slowly. "Six ways till Tuesday," Georgie whispered.

The voice in his head was gone.

The sun arced across the sky, and Georgie sailed slowly through the sparkling waters. He never heard Flint's voice inside his head again.

Because the next time Flint Eldritch spoke to Georgie, he was standing right in front of him.

Chapter 35

Waiting for the Signal

Dusk was descending into night by the time Georgie saw Fumbluff's landmark: a jutting shelf of rock that looked like three knuckles a mile south of Scatterplot. When Georgie was about fifty feet from the shore, he abandoned the narrowboat and waded through the knee-deep water.

By the time he reached the outskirts of the city, the last arc of sun had disappeared behind the mountains. Night had fallen, and the Dregs of Mishap swarmed Scatterplot like an infestation. Flint's men, in their black boots and black leather armor, clomped along the cobblestone streets.

Georgie approached the city from the south, moving like Rollie taught him: on the balls of his feet, *never* on his tippy-toes like an amateur, his eyes always trained on the next safe place to stop.

Thunder rolled in the distance. The air was thick and still. A storm was coming.

Georgie crept low along the backyard fences at the city's perimeter, climbing and hopping one after the other. He snaked his way through the shadows between smaller shops and apartments. As he drew closer to the center of the city, the sound of the Dregs of Mishap pillaging whatever was left of it grew louder.

Georgie rested against a short stone building, catching his breath and wiping sweat from his forehead. Thunder clapped again, this time closer. He peered around the corner and saw a group of Flint's men stomping away. One of them pried a loose cobblestone from the street—which was already so chopped up it looked like a mouth missing half its teeth—and tossed it through a low window. Glass shattered.

Flint's men cackled, and Georgie crept on.

He took dark alleyways (less likely to be teeming with Flint's men) toward the city center, past more shattered windows and broken balconies.

It took Georgie nearly an hour to travel the next three blocks. The Dregs of Mishap were everywhere now, and he kept having to duck into an archway or hide beneath a porch. Some of Flint's men walked the streets aimlessly like drunkards. Others were smashing shop windows, ransacking what little spoils remained of Scatterplot's handmade merchandise.

Rollie had been right. There was no way Georgie would have made it to Stone's Blacksmiths, Bladesmiths, and Problem Solvers without a diversion.

Georgie turned left, then right, and then into a narrow alleyway. The building straight ahead was built of giant rounded stones, with iron balconies outlining the arched doorways on every floor. *That building has the tallest rooftop in Scatterplot,* Charlie Fenton had said. *From there you'll wait for our signal.* Georgie found the ladder in a small wooden shed at the end of the alleyway, just as Shepherd the blacksmith had said he would. The ladder was rusty and heavy and made of metal, and as Georgie carefully carried it to the back of the building—

SCRAAAAPE.

—the ladder legs scraped loudly against the stone.

Angry voices echoed from the front of the alleyway: "Who's back there?!"

Now wasn't the time to be afraid. Now was the time to haul buns. He leaned the short ladder against the building as quietly as he could and started to climb. The ladder took him just high enough to reach the first balcony. He balanced on the narrow railing and from there was able to hoist himself onto a second-floor window ledge. As he climbed, from ledge to balcony to railing, the ground below and the angry voices of Flint's men sank further and further away.

Georgie's fingertips were scraped and numb. Sweat dripped from his forehead and stung his eyes. But Georgie climbed on, careful and slow, until finally he swung his leg onto the roof, rolled over, and caught his breath. He'd made it. The roof's perimeter was built like a castle, with stone merlons shaped like teeth with wide, empty spaces between them. From way up here, Corrigendum was just a shadowy speck on the grim horizon.

Now all he had to do was wait. Wait for Rollie and Fumbluff and Roscoe and everyone else . . . for the signal. For the diversion. He scooted away from the ledge and found a stone structure in the center of the roof, shaped like a box. Georgie circled it, finding an arched iron door on the far side. He slumped down beside the door, resting his back against the rounded stone, until—

BAM!

The door slammed open, nearly squashing Georgie into a pancake.

Three of Flint's men strutted onto the roof, not noticing Georgie. They stopped between two of the tooth-shaped merlons to light their cigars.

Georgie pulled his feet into the shadows, his heart whamming against the walls of his chest. There were three of them. He could use his slingshot, but did he have time to fire off three perfect shots before one of them got to him?

Georgie had an idea.

There's extra meat in there, Rollie D had said back at camp. *Some extra lighter fluid and fishing wire . . . just in case.*

Georgie grabbed the fishing wire and lighter fluid from his rucksack and slithered silently on his stomach behind Flint's men until he reached the edge of the roof. He tied the fishing wire between two merlons and gave it a light flick to make sure he had tied it taut enough to work.

He took a deep breath, stood up tall, tried to steady his shaking hands, and then walked slowly across the roof toward the three Dregs of Mishap.

"Excuse me!" Georgie said when he was just three feet away from them.

Flint's men turned in unison, all three with lit cigars popping from their mouths.

"Good evening," Georgie said, and then in a swift arc squirted a thick stream of lighter fluid at their faces.

The three cigars erupted in three balls of flames.

The Dregs of Mishap screamed and batted at their bearded faces, which were now smoking and catching fire quickly.

Georgie backpedaled across the roof and stopped three inches from the ledge. Another foot backward, and he'd free-fall ninety feet and splatter against the cobblestone.

The Dregs of Mishap ran wildly at Georgie, screaming as their skin singed, and when Georgie dropped flat on his back, they tried skidding to a halt . . .

But none of them even had a chance of noticing Georgie's tripwire, and all three tripped right over it. They pinwheeled their smoking arms, gave final shrieks for help, and fell off the roof. They screamed all the way down.

THUMP. THUMP. THUMP.

Georgie rolled over and looked over the ledge.

The noise had drawn attention. Flint's men gathered around the bodies, looking up at Georgie and pointing.

More Dregs came, from apartments, from shops, from *everywhere*, looking to the roof, pointing, and crying out.

So much for my great idea, Georgie thought in a panic.

Down below on the street, Flint's bearded men hoisted each other onto the first-floor balconies.

They started to climb.

The rooftop where Georgie was supposed to have waited safely for the signal had become a killing zone.

And the killers were coming for him.

Chapter 36

Every Color of the Rainbow

*B*A-BOOM! CRAAACK!

A great big thunderclap slammed across the sky, and the rain came immediately, falling in torrential sheets. Georgie could hardly hear the Dregs of Mishap over the roar of the storm. He squinted through the rain and the darkness as he loaded his slingshot.

A blast of lightning lit the sky in a spider web of electricity and, for a moment, Georgie could see Corrigendum in the distance, a black cardboard cutout against the strobing light.

Another lightning blast struck, and in the flash of light, Georgie saw a huge, bearded face crawling toward him over the roof's edge.

THIP-TWANG!

Georgie heard a dull CRACK as his marble connected.

One for one, Georgie thought. He stuck a hand into his pocket. Six or seven marbles left. Eight at most.

The lightning came, and so did Flint's men, their white faces lit up like electrified ghosts as they rolled themselves over the roof's ledge. Georgie rolled to his left, using the temporary darkness for cover. *If they can't find me,* Georgie thought, *they can't kill me.*

Lightning struck again, and in the brilliant, momentary strobe, Georgie saw six of Flint's men rushing across the rooftop, murder in their eyes. Georgie could almost feel his father reaching out and adjusting his wrist just a millimeter. *You don't aim at where the target is. You aim at where the target is* going.

Georgie released his breath and fired off six shots in rapid succession.

Were his hands as fast as Rollie's? No one could say for sure, but it was definitely close.

Crack. Crack. Crack.

A Scribe sees with his heart and writes with his mind.

Crack. Crack. Crack.

But Georgie Summers shoots like a gunslinger.

When lighting struck next, he could see the six bodies of Flint's men lying motionless in the rain, on the lip of the roof.

But more were coming. Up the stairs, getting close. There were too many of them—even with perfect aim, he only had two marbles left.

And just as Georgie was sure he'd feel two meaty hands grabbing his neck in the darkness—

AAA-HOOOO-GA! BLAA-RUUUMP! AA-HOOOO-GA!

A tremendous horn blew, louder and longer than any clap of thunder Georgie had ever heard.

Georgie could hear the Dregs clomping across the roof, but they were no longer coming toward him. They were going *away* from him! A moment later he heard the Dregs of Mishap scrambling down the side of the building.

Georgie took one step toward the roof's edge and saw lights twinkling in the distance.

Twinkling *firelight*. There were hundreds upon hundreds of these moving lights. *Thousands.*

And these lights were moving. Moving *fast.*

Georgie's skin broke out in goosebumps. The good kind.

They streamed from the forest's edge, at least a mile away, blanketing the long, sloping hill in a wavy quilt of two thousand torches moving in perfect synchrony.

Like an army.

The horn blared again, long and clear, slicing through the thunder.

Georgie crawled to the edge of the roof. The streets of Scatterplot all swarmed with Dregs of Mishap, running with great enthusiasm toward the sound of the horn.

He grabbed Ore's binoculars for a better look at the speeding army of torchlights.

Rollie had been right. Even through binoculars, in the pitch black, the speeding balls of flame bobbing up and down looked *exactly* like an oncoming army of warriors on horseback.

Between the trees at the edge of the forest, so close through Ore's binoculars, Georgie saw the Altercockers and Scatterplotters, waiting in shadow. He could just make out Yooker Tenderfoot and Blaze Nelson, standing side by side. He found Roscoe, a long sword in his hand. Further up, he found Fumbluff just a few feet from the tree line, watching the birds descend upon Scatterplot, the blazing chunks of wood soaring beneath them.

Georgie pumped his fist. The diversion was working! The Dregs of Mishap were rushing from the city toward the ridge, racing to defend the Seminary.

Time to move.

Georgie slung his rucksack over his shoulders and climbed down the side of the building, jumping from the last balcony railing to the cobblestone. The streets were deserted, and it took him no time at all to reach Stone's Blacksmiths, Bladesmiths, and Problem Solvers, with its gigantic bluish-green arched door. He wrapped his hand around the doorknob and began to turn it . . . then he heard hoofbeats.

Georgie whipped his head left and right.

He thought he saw a trail of green fabric disappear around the corner. His heart thudded in his chest as he squinted down the dark and rainy street, straining his ears. He heard only the tapering rain and his own thumping heartbeat.

Georgie was turning back to the workshop's door when a hand fell on his shoulder. He spun around and met a pair of eyes that seemed to contain every color of the rainbow.

He remembered something his father once told him: Artists see *more* colors at night than during the day. Now, Georgie finally understood what his dad had meant. All of a sudden, the darkness around him—the cobblestone street beneath his feet, the limestone buildings, the brass and oily doorknob—bloomed with rich nighttime colors.

Perhaps the most sensational color of all was the returning hue of *hope*.

"Hey, Georgie," Apurva said.

She was there. *Really* there. Standing a foot away, within arm's reach. Georgie wasn't sure what he wanted to do— hug her or pull her hair.

Georgie exhaled. "You . . . you came back."

Apurva shrugged and smiled. "Rollie came to get me." Her hair was pulled up in a high ponytail and she wore a pair of dark purple jeans and a faded yellow hoodie over a t-shirt. "I don't know how she knew my address—but there she was, knocking on my front door."

Georgie nodded, trying to process everything. "How's . . . how's your mom?"

Apurva split her pony in two equal halves and pulled it tight. "It's not good, Georgie. She's worse than before." Apurva took a stuttering breath. "Now that I know the pills I've been giving her aren't what she *really* needs . . . I thought I'd be of more use here. With you . . . and Roscoe, of course.

Rollie actually brought my mom this horrible-smelling tea. She said it'll make her feel better, at least for a few days."

Georgie was happy Apurva was back. *More* than happy. It felt as if a giant stone had been lifted off his chest. He had been more terrified than he'd care to admit since leaving Rollie D back in the forest. He had been terrified of going underground to find Fumbluff's hidden piece of whisperleaf. He had been terrified of failing, but more than that, he had been terrified of failing alone. But now, he had someone to go with, and it wasn't just *anybody*. It was Apurva.

But he also felt bad for Apurva. What she wanted most of all was to help her mom, but they had to defeat Flint Eldritch first. It was weird feeling happy for yourself and bad for someone else at the same time.

The door to the blacksmith's shop was unlocked and the doorknob was well oiled. Moonlight reflected dully off the scattered nails and horseshoes the Dregs of Mishap left behind.

In the back of the cool, damp room was a giant forge that looked like a portly round well.

Georgie and Apurva first removed the stones from the wall of the forge one by one, just like Shepherd had instructed. Georgie worked quickly, feeling like he had enough energy to disassemble a hundred forges built with stones a hundred times heavier if he needed to. They used shovels to clear the coal away, revealing a circular wooden door capped with iron planks at the bottom of the forge—just as Fumbluff had described.

They pulled open the trapdoor together, and with their hands on their knees and soot all over their faces, Georgie and Apurva tried to catch their breath. They looked at each other and smiled. Then they giggled, which only made them wheeze and pant harder, which sent them both into hysterical laughter.

When their laughter had died out and the sweat had dried on their foreheads, Georgie stared into the black hole beneath the trapdoor. He lowered himself onto the first rung of a ladder that descended into the darkness beneath the workshop's floor—the last remaining passage to Scatterplot's original Library . . . and Fumbluff's hidden piece of whisperleaf.

Apurva laid down on her stomach, her forehead touching Georgie's.

"Let's go save your father," she said, her breath warm and sweet on the tip of Georgie's nose.

The Aetherquill throbbed warmly in his pocket.

Georgie descended into the darkness, and Apurva followed.

Chapter 37

Let Me Hug You

*P*link plink plink.

Water dripped somewhere unseen. They were in a tunnel with damp dirt walls on either side. They followed Apurva's iPhone flashlight for what felt like a mile. Just when Georgie was starting to wonder if they were lost . . . if they were ever going to find the archway of ancient stone Fumbluff had told them about . . . they saw it dead ahead. The whisperleaf characters carved into the keystone at the top of the archway may have once spelled something, but the shapes and patterns had eroded with time. The stones along the archway were chipped and crumbling, and

Georgie wondered how long they'd been here . . . and how much longer they would hold.

Georgie pointed down the dark tunnel and he and Apurva picked up their pace.

They both gasped when they stepped through the archway. Apurva's iPhone cast a cone of light around a room at least three times the size of a movie theater. Two rows of crumbling pillars stretched out in front of them, and along the ancient stone walls, row after row of empty shelves, covered in dust and cobwebs. An underground ruins! The ceiling soared high above their heads, lined with giant spikes of limestone buildup.

"Whoa, Georgie," Apurva said, her voice echoing throughout the great chamber, "this must be the old Library!" Georgie turned slowly in place, amazed. He wanted to explore the ruins of Scatterplot's original Library, but Apurva was tapping his shoulder and pointing across the room, where a faint yellow light flickered beyond another stone archway.

Apurva led the way through the second archway and into another narrow tunnel. As they walked, the faint flickering light became brighter, even as the tunnel narrowed to the point they had to sidestep with their backs pressed against the dirt wall.

Finally, the tunnel deposited them on a wide, rocky platform.

Up ahead, where the ceiling sloped downward, three glass panels jutted from the cave wall, making a box-like room sealed off from the rest of the cave. In the middle of the glass room was a wooden table, and on the table sat a flickering oil lamp beside a single piece of paper. A single piece of whisperleaf. Georgie stared at the shadows the oil lamp cast on the craggy cave wall. The shadows danced along the walls like reaching hands . . . hands that were trying to catch something moving too fast.

Don't aim at where the target is. Aim at where the target is going. That nagging at the back of his mind resurfaced—just as it had the moment before Eldritch and his men appeared on the horizon during the Coronation Ceremony. What *else* had this father said? If only Georgie could remember . . .

"Are you ready?" Apurva whispered.

Georgie exhaled and told her the truth. "I don't know."

The glass room had a single glass door, except there was no door handle or keyhole.

"What's this?" Apurva asked, rubbing her fingers against an indent in the door, just about where a doorknob would usually be.

The indent was oval-shaped, tall, and thin.

It was the shape of a narrow cigar.

It was the shape of a piece of chalk.

It was the shape of an AA battery or a middle finger.

Then Georgie's hand was in his pocket because what the glass indent was *really* shaped like was the Aetherquill. It buzzed against his skin as he placed it into the indent—

Click. The Aetherquill snapped into place.

The door swung outward with a hiss.

Georgie and Apurva stepped slowly into the glass room, and when Georgie took the Aetherquill back, the glass door swung shut, sealing them inside. Georgie pushed against the door, noticing an identical indent on the inside, and found the door locked. It didn't even wiggle an inch.

They stepped to the table, Apurva hugging herself even though it wasn't very cold and Georgie wishing he had Roscoe's dinosaur blanket . . . the one Roscoe said fended off demons and monsters.

Georgie stared down at the blank, pulpy page of whisperleaf, his mind racing and his heart throbbing. Would he just be repeating his mother's mistake? Putting people's lives in danger? What was he going to write, anyway? Using the Aetherquill in a lower realm was dangerous— *unpredictably* dangerous. Just like when his mother used it on his father all those years ago . . . when she tried to make his dad believe the little girl Rollie D had met in New York was still alive.

Georgie unscrewed the Aetherquill's cap, but his hands were trembling so badly that he only managed to drop the cap on the floor.

The Aetherquill's fiction . . . didn't fully stick in your father's mind, Fumbluff had said during dinner at Corrigendum. *Part of him KNEW the Aetherquill's story was not true . . .*

"Breathe, Georgie," Apurva whispered, even though Georgie *was* breathing. Breathing *heavily.* Apurva handed the cap back to Georgie and wrapped his hand in hers. "A Scribe does not write with his hand."

Georgie looked into Apurva's chocolate-brown eyes. "He writes with his mind." He gripped the Aetherquill tight, feeling the individual ridges along the pen's ancient brass barrel against the palm of his skin.

And Georgie *remembered.*

In his mind's eye, he saw himself sitting in his backyard with his father, his Xbox and candy tray open beside them on the grass. *Don't aim at where the target is,* his father said. Georgie could hear his dad's voice as if he was standing right next to him. *Aim at where the target is going.* John put an arm around Georgie and pulled him close. Georgie, a hundred feet beneath Scatterplot's surface, could almost smell his father's sandalwood and grapefruit cologne. *It's the same thing with stories.*

Georgie had thought his dad had been going off on something totally random. But he was a Scribe now, and his heart was telling him that *nothing* was random. His mind slowly lit up with a kaleidoscope of shapes and nodes and connecting lines, like the sky above Scatterplot had lit up when the realms aligned.

Yes, stories, his father said. *The stories we believe are the stories that show us a path to where we most truly want to go. To where we believe we're going.* The Aetherquill's golden nib hovered above the blank page of whisperleaf.

And where did Flint Eldritch believe he was going?

Georgie drew in a deep breath, his eyes still closed, and when he exhaled, it was Rollie D's voice he heard: *If Eldritch has one weakness, it is this: Now that he's conquered Scatterplot, he thinks it's over for the Scribes. He believes his victory is a sure thing. Use that belief against him.*

But use it how, Rollie? Use it *HOW!?*

Another bright line in his mind's eye connected, and Georgie had an idea. The idea did not come to Georgie slowly, rough around the edges, the way most ideas develop. It crashed into Georgie's mind fully formed, in a single, brilliant flash.

Aim at where the target is going . . .

The stories we believe are the stories that show us a path to where we most truly want to go . . .

No, *not* a memory of utter defeat.

But instead . . .

The Aetherquill was hot in Georgie's hand as he lowered it toward the whisperleaf.

But just as the first drop of ink bled into the gauzy paper, Apurva's fingernails dug into Georgie's arm. He turned to her, his concentration now shattered, and saw that her face had gone white.

Georgie followed her wide-eyed gaze through the glass wall.

Someone . . . or *something* . . . was shuffling out of the narrow tunnel.

The figure stepped into the light. He wore his usual checkered button-down shirt and his usual dark jeans. He had no cane, but still walked with a limp.

Georgie felt suddenly weak all over. "Daddy?"

John Summers stood half in and half out of the light, just a few feet from the glass room. He took another step forward, his gray-blue eyes still wrinkled around the edges.

"Georgie, buddy."

But his voice didn't sound right. It sounded like a stuffed

animal preprogrammed to talk when you pulled the ripcord in its back.

"Dad," Georgie whispered again. Could it *really* be his father? But his voice, that creepy stuffed-animal voice . . .

"I need you to open that door," John Summers said, limping another step forward. "I need you to put down that pen." Then, after an awkward pause, "Please."

Georgie stared into his father's blue-gray eyes. John's face seemed to *shift*, ever so slightly, like the bones beneath his skin were made of clay. Georgie brought his mother's pen toward the door, overwhelmed by his father standing so close, even though a distant part of his brain was screaming in protest.

"Do it now, Georgie," his father declared, in that same stuffed-animal voice. "Let me hug you."

And just at that moment, like an unexpected gale of wind, Apurva was there, knocking the Aetherquill away before Georgie could unlock the door. Georgie tried to catch it as it fell, but Apurva slammed into Georgie's side, sending them both tumbling to the ground.

"That's not your father!" Apurva screamed, pinning him down. "Can't you *smell* it?"

Georgie could. Stale fish and rotting carcasses and many worse things. The awful stench must have been seeping through the glass panels.

Apurva let Georgie go, and Georgie stood up slowly. He was shaking all over, but his mind was working again. *He's limping with the wrong leg*, Georgie realized. *He needed a cane for his LEFT leg, but he just limped on his—*

John Summers had his palms against the glass door now. He exhaled, and the glass between him and Georgie fogged up.

When it cleared a second later, Georgie's blood ran cold.

It was the *eyes*.

Like a camera shutter, his father's eyes flipped from blue-gray to black.

Black as an oil spill, and just as lifeless.

Flint Eldritch's eyes.

Chapter 38

Flint Eldritch's Victory

The bones beneath his father's face more than shifted now . . . they began rearranging themselves like cogs in some nightmarish machine.

Georgie screamed.

His father's gray hair receded, revealing a splotchy bald scalp, except for a few ropy tufts slinking from his temples. His cheekbones jutted to points, stretching his skin like scissors about to puncture a rubber ball. His father's clothing became translucent, then disappeared, and in its place was Flint's skeletal frame, black vest and pants, leather boots, and frayed scarf.

Flint had *come forward* entirely, his eyes sunken into ice-cream cone hollows in his skull.

Georgie staggered backward. He would have tripped over his own two feet and maybe cracked his head against the table if Apurva hadn't been there to catch him.

"*Oh my God,*" Apurva panted. "*Georgie, oh my God!*"

BAM! BAM! BAM!

Flint pounded on the glass. His mouth was pulled back in a sneer, revealing teeth eroded with decay. Bubbling black sores covered his gums. "Open the door," he said. "I'm going to kill you now."

Georgie closed his eyes.

He could smell the ancient dust and the overpowering stench of rotting fish. But beneath it all he could smell his father's sandalwood and grapefruit cologne.

Georgie frantically thought about his plan. Was it too late? Did he have enough *time?*

"OPEN THE DOOR!" Flint thundered. He flung his open palms at the glass wall, and it buckled violently against the blast of dark energy. He snarled, his skin peeling further away from his black gums and rotten teeth.

Georgie looked down at his hand, which was still holding the Aetherquill. The pen pulsed with a warm heat, almost urging to be written with, like it had words—no, *a story*—trapped inside, screaming to be let out. A tremendous surge of power coursed up his arm. The room fell away and Georgie felt weightless, almost like he was back inside the Writer's Orb. It was just Georgie, Apurva, and the single page of whisperleaf.

Georgie took two steps toward the table, barely noticing when the glass wall spidered with cracks under Flint's next blast of purple energy.

He barely heard Apurva's shriek.

"DON'T YOU DARE!" Flint howled. "YOU MAY NOT USE THE AETHERQUILL!"

One of Flint's sores popped and black puss oozed thickly over his front teeth.

Georgie uncapped the Aetherquill, this time his hands steady as stone.

He had a plan, and he was going to give it his best shot, even if it was the last shot he ever took.

The Aetherquill's gold nib touched the paper.

Ink flowed.

At first his arm felt as heavy as one of the blacksmith's anvils, but then the words came, in the patterns and shapes and figures of Whisperloom.

A Scribe sees with his heart and writes with his mind.

And if a Scribe, or a talented apprentice, were to happen upon this particular page of whisperleaf, this is what they'd read:

You've won, Eldritch.

You stand on the highest balcony of your black tower, the Aetherquill in your hand.

You look down at the people—now your people—refashioned in your image.

Every shadow has become detached from its light.

Every soul is an island, untouched.

Untouchable.

Because you've won.

Every heart now beats alone.

No tears stain any faces, for no bonds are formed
to be broken.

This is your victory.

The sky above you and the ground below you are
gray and soulless.

The winds carry no laments.

The rivers are still, no longer aching to belong.

Nobody will ever again be abandoned, because
never again will anybody be loved.

You gaze out upon this absence of suffering.

And you rejoice.

This is your victory, Eldritch.

You rule over this utopia, where there are no
friends around to help fix you when you break.

You are a wise soul, Eldritch.

Exult in your victory.

You've won.

An amber glow around the Aetherquill grew brighter and hotter as Georgie wrote, until the amber light flooded through the gaps between Georgie's fingers. He lifted his hand from the whisperleaf, his heart beating like a locomotive, and the amber light dulled to a faint throb. The pen cooled.

Don't aim at where the target is. Aim at where the target is going.

And if the Aetherquill's story made Flint believe he'd

already gotten everything he wanted, Flint just might loosen his hold on John Summers. And if Rollie was right—that his father still had the fight in him—it might just be enough.

He looked over at Apurva, understanding she couldn't read what he'd written, and nodded. *I gave it my best shot.*

And later, if they made it out of here alive, Georgie would translate it for her.

But he *wouldn't* tell her that the words came easy to him because in some buried compartment in Georgie's own heart, he understood why a creature like Eldritch would want a world where pain and suffering no longer existed. He understood what it was like to grow up wishing for a mom and dad to tuck him in at night. He understood what it felt like to be abandoned by a friend you loved. The pain of loneliness might not show up on an X-ray, but that didn't make it any less real.

Georgie looked up at Eldritch, wondering what was supposed to *happen* now . . . wondering what would happen now that he used the Aetherquill in a lower realm.

"STOP WRITING!" Flint roared, his voice now filled with fear. The spider web of cracks had spread from floor to ceiling, and, with each blast of Flint's power, tiny chips of glass went spraying. "WHAT HAVE YOU DONE?"

Flint pulled back one shiny black boot and swung it forward. This time, the wall exploded. Shards of glass rained down all around them.

Flint Eldritch leaped forward.

Chapter 39

The Everything

lint Eldritch flew to the table, grabbed the page of whisperleaf, and held it to his face. His eyes shifted like an insect's, back and forth and back and forth over Georgie's words.

Apurva held Georgie around the waist and pulled him backward until their butts collided with the craggy cave wall.

Did it work!? Georgie wondered frantically. *Is something supposed to happen now?*

Then something did.

Flint began to blink rapidly, like there was a piece of hair or dust caught in his eye. He shot a look at Georgie, then back at the whisperleaf drooping from his hands. The terror in Flint's face slowly slackened into something resembling wonder. His mouth, just a lipless slit above his chin, hung agape. Flint's eyes rolled in his sockets until they settled on Georgie. He shuddered, a small seizure rippling through his body, and his mouth opened wider.

Black puss covered his lower teeth.

Georgie looked down at the Aetherquill, still in his fist, and saw that deep, amber glow once again surrounding the barrel. It thrummed gently.

Something was happening.

Georgie squeezed the pen in his fist. Whatever happened next, he would not let go.

Flint's smile widened into a nightmare. He let out a heehaw of laughter. Just one trumpet blast of insane glee. He dropped the whisperleaf to the floor where it landed silently.

Flint started to cackle, throwing his head back as he uncoiled his scarf.

He took a step toward Georgie and Apurva.

Georgie held his hand out. The Aetherquill's amber light shot through his fingers.

"I'm going to kill you now?" Flint said. Or was it a question? He sounded terribly confused.

"NO!" Apurva shrieked. She stepped between Georgie and Flint. "DON'T TOUCH HIM!"

Flint swept his arm back and brought it rocketing down. His hand met the side of Apurva's face with the sound of a wet t-shirt slapping against concrete. She went flying and landed on her back a few feet away, her hands limply splayed out beside her.

Georgie sprang toward her, but Flint kicked him square in the chest, sending him crashing back against the cave wall. Flint's arm shot out like a cannon and his long, bony fingers clamped around Georgie's neck.

His grip was like steel wire, crushing Georgie's windpipe. He couldn't breathe.

Come on, Dad, Georgie thought as his vision clouded around the edges. *COME ON! FIGHT!*

The Aetherquill's amber light soaked through his fingers. It was beautiful and warm and there was—strangely, *very* strangely—a scent of mangos.

All Georgie could hear now was a faint buzz, like a swarm of insects hovering beyond the trees. Like static. Like his fan that kept him cool during the muggy summer nights.

So sleepy.

I'm sorry, Apurva.

Georgie closed his eyes.

Inkblots joined together, forming a purple veil.

I'm sorry, Dad.

Georgie slipped below the surface of a breathless black ocean as a monumental wave of exhaustion washed over him, hugged him, cradled him.

Then, coming from a thousand worlds away, like Edie and Ore's fragmented voices through his garage wall for the first time, Georgie heard a scream.

Then another scream, warbling down through the darkness.

Beyond his closed eyes, he saw light. A moon. Or *some-thing*. The light pulsed and bloomed, then, before his brain could even register the sensation, his lungs filled with air. It traveled through him, hot and fast, burning down his legs and into his toenails, through his belly, around the tips of his ears, and into the soft folds of his eyelashes.

WHAM!

Georgie's eyes flew open.

Apurva still lay motionless on the cave floor. He sucked in another huge wallop of air.

"*LET GO!*" Flint Eldritch screamed. "*LET GO, OR I'LL KILL OUR SON!*"

Flint's hand was no longer wrapped around Georgie's neck. Instead, Flint's hand was wrapped around his other wrist.

Then Georgie looked down, and realized it wasn't *Flint's* wrist at all. It was his *father's* wrist. It wasn't Flint's bony fingers with his sharp fingernails. It was his *father's* hand, his *father's* smooth skin touching Georgie's as they gripped the Aetherquill in their fists, holding on to it with all their might.

"*LET GOOOOO!*" Flint screeched. He was wheezing, and trails of cold sweat were dripping down his pale brow.

"*DAD!*" Georgie screamed. "*DAD! HOLD ON!*"

John Summers held on.

Georgie watched in amazement as Flint's bony, bare arm slowly thickened with healthy muscle. Then, at first trans-parent but opaquing rapidly, a shirt appeared, dressing the arm. It was the same faded blue checkered shirt his father had been wearing the morning Flint first appeared in their driveway.

John's shirt, and his arm, stopped just short of Flint Eldritch's shoulder.

"*LET GO OF IT NOW!*" Flint howled. It was unclear if he was screaming at Georgie or his dad. Or both.

It didn't matter. Georgie *knew* he had to hold on.

"*NO!*" Georgie gasped, the cords in his neck straining as he held on with every bit of strength he had left. The Aetherquill grew hot, like an iron, and a whamming jolt of energy shot through him. Georgie's stomach jumped clean out of his mouth like a roller coaster whipping over a hill. His hips thrust forward.

He felt weightless.

He *was* weightless.

He floated up and out of his body.

He could see the scene in the cave from above now: There was Apurva, lying on her back, her long dark hair fanned out around her head. There was the small table and there, on the floor in front of it, was the page of whisperleaf. And there was John Summers/Flint Eldritch, locked in a battle of wills.

Strangest of all, Georgie could see *himself,* holding onto the Aetherquill for dear life.

Up.

Through the cave ceiling and above ground now, floating higher and higher with increasing speed. He saw twinkling torchlight moving around the Seminary where the

Altercockers and Scatterplotters were battling the Dregs of Mishap.

Up.

The mountains looked like guitar picks now.

A faint blue light outlined the horizon's unbroken arc; marking the border between this realm and the others beyond it.

Up.

Into the eternal galaxy. It was dark, but it wasn't black. It wasn't empty.

It was *Everything*.

The realms detached from one another, like a stack of plastic bowls all separating at the exact same time. He could see portals between the realms, tunnels of multicolored streaking lights rotating like a galactic Ferris wheel. And through some of them, like shooting stars, beautiful creatures of gold and purple flew gracefully. Glittery strands of color trailed behind them.

Georgie floated in the stillness and the silence, feeling its unfathomable force. Then, coming from inside and without—coming from *everywhere*—his father's voice boomed:

Kiddo, can you hear me?

Chapter 40

Shadow and Light, Again

*D*ad! Where are you?

I'm here, Georgie. The memory of victory . . . wow! That was brilliant!

Did it work!? Did he believe the story?

There was a long pause. Georgie thought his father was gone. Then: *Yes. It . . . Flint . . . loosened his hold on me. I came forward. I'm still* trying *to come forward. But Eldritch is strong. It's not over yet. You need to finish this.*

Dad? Are . . . are you alive?

Do I sound dead? Yes, I'm alive. Now listen to me and listen closely. I'm going to recede again. On purpose.

No, Dad! Keep fighting . . . keep—

Go for the hole in Flint's neck, Georgie. Seal it. Completely.

But . . . won't that hurt you?

It will only hurt Eldritch. Apurva will help you . . . she's something else, isn't she?

Yeah, Dad, she really is.

Georgie, look around. This beats the Grand Canyon, let me tell you. Beats it by a mile. Isn't it beautiful?

It's beautiful, Dad.

I love you, Georgie.

Daddy—

I've always loved you.

Dad!

Do it NOW, Georgie! Do it NOW!

No! Wait, DAD—

◇ ◇ ◇

A million miles away, at least a hundred ladder rungs beneath Scatterplot's surface, John Summers let go of the Aetherquill.

Georgie rocketed through the cosmos like a torpedo, picking up speed as he plummeted. He slammed back into his body, causing him to bite his tongue hard. He could taste his own salty blood now.

Georgie was back, alright.

His father's hand and arm and clothing were gone. It was just Flint Eldritch now, stumbling back and banging into the wooden table before he could catch himself. Georgie wondered if his dad had dragged Eldritch backward like that when he *receded*. Georgie hoped so.

Apurva stirred, moaned, and tried to lift her head.

But Flint was advancing on Georgie now with murder in his eyes.

The hole.

Flint's scarf was completely unraveled now, and Georgie could see that the hole in his neck was infested. Maggots squirmed and slithered around its inner lip.

Georgie felt it now: the calm that descended upon great warriors in the moments before battle. He drew his slingshot and his second-to-last marble from his pocket. He placed the marble in the leather pouch and pulled tight.

Flint Eldritch roared, and then the first beetle came as if rushed along the tunnel in Flint's throat on the current of his scream. It tumbled out, fell to the floor, and landed on its back. Its legs twitched, and then it flipped itself right side up and took off straight for Georgie.

Georgie watched the plump beetle racing toward him. You don't aim *at* the target; you aim at where the target is *going*. And with that thought, Georgie lifted his leg and brought his foot down hard. The beetle crunched beneath his sneaker like a pile of dead leaves and slender twigs. Yellowish liquid, thick and warm, squirted everywhere. A syrupy strand of guts twirled through the air and landed with a splat near Apurva's thigh.

Flint screeched, but Georgie ignored him. He aimed his slingshot.

THIP-TWANG!

The marble flew like a bullet straight into the hole in Flint's neck and embedded itself there halfway with a wet, sucking pop.

"THAT *HURTS!*" Flint screeched, stopping in his tracks, the furious buzzing coming from inside him growing louder and louder. Then, against the rushing weight of a hundred more beetles, the marble popped right back out of the hole like a champagne cork.

They came.

Gurgling from the black hole like sewage. Some fell straight to the floor, landing on their backs before flipping themselves over and taking off toward Georgie, but the rest— Cheez-Its, Mary, and Joseph Stalin—*leaped* from the edge of the hole. They landed on Georgie's sneakers and his ankles and his legs. A few particularly large ones flew through the air and landed on his hands. He felt them now on his wrists and scurrying up his forearms.

Georgie screamed. It was a cry so full of fury that he hardly recognized his own voice. He flipped his slingshot in the air and caught it by the shooting end. He held it like it was a blade as he lunged at Flint, swinging his arm forward, aiming for Flint's chest.

Flint ducked, just as Georgie expected he would, and the slingshot handle went where Georgie was *really* aiming: straight into the hole. The wooden handle sank into Flint's flesh like butter.

The beetles trapped inside kept coming, but now they gouged themselves against the slingshot handle. Twitching antennae and legs jutted out around the hole like nose hairs. Then a gush of thick yellowish puss sprayed around the wooden hilt all over Georgie's hands like water from a thumbed hose.

But the beetles that had escaped before Georgie had clogged the hole—hundreds of them—continued to climb briskly up his arms.

"GEORGIE SUMMERS! KILL! KILL! KILL!" Flint screeched. "*EAT HIM!*"

Georgie wanted to shake and shuck. He wanted to dance the hula-hoop until every one of those awful, bloated beetles was off of him. And then he wanted to run. Straight back to his bedroom.

But then he'd be running away from everything he'd ever loved.

"YOU PICKED THE WRONG SCRIBE TO MESS WITH!" Georgie roared, tears coursing down his cheeks, and drove the slingshot hilt even deeper. He would not let go, no matter what, even though his hands were covered with beetles twitching and scurrying madly, hundreds of tiny beetle feet needling his skin.

The hole began to smoke.

Flint Eldritch screamed in agony. "*STOP! LET ME GO AND I'LL LET YOU LIVE! LE– UGH– OH– EEEEE!*" His voice became garbled. His skin turned whiter than cheese and it started to sag all around his face. Flint's eyes rolled up in their sockets until just the veiny whites remained visible.

The beetles on Georgie's shoulders started up his neck now. He felt their antennae twitching anxiously against the skin below his chin. But he wouldn't—*couldn't*—let go of the slingshot handle. If he did, Eldritch might still be able to pull it out. He squeezed his eyes shut as the first beetle crawled over his lower lip.

Then he heard a sound on his left and turned to see Apurva standing beside him. Apurva, who'd had the courage to run headlong at the Dregs of Mishap. Apurva . . . who'd come back. She flicked the beetle off Georgie's mouth with a cry of disgust. Then, with more courage than Georgie could possibly imagine, she plunged her hands into the thick layer of scurrying beetles and puss, wrist deep, and found Georgie's hands.

She screamed in revulsion as the marching army of beetles branched like they'd met a fork in the road, half of them scampering up Georgie's arms and the other half now racing past the ticklish crease in Apurva's elbow.

Some of the beetles on Georgie's shoulders turned and leaped, landing in Apurva's hair.

"Push, Georgie!" Apurva cried. "*PUSH!*"

She closed her hands tightly around Georgie's, and together, they pushed.

For a moment, Georgie thought they were still too weak, that the slingshot handle just wouldn't go any further.

But then the handle *did* move. Georgie grunted without opening his mouth (the beetles would surely run down his throat if he did), and the slingshot handle sank all the way until a knobby knot of wood in the handle plugged the hole in Flint's neck with a perfect seal.

Flint's screams choked off into a high-pitched wheeze. His back arched violently, and his head flung back with a snap, like a tree branch torn from its trunk in a hurricane. His chin was pointing almost vertically at the cave's ceiling.

Georgie heard a squishing, sucking pop and watched in horror as one of Flint's eyeballs exploded from its socket and dangled off the side of his upturned face. It swung there lazily, like a yo-yo.

Apurva shrieked and stumbled backward, shaking wildly, swatting beetles out of her hair.

Georgie stumbled backward too now, leaving the sling-shot protruding from Flint's neck, mindlessly slapping beetles from his face.

More black holes opened in Flint's flesh.

The melted gorges appeared on his legs, his shoulders, and his skinny, pale chest. Swarms of beetles cascaded from each cavity, but these beetles exploded as they arrived, in blasts of black smoke.

All of a sudden, Georgie and Apurva were surrounded by exploding beetles, each leaving a twisting cloud of black smoke in its place. Those that remained on Georgie's face exploded too, burning his skin like acid and leaving welts that wouldn't begin to fade for days.

Flint screamed again, and the sound was almost too hor-rible to bear. It sounded like a handsaw scraping back and forth against a rusty metal pole. Like claws dragging against a blackboard.

Georgie and Apurva clapped their hands to their ears. The two remaining glass walls shattered, raining shards of glass down all around them.

"*NOOOOO!*" Flint screeched. "*I HATE YOU! I'LL GET YOU! I'LL KILL YOU!*"

Flint's arms shot out like scarecrow arms. But he was

falling backward now, flickering like a frozen computer game. And as Eldritch flickered, Georgie could see his father's dark jeans and checkered button-down shirt. He even caught a glimpse of his father's gray hair—which was no longer messy but brushed neatly behind his ears.

The exploding beetles slowed down the way a bag of popcorn does when it's almost done. The last of them went (*pop pop . . . pop*), and for a moment, Georgie couldn't see anything but a thick black curtain of smoke.

The cave became utterly silent.

Georgie could hear only Apurva's shaking sobs and his own heaving breath.

The black fog slowly dissipated.

"*Dad?*" Georgie whispered, a wave of dread rising inside him.

His father was dead, he was sure of it. And just like Rollie D and that little girl from New York City, Georgie had killed him.

"*Georgie?*"

John Summers was lying in a heap on the floor, his head resting on a pillow of broken glass, his knees curled gently toward his chest. The sleeves on his blue checkered shirt were rolled up, and Georgie saw muscles on his arms that he'd never noticed before. Or, maybe, they'd never *been* there before.

Georgie ran to him.

Chapter 41

The Best Things in the World

"**D**ad!" Georgie dropped to his knees and grabbed his father's head in his hands.

John Summers coughed and opened his swollen eyelids. He looked tired and beaten, battered and bruised—but he also looked *different*. Fuller, stronger . . . *wholer*.

"*Dad*," Georgie choked, still certain his father was dead, that this was all some crazy illusion. "*Where are you hurt?*"

"I'm not hurt, Georgie," John Summers said, and his *voice*—his voice had changed, too. Whereas before it had sounded flat, now it vibrated with warmth and depth. "Hey, kiddo, why do golfers wear two pairs of pants?" John Summers smiled, and for the first time in Georgie's life, that smile reached all the way up to his eyes.

"Dad!"

John Summers slowly got himself into a sitting position. "In case they get a hole in one!"

Georgie brought his cheek against the backs of his father's hands. Just to feel his father's skin—to make sure this was all *real.*

"You did it," John Summers whispered. He looked at Apurva. "You *both* did it. I'd say thank you but 'thank you' doesn't even come close to cutting it. Rock and roll, you two. I'm . . ." He flipped his hands over, back and forth, inspecting them. " . . . *Me.*"

"It worked?" Georgie asked, tentatively. "It really worked!?" He had a million other questions and a billion conversations he wanted to have with his dad. This dad that looked and sounded so strong. This dad, with eyes that blazed with life and love. But there would be time for all that.

Later.

"Yeah, it worked," John Summers said. He held Georgie by the shoulders, and his grip was as strong and firm as a clamp. "I love you, kiddo. To infinity and beyond."

Georgie crumpled against his father. He hugged his dad with both arms, *hard*, because he no longer had to worry about hurting his dad.

And this time, his dad was able to hug him back.

Georgie stayed there for a while, feeling his heart beat

against his father's chest. *THIS is what I call winning,* Georgie thought while his face was pressed against that soft and faded flannel button-down.

That no two people exist on their own islands.

That no two hearts beat in solitude.

That it's worth loving someone so much, even if tears stain your face when you lose them.

Georgie looked over at Apurva and put an arm around her.

And that the absolute BEST thing in the world is having friends around to fix you when you break.

◇ ◇ ◇

Georgie pulled his head away from his father's chest. "Dad?"

John Summers looked down at Georgie and smiled brightly. "That's me."

"Dad," Georgie repeated, "Fumbluff said using the Aetherquill in a lower realm is really dangerous. Like what happened between you and mom. But nothing happened this time? Everything's okay?"

John Summers scratched his stubbly cheek. "When you wrote Eldritch that story of his victory, I *felt* it work. He believed he'd won. He got . . . *stronger,* somehow, almost ecstatic, but in the same moment he weakened his hold on me. That's when I came forward and grabbed the Aetherquill." John Summers closed his eyes. "But then—"

John Summers couldn't finish because a loud rumbling crash came from somewhere deep in the cave. It sounded like bookshelves toppling, and Georgie wondered if that's exactly what it was—if the ancient bookshelves in the old Library they had passed through earlier were crumbling.

A fine band of dirt and sediment landed on the back of Georgie's neck. He looked up and saw the craggy ceiling was rumbling. Maybe it was Flint Eldritch's dark blasts of energy that had disrupted the cave's foundations. Maybe it was just the unyielding passing of time, and the cave was just ready to collapse. A block of limestone shaped like a dinosaur tooth cracked off the ceiling and landed with a tremendous thud a few feet from where Georgie, Apurva, and John Summers were huddled.

"*WATCH OUT!*" John Summers shouted, shoving them both out of the way as another stalactite came crashing down. He gathered Georgie and Apurva in his arms and took a block of limestone straight in the back. "*IT'S COLLAPSING!*"

Dislodging debris was falling everywhere now like a meteor shower.

John Summers roared as he carried Georgie and Apurva away, through the narrow tunnel, through the ruins of Scatterplot's original Library, all the way to the ladder leading up to Stone's shop, their feet barely touching the ground.

He roared like a lion.

He roared like a father protecting his son.

He roared like a light in control of its shadow again.

◇ ◇ ◇

Later, when Georgie would be too delirious with fever to think much of anything, he would remember the moment he'd grabbed the first wrung of the ladder. It was then that he felt the first signs of illness. An itch of the throat and the dull ache of bones, like the onset of a bad flu.

But right now, he was so pumped with adrenaline that those symptoms went unnoticed.

On the cave floor, scuttling between the falling debris, was a shiny black beetle.

Its antennae twitched and its pincers clicked as it scurried away into the shadows.

It, too, went unnoticed.

Chapter 42

Funerals and Celebrations

Georgie awoke the very next morning to find the dull ache in his bones was now a throbbing soreness, but he chalked it up to all the adventure over the past few days. He rolled over in bed and looked out Corrigendum's third-floor balcony doors. A thick fog had rolled in from the mountains and blanketed the landscape, rolling across the hills and forest all the way to the Seminary, where the tent beams that hadn't collapsed rose up through the mist.

Roscoe stirred and stretched his arms out from beneath a bundle of quilts on the floor. "Rise and shine, you miserable toenail-nibblers!"

How many hours of sleep had they gotten? Not many, that's for sure. Georgie, Roscoe, and Apurva had stayed up most of the night talking about everything that had happened. Roscoe had been especially jazzed, boasting to Georgie and Apurva of his bravery and marksmanship during the battle with the Dregs of Mishap. *You two shoulda BEEN there!* He'd said at one point, to which Georgie thought, *We were sorta busy ourselves.*

"*Shhhhh!*" Apurva moaned from her bed and shoved her head beneath her pillow.

Georgie, Apurva, and John Summers had emerged from Stone's blacksmith shop safely, finding the streets of Scatterplot deserted. They had met up with Rollie D and Fumbluff on the Seminary's Great Lawn, just as the last few remaining Dregs were running toward the mountains like their pants were on fire and their butts were catching. When Roscoe had told Georgie that at some point, smack in the middle of the battle, the Dregs just stopped fighting, like whatever or whoever was controlling them had run out of batteries, Georgie had a horrifying image of his slingshot handle sealing the hole in Flint's neck. Of course, Roscoe took the credit (he said the Dregs were scared of his aim and his accuracy), and while Georgie knew otherwise, he didn't feel the need to say so.

Everyone had been astounded to see John Summers again, but none more so than Rollie D, who had taken the Seminary's stairs by four and flung herself into John's arms. When they'd reached Corrigendum, Rollie, Fumbluff, and John Summers headed for Fumbluff's chamber to meet in private while Charlie Fenton (who had been feeling well enough to remove his bandages) helped Georgie, Apurva, and Roscoe settle into their bedroom.

Soon the three of them were all up and dressed, heading down Corrigendum's third-floor hallway, where John Summers and Rollie D were given their own quarters not too far from Fumbluff's.

◇ ◇ ◇

An hour later, Scatterplotters and Altercockers gathered as one on the Seminary's Great Lawn. Soon they'd begin rebuilding all that had been damaged and burned, but not yet. There were fallen soldiers to bury first. Those who'd died at the Coronation Ceremony, and those who'd fallen in battle against the Dregs of Mishap.

Rollie D had been up all night decorating the coffins by hand, inlaying her designs with pearl. Her artwork told tales of battles and grief and love.

A stray leaf blew across the lawn, flipping over Georgie's feet.

He looked at all those shallow graves. The people standing around them, weeping silently, had lost parents, friends . . . children.

Those memories were going to be very painful for a very long time.

Georgie felt a squeeze on his shoulder. He looked up into his father's sorrowful eyes.

"Aren't some memories *good* to forget?" Georgie asked in a

whisper. He thought about that piece of peanut butter sand-wich stuck to his butt. How everyone had laughed at him.

John Summers put an arm around Georgie. "No, kiddo. Because it's not about who or what you've become, but *how far a distance you've traveled.* And remembering where you started is the only way to judge that distance."

A sharp wind whipped up, bending the tall stalks of feather grass.

Apurva wiped her eyes with the back of one hand and held Georgie's with her other.

Roscoe, Edie, and Ore stood in a row on Apurva's other side, their eyes cast downward.

It was early afternoon when the wind finally died down and the sun broke through the clouds. A sizable cemetery now stood on the Great Lawn, each grave marked with a tombstone shaped like a book.

◇ ◇ ◇

"Jeez, Georgie," Roscoe said once the funerals were over. They were heading away from the cemetery toward the Timbernotch Tavern, where Rollie, Yooker, and Toots were getting started on the repairs. "Have you seen your dad? *Sincerely!*"

"Nope," Georgie said sarcastically, then rubbed his temples. His headache was pounding. "Haven't seen him."

"I can't believe that's really Mr. Summers . . . he looks so *good!*" Roscoe punched Georgie in the arm. "For his age, obviously."

Georgie smiled and had a sudden image of Roscoe standing over him on the embankment across Jericho Road. *The crowd is going absolutely WILD!*

They had all grown up a lot since that day. Not so long ago.

And there was Roscoe now, sauntering toward the round-about above the ridge, his swords and arrows and handmade wooden bows swaying in their scabbards and sheaths around his back and waist.

"And Flint?" Roscoe asked. "Is he really . . ." he spoke slowly, like it was a dangerous question.

"Yeah," Georgie said. "Didn't we go through this all last night?"

Roscoe looked suspiciously at Georgie. "*Inside your dad?*"

Georgie nodded and smiled weakly. "Light and shadow. Just like I told you." Georgie rubbed his forehead. The feverish ache in his bones was getting worse. "Shadow and light."

He wanted to hear about the battle with Flint's men again, especially the part when all the Dregs dropped their weapons and ran for the mountains, it was his favorite part . . . but not now.

Right now, he wasn't feeling good at all.

◇ ◇ ◇

That evening, dusk painted Scatterplot in warm golds and purples. Three enormous tents had been built on the Great Lawn, each illuminated by lanterns hanging from criss-crossing ropes overhead. The party was about to begin.

Rollie stepped out from one of the tents, her red hair tied up with leather straps, and approached Georgie, Apurva, and Roscoe. "Georgie, you okay, kid?" Rollie asked. "You don't look yourself."

I don't feel like myself, Georgie wanted to say. *Not one bit.* He thought about what had happened when his mother had used the Aetherquill. If he told Rollie how sick he was feeling, it would get back to his dad, and he didn't want his dad to freak out.

Maybe it *was* just a bad flu.

"I'm okay," Georgie muttered, casting a look at Roscoe, who raised his eyebrows in return. Friends always knew.

The three of them followed Rollie to a smooth ledge of rock overlooking rolling valleys behind the Seminary. Wooded foothills unfolded into the distance. "Listen, kids," Rollie began, "I'm proud of you. All *three* of you. I'm not the sentimental type, I guess you know that about me by now, but I did make . . . a little gift for each of you. Don't let it get to your heads."

Georgie took a deep breath. The air was crisp and fresh, no storms on the horizon—and subtly, beneath the pine and the moss and the fresh salt from some distant river, Georgie smelled the scent of mangos again.

Rollie untied Roscoe's two swords and three wooden spears slung around his waist. "Poorly fashioned weapons are more apt to get you killed than anything," Rollie said. Then she pulled a long, slim dagger from her rucksack. "Take this instead. It's good. I made it for you."

Roscoe beamed and slipped the dagger into a sheath at his hip.

Rollie turned to Georgie and held out a handmade leather pouch. She tied it around Georgie's waist. "For your ammunition. Gives you a quicker draw."

Shepherd the blacksmith had given Georgie an entire bucket of new ammo last night, and now Georgie loaded a handful of the metal balls into the leather pouch. "Thanks, Rollie."

Rollie reached into her rucksack once more and pulled out a large scroll wrapped with red string. She unrolled it and handed it to Apurva. "Been saving this one for you, especially."

Apurva held the tall parchment with both hands. She turned, and the charcoal constellations on the map moved with her, like particles settling in a snow globe. "Is it a map of the stars? It's so . . . *different.*"

"It's no ordinary map," Rollie said.

"Whoa!" Apurva gasped, tilting and rotating the map and watching everything move and shift and—"*The Department of Recovery and Reclamation!* But . . . it's gone now! It was right there!"

"You'll find it again," Rollie said.

"Promise?"

Rollie smiled, and then she wrapped all three of them in a hug and held on for a long moment before stepping back.

"The party's starting—and while I despise parties, I do value punctuality."

Georgie looked from Roscoe to Apurva, and although his head was pounding and his bones were aching terribly, his heart was full. He was with his friends, and they were with him.

"Ahhh, you *wets!*" Roscoe cried.

A dying ray of sunlight flicked off an outcropping of smooth black rock way out in the distance.

The three of them went to the party.

❖ ❖ ❖

Georgie stood at the edge of the dirt-swept dance floor, hardly believing his own eyes.

John Summers and Rollie D were *dancing*.

Rollie's cloak, which was once Penelope Summers's cloak, fanned out all around her as she spun and dipped with the music. Fiddles and flutes hurtled above the bongos, and everyone clapped their hands with the rhythm.

Roscoe slapped Georgie on the back and pointed to Georgie's dad. "Guy can *move*," Roscoe said, but it came out "*Eye uh mooof*" because his mouth was stuffed with three chocolate banana pops.

"You're disgusting," Apurva said, holding two frosted candy apples of her own.

The music got louder and faster, and the crowd shouted *HEY! HEY! HEY! HEY* with every beat. John Summers folded his arms across his chest, squatted low to the ground, and alternated kicking his legs out from under him.

The crowd went absolutely wild.

The music went faster.

John's legs became a blur.

HEY! HEY! HEY! HEY!

Fumbluff, who had been talking with Fenton and Scribe Hambrey, joined Rollie D and John Summers on the dance floor. His legs kicked out like pistons, and before long, it was hard to tell who was moving faster.

The song ended in a crescendo, and the tent rocked with applause and stomping feet.

Then, quietly at first, Georgie heard his name being whispered throughout the crowd.

Geor-gie! Geor-gie! Geor-gie!

The whispering chant grew louder and louder.

Everyone's eyes fell on him.

The ground shook with a thousand or more men and women declaring his name.

GEOR-GIE! GEOR-GIE! GEOR-GIE!

Apurva grabbed Georgie's hand. "Dance with me!"

Georgie gulped. "Oh. Oh. No. Really, not here, please. Not ever."

Then Ore was behind him, shoving him onto the dance floor. Georgie looked for an escape route, but found none. Just a dense ring of happy faces yipping and hooting.

Then Apurva was there, her hair tied back in a high ponytail. She guided Georgie's hand to the side of her waist. He felt her silk dress beneath his skin. Somewhere far away, Georgie heard Roscoe laughing like a madman.

They moved to the music, and for a brief moment, Georgie forgot how ill he felt.

Apurva laughed when Georgie stepped on her toes, and then the dance floor filled up.

Yooker Tenderfoot slapped his giant beer mug down on a table and grabbed Emma Hambrey's hands. "Oh my!" Emma exclaimed, turning very red in the face.

Georgie danced, despite feeling sicker than ever, the crowd just a colorful streak of motion all around them. He began to feel dizzy. He was hot and itchy and sweaty all over, and very relieved when Roscoe shoved him aside to take his place on the dance floor with Apurva.

Georgie slumped into an open chair next to his father. He wondered if his face was as red and splotchy as it felt.

"Hey, buddy, you okay?" His dad smiled.

No, I'm not okay, Dad. I think I'm sick, and I'm pretty sure it's not something a couple of Advil is going to cure. He felt like lying down. Maybe even right here, on the cool, damp ground. He'd surely get stomped on by some drunk Altercocker, but he didn't care.

"Dad?" Georgie looked into his dad's eyes. "I'm . . . I'm scared."

Georgie brought the Aetherquill out of his pocket. It was cool to the touch, the ancient brass barrel dull and grimy. Georgie tried to squeeze the Aetherquill and found that he could hardly make a fist. "Are you *sure* nothing happened this time?"

The band was playing softly now.

A billion bright stars and constellations lit up the night sky bending endlessly over Scatterplot. "You were going to say something last night," Georgie urged. "Right before the cave started to collapse." He was feeling *very* sick now. The smell of meat was making him nauseous.

John Summers stared intently into Georgie's eyes. "It happened right after I came forward and grabbed the Aetherquill. Flint *felt* me coming forward. Like I was an

intruder. An uninvited guest at his party. He fought me.
Fighting the story you wrote him. On one hand, he knew
the memory you gave him was real. On the other hand, he
knew it wasn't. That's what we call a paradox . . . when two
things are true at the same time. But a paradox so real, one
caused by the Aetherquill, can tear your mind apart." John
closed his eyes and pinched the bridge of his nose with his
thumb and forefinger. "I know how that feels."

"But is everything *actually* okay?" Georgie asked again.
"Nothing's gonna . . . blow up?"

"Everything *seems* okay," John said.

Nothing's okay, Georgie thought frantically. His headache had become a migraine.

John Summers looked around at all the happy
Scatterplotters and Altercockers. "Everything seems under
control, doesn't it?"

Nothing's under control. Georgie thought. *I'm not in control.* He wiped more sweat from his forehead.

Control.

"Hey, Georgie?" John asked anxiously. "You're *sweating.*
Buddy! What's wrong?"

Control.

"Dad," Georgie choked. "I don't feel so good—"

Someone get me outta here.

Then Georgie collapsed in his father's arms.

Chapter 43

Homecoming

The rest of the night passed like slow-rolling thunderclouds; Georgie couldn't tell where things started and where they ended. He was back in Corrigendum, he knew that much, lying on the couch in Fumbluff's private chamber. Portraits on either side of the wall Flint Eldritch had smashed through hung askew.

There were no thermometers in Scatterplot, but his fever was now a bonfire.

Rollie D brought him something to drink every few minutes—a spicy liquid that burned his throat on the way down. Georgie tried fighting it, but Rollie forced the brew down his throat. Was it helping the fever? Was it the same tea Rollie had brought for Apurva's mother? Georgie had no idea.

Apurva and Roscoe were there, somewhere, in and out.

At some point, Georgie saw the fuzzy shapes of Charlie Fenton and Scribe Hambrey whispering worriedly to Fumbluff.

John Summers was by Georgie's side, dabbing his forehead with a soaked rag. Trying to cool him off.

It wasn't working.

Georgie dozed off.

And dreamt.

◇ ◇ ◇

Georgie flaps about in the lake.

He pinches his nose and dunks his head underwater. He emerges, spitting and smiling. Georgie waves to his mother. She is standing on a narrow strip of pebbles and sand. Her long dress blows sideways in a comfortable wind.

She waves back, clapping a hand to her hat to keep it from blowing away.

"Not too much farther!"

Georgie dunks under again. This time, the water is much colder.

He emerges and the day has grown impossibly dark. A freezing gust of air makes Georgie shiver. His lips turn purple.

He squints across the lake and sees a wave taking shape. The water around Georgie begins to churn violently. The wave in the distance picks up speed, growing taller all the time.

Georgie turns to rush back to his mother but he loses his footing and comes down in the shallow water on his back.

He is underwater.

He can't breathe.

◇ ◇ ◇

Georgie stirs and moans.

He cracks his eyes open, nearly delirious with fever.

He's on his back still, but now he's moving.

Outdoors.

He could see the millions of geometric shapes the gaps between the trees make, and the blue sky beyond.

He is on some sort of stretcher made of wood planks, being carried through the woods by Rollie D, Roscoe, Apurva, and his father. His father, who won't leave his side.

Where are they taking me? He's shivering with cold sweats, shaking all over. He wraps the burlap blanket tight around him, noticing jagged red lines climbing up his arms like vines. Like poison.

And all over, on every inch of skin, he itches.

Oh, how he itches.

He could hear fragments of conversation. Rollie D, his father. Arguing? Planning? Hard to tell.

Who cares.

He hears the words "New York."

He hears the word "hospital."

So that's where they're taking him.

Georgie dozes off again.

And dreams.

◇ ◇ ◇

Georgie is tossed this way and that way underwater, until he manages a gaspy gulp of salty air. His mother is running into the lake, screaming. Her hat blows off.

"GEORGIE!" Now she is waist deep, thrashing her arms madly.

"Mommy!" Georgie screams.

The current pulls him under and his lungs fill with water. It's pitch dark, and Georgie doesn't know which way is up or down.

Then there is an arm around his waist.

Georgie's mother pulls him out and cradles him.

"Mommy," Georgie sputters. "I'm so itchy."

His mother carries Georgie back to shore. She lays Georgie gently on the pebbled shoreline. "Almost there."

She turns back to the lake. The gigantic wave is very close now.

"Lay him down! Lay—"

"—him down," Rollie D says sternly. "And stand back."

Georgie is jostled as he is laid down. He sees Apurva's and Roscoe's feet out of the corners of his eyes.

He knows where they are now.

The portal.

Georgie shivers again and looks down at his arms. The

streaks of infection have turned an ugly shade of red, with fine veins of purple now shooting all the way to his shoulder. He scratches at them, digging his fingernails into his skin hard enough to draw blood.

"Don't scratch," John Summers says, kneeling down and grasping Georgie's wrist in his hand. "Please, don't scratch."

Georgie moans and struggles, but his father holds tight. "Hang on, kiddo, we're going to get you help."

Apurva and Roscoe are beside him now. Apurva puts her hands on Georgie's shoulders.

Roscoe mutters something. Georgie thinks it sounded like *wet noodle*.

Rollie is just a few feet away, rolling her arm up and down like she is unzipping a six-foot-tall hoodie.

Georgie's eyes close.

◊ ◊ ◊

The gigantic wave is nearly upon them now.

"Mom?" Georgie asks, his chest heaving up and down, his nipples as purple as a bad bruise.

But it's too late. His mother has turned back toward the oncoming wave. She walks slowly into the lake, the water moving around her legs as if to welcome her.

A gray hand shoots from the gigantic wave that is now so tall Georgie can't see anything above or beyond it. The hand opens and stretches and grabs Georgie's mother around the waist. It pulls her toward a hole that has opened like a mouth in the middle of the wave.

Georgie screams.

He runs into the lake after her, but the moment his feet hit the water, two hooks grab him by the armpits and—

—thrust him through the doorway between Scatterplot and New York.

Georgie is breathing heavily, the air coming in fits and spurts.

He is home now.

But . . . the garage.

The garage is gone.

The concrete stairs are still there, and so is the doorframe. But everything else is in ruins. Where the garage ceiling used to be, Georgie looks straight up into the ash-gray sky.

Roscoe, Apurva, Rollie D, and John Summers lift his stretcher again and carry him carefully up the stairs.

He picks his head up an inch, which feels like a bowling ball rolling around in his skull—

Where his house used to be is a crater in the earth, littered with beams and shingles and glass. From the wreckage, a column of black smoke rises into the sky.

Why isn't anyone saying anything?

Georgie tries to stand, but his legs are so weak and wobbly that they won't hold him.

But his father could hold him, and he does, lifting Georgie from the makeshift stretcher.

Now Georgie can see more columns of black smoke rising from the direction of Main Street. Across Jericho

Road, Roscoe's house is on fire. Flames lick from the shattered windows. From where they stand, he can see straight into Roscoe's charred bedroom. A large burnt square of Roscoe's dinosaur blanket flips across Roscoe's lawn like an ember.

Georgie looks to his left, and there is Rollie D, her bow and arrow slung around her back.

Georgie looks to his right, and there are Roscoe and Apurva, his friends, still with him after all this time.

Georgie looks up, and there is his father, his thick hair combed, his jaw set, his eyes blazing.

Georgie looks down, and there, on his arm, inching slowly along the dark red streaks of infection, is a shiny black beetle.

The beetle pauses, twitching its antennae along the inside crease of Georgie's elbow.

Georgie stares at it, and it stares back, neither of them paying attention to the trail of yellowish slime running down to Georgie's wrist. Worse than the fever, worse than the throbbing migraine, was a screaming storm of terror coursing through Georgie's body—a storm where monsters more deadly than anything his worst nightmares could conjure stumbled out of the fog.

And *come*.

Georgie pulls his sleeve down over the beetle, but it does not hide the small bulge slithering slowly up his arm.

"Georgie?"

From a world away, Apurva's hand touches his shoulder. "Come. Lie down. We have to get you to a hospital."

Georgie has a sudden monumental urge to scream. *LOOK AROUND! WHAT HOSPITAL? EVERYTHING IS GONE!* To scream it so loud that everyone between here and Main Street would go deaf.

But he doesn't. He *can't*. His throat feels shrunken to the width of a needle, and he can hardly draw any breath into his lungs.

Another small bulge appears high on his arm, an inch from Apurva's fingers.

He looks up at Apurva. Her hair is tied high and tight in a ponytail with her blue scrunchie.

I'm sorry, Georgie thinks. *Oh, God, I'm so sorry.*

And when his knees give out a moment later, John Summers catches him, and when Georgie speaks one last time, it doesn't sound at all like his own voice.

"Daddy?"

It sounds like the voice of a stuffed animal when you pull the cord in its back.

Epilogue

If you were to travel to a realm higher than Scatterplot—a realm the Scatterplotters call Quillethra, although there are other names for it, depending on who you ask—navigate across the Black Sea, and then survive many days of treacherous climbing, you'd reach a magnificent castle.

Inside the largest room of that castle is an enormous throne studded with jewels the size of oranges.

Upon that throne sits a woman with golden-brown skin. A woman of unimaginable beauty.

So beautiful, in fact, it's said that men have lost their breath just by gazing upon her. Words would be stolen away, and all they could think was how her hair looked precisely like a chocolate waterfall. Draw close enough (though few did) and take a deep breath (though few could), and you'd think you were no longer in a castle, but a mango orchard.

In the polished armrest of the bejeweled throne is a hidden compartment, and in that compartment lies the creased photograph of a young boy.

In his hand, the boy holds a toy slingshot.

Whenever she could, which was almost whenever she wanted, this beautiful woman, known to most as the Librarian, would take out the photograph and gaze upon her son.

◊ ◊ ◊

Now, the door to the Librarian's chamber opens and in walks a man with receding gray hair. His cloak has a tear down his right sleeve, which had been repaired with red thread.

"Dullwick, dear," the Librarian says. "Dullwick Ratriot."

Dullwick bows low to the ground, keeping his usual, healthy distance from the Librarian.

"Tell me," the Librarian continues, unscrewing the cap of an ancient fountain pen hanging from a golden chain around her neck. The pen is shaped like a bullet, with inlays of black shale decorating its polished chrome barrel. "What news from Scatterplot, Dullwick? Tell me *everything*."

Only Scribes
May Enter Here...

So, you learned to read in Whisperloom? Impressive indeed, young Scribe! Upload the hidden message at www.GeorgieSummers.com or send it straight to me at isaac@georgiesummers.com for a chance to win incredible prizes and giveaways!

_____,

_____.

_____,

_____.

_____,

_____.

_____,

_____.

_____,

_____?

_____,

_____?

_____,

_____?

Acknowledgments

Thank *you*, mainly.

Here's something I think a lot of writers (no, I'm not ready to call myself an *author*) feel but aren't so quick to admit: *They really want people to read their stuff.*

To a fault? Maybe.

And maybe you're thinking I should just speak for myself. Fair enough. I didn't write this book because I love writing. I write because the idea of a stranger enjoying my stories excites me.

It's not very artistic, but it's the truth.

So, if you've read this far, thank you. *Sincerely.* And if you just flipped to the acknowledgments like I do sometimes, get outta here right now.

Another thing most writers feel and probably *would* be quick to admit: Writing is an unbelievably lonely ordeal. It's just you, the blank page, and all the voices in your head telling you how badly you suck. But while I *did* write this book alone, some people made the process a lot less lonely than it otherwise would have been.

Now, this is the part where writers (especially writers of children's fiction) thank their kids for all their inspiration . . . how, without them, they could have *never* written their book. But there'll be none of that here. I wrote this book *despite* the best efforts of my three little psychopaths. It is *they* who should be thanking *me*. Fat chance, though.

A special thank you to Web Stone, my first editor and also the first person to give it to me straight. I met Web over coffee in New York City twelve years ago. I had four hundred written pages and less than five hundred bones to my name. Web was kind enough to spare me his usual editorial fee and instead had me study Vogler and McKee. By the end of all that, I agreed with Web's assessment: that my four hundred pages were *notes* for a book—and not very good notes at that. Disheartened (but at least disillusioned), I put the manuscript (notes) in my desk drawer and founded an advertising agency. Nine years later, I reached back out to Web, and the rest is this-story (sorry, I had to).

Thank you to Sam Copeland, agent extraordinaire, whose editorial insights helped streamline the narrative. And for her sharp eye and discerning ear, thank you, Jenny Pearson.

A very special thank you to my developmental editor, Jim Thomas, who helped me kill the darlings (52,000 darlings, to be precise). Jim, the final drafts of this book have your fingerprints all over them, but what I appreciate most is your indefatigable belief in me. You're more than an editor; you're a dear friend. I'm lucky to have found you.

A special thank you goes to Jim Madsen, whose brilliant artwork brought the cover to life.

To Neil Blair, whose generosity of spirit and timely advice helped me bring this book to market with a supporting cast most authors don't have the opportunity to collaborate with: Thank you, brother.

Marc Maley helped design and orchestrate this book's launch strategy. His marketing savvy and creativity have been invaluable. Thank you, Marc.

Thank you to Shira, my sister-in-law, who was a weirdly perceptive (and dare I say helpful) early critic.

Thank you Nina, Andrew, Esti, Bruna, and Kirsten for your brilliant, creative marketing. I have no idea how many copies we're going to move—but wherever we land will be thanks to your support and enthusiasm.

Patrick, your integrity and honest leadership at AdVenture's helm afforded me the headspace to bring this to the finish line. Thank you. Besides, I could only let you be the only published author for so long.

To my team at Greenleaf Book Group: Tanya Hall, Emma Watson, Elizabeth Brown, Justin Branch, Leah Pierre, Kristine Pcyre-Ferry, Madelyn Myers, and Neil Gonzalez. Thank you for navigating through all the chaos and keeping this project on track.

Hope is the greatest gift a parent can give a child, so thank you, Mom and Pop, for raising me with a streak of idiotic optimism ... an irrational belief in the goodness life has to offer. I love you both—to infinity and beyond.

And a most resounding thank you to my wife, who was on the train to Deloitte at 6:00 a.m. while I was home working on a novel that I had no business writing and had no reasonable shot at ever being published. I don't know why you encouraged me to stick with it, to *finish* it, to spend our very last dollars all those years ago on editorial fees—but you did. You could have told me to stop and get a job (and yeah, you did, *eventually*), you could have told me that my writing wasn't very good (I'm *sure* you were thinking it), but you encouraged me to carry on carrying on, and it fills me with appreciation whenever I think about it (which is often). The last thirteen years haven't always been smooth or easy, but they've been the best thirteen years of my life.

About the Author

After earning his master's in industrial psychology, Isaac Rudansky founded AdVenture Media, an award-winning advertising agency that has written campaigns for AMC Networks, Sports Illustrated, Forbes Magazine, Hanes, Nasdaq, and many others. His online courses have attracted over 300,000 students worldwide. He writes for industry-leading publications and leads workshops at marketing events around the world.

Isaac married up (*way* up), and he and his wife live in Long Island with their little anarchists who operate on a sugar-based economy. For Isaac, writing isn't just escapism; it's a tactical retreat from those insurgent kids. Besides, it's the only time he gets to decide what happens next without a cacophony of dissenting opinions.

Reach Isaac at isaac@GeorgieSummers.com. He likes critical feedback, but he likes compliments even more.